Praise for *We're All Damaged*

"In *We're All Damaged*, Matthew Norman has crafted a fast-paced, funny, and touching story. Comparisons to Tropper and Hornby will be made, and deservedly so, but Norman's voice and characters are fresh and all his own. A winning novel that is sure to make you laugh, cry, and nod in recognition as all the best books do."
    —Catherine McKenzie, bestselling author of *Hidden* and *Smoke*

"*We're All Damaged* is explosively funny and fast-moving; a wild whacked-out romp that travels from New York to Omaha and back again. In the end, though, Matthew Norman has written a sweet story about family and love and how they sustain us."
    —Jessica Anya Blau, author of *The Trouble With Lexie*

"In *We're All Damaged*, Matthew Norman takes humor and heartache, pathos and pop culture, love and loss, family and friends, Cubs and Cornhuskers, marriage equality and male blow-up sex dolls; blends them into a sublime literary margarita; and serves it on the rocks with salt. There's just so much to savor here, it's impossible not to enjoy."
    —Greg Olear, author of *Fathermucker* and *Totally Killer*

WE'RE ALL
DAMAGED

ALSO BY MATTHEW NORMAN

Domestic Violets

WE'RE ALL DAMAGED

MATTHEW NORMAN

Little
a

Published by Little A, New York

www.apub.com

Amazon, the Amazon logo, and Little A are trademarks of Amazon.com, Inc., or its affiliates.

ISBN-10 (hardcover): 1503933377
ISBN-13 (hardcover): 9781503933378

ISBN-10 (paperback): 1503933385
ISBN-13 (paperback): 9781503933385

Cover design and illustration by Joan Wong

Printed in the United States of America

For Hazel

WE'RE ALL DAMAGED

I

It's scary how many details I remember about the night Karen left. That's the thing I hate most about my brain, the way it stores and catalogs things, all this dumb shit on a giant hard drive in my head, so I'm forced to obsess over it all like a crazy person.

Here's a perfect example.

Our waiter had a button stuck to his apron that said "Ask Me about Bacon Time!" Why in the hell would I remember that? He had to have been wearing, like, thirty buttons—they always do—but that's the one I remember. He brought us our food, I saw the button, and I wondered if he was ever tempted to wear it outside of work, like with jeans and a T-shirt, just hanging out with his friends.

Hey, everybody—you guys—ask me about Bacon Time!

There was an old couple at the table next to ours drinking these enormous novelty margaritas, like a pair of drunks on a cruise. The lady kept touching her husband's hand across the table. It was nice. I remember thinking that. They wore matching Velcro sneakers.

"Wake Me Up Before You Go-Go" by Wham! was playing. Blast from the past, I know, but talk about a jagged little piece of pop music irony. I suggest Googling it. It's the single most upbeat fucking thing in the history of recorded music. In five thousand years, archaeologists will unearth it on someone's long-lost computer. *Jesus, were these primitive people really that happy?* they'll ask in their high-tech future language.

Karen was wearing her green sweater, the one I got her for her birthday. She really loves green. Green throw pillows. Green socks. She painted an accent wall green in our dining room once when I was away. It was kind of weird—her green obsession—but I went with it, because she was my wife. I saw the sweater on one of those creepy headless mannequins at the Gap, and I knew she'd love it.

Here's the worst detail of all—worse than Wham! even, if you can believe it. It all happened at Applebee's.

Don't get me wrong. I'm not a snob. I don't have a problem with Applebee's per se. But I think we can all agree, as a civilized society, that lives shouldn't change there. Significant things shouldn't begin or end at Applebee's. You shouldn't walk into Applebee's as one thing and then leave as something else entirely.

She was eating chicken fingers and fries, and I was eating Sizzling Chili Lime Chicken off the 550 Calories menu. I was a lot healthier back then.

She was being so quiet.

This had been going on for months—the quiet game—but that night was pure radio silence. Nothing. She just stared out into the parking lot, out toward Home Depot, while I asked her all those idiotic questions husbands ask their wives when they're not saying anything.

How was traffic this morning?

Is the pollen count higher than usual today?

Who's hosting SNL this week?

Can you see my nipples through this shirt?

How many of these people do you think are actually spies from TGI Fridays?

And then, this is what she said. She said, "Andy, I don't want this anymore."

I've been over this in my head a few times, and I've come to the conclusion that it's perfectly reasonable that I thought she was talking about her chicken fingers. They were just sitting there; she'd hardly even touched them. I saw the opportunity to do something intimate and husbandly, so I cut a little triangle of my Sizzling Chili Lime Chicken and held it out to her. "Well, you should totally try this," I said, the World's Most Oblivious Living Human Man.

She looked at it glistening there on my fork.

We were never the kind of couple that feeds each other. Maybe that's the ultimate litmus test for marital stability. Maybe all those horrible idiots you see sensually feeding each other in public are doing it right, and the rest of us are all doomed to studio apartments and eHarmony.

"No, Andy," she said. "Not *this*. This. I don't want *this* anymore."

And then everyone started clapping.

The entire waitstaff came marching out from the kitchen, huddled around a cake and candles. A few tables over, a teenage girl with braces blushed. It was the girl's birthday, but for a few seconds, I imagined that it was all for me—the cake, the candles, the singing. I imagined that Karen had called Applebee's from work and set the whole thing up. *Got you,* she'd whisper from across the table.

The birthday girl's name was Bailey, like someone's pet, and by the time the waiters and waitresses were done singing, Karen was crying. I just sat there, shell-shocked and numb, the victim of sudden domestic terrorism.

"Can I help you folks with anything else?"

It was our waiter. He was smiling in that maniacal way that waiters at places like Applebee's smile, like they're all doing methamphetamine back in the kitchen.

Believe it or not, the thing I regret most about the whole shitty evening is that I didn't have the presence of mind to look our waiter in the eyes, clear my throat, and say, "Yeah. Question. Can you . . . tell me about Bacon Time?"

Stupid, I know. But maybe it would've given Karen a small glimpse of what she was in the process of leaving behind. Maybe she would have had second thoughts. I didn't say it, though. Instead I told him probably the biggest lie I've ever told anyone in my life. "No," I said. "We're fine."

2

That was a year ago.

Two thousand fourteen. The year of the Great Applebee's Massacre.

It seems longer than that, like a decade at least. Long enough for a lot of things in my life to change. For starters, I live in New York City now. That's something I never thought I'd say. Exactly how that came to be true is a long story, one I'll get to, probably. But for now, I prefer to focus on what's happening at this exact moment.

I'm in a bar. It's a place called Jerome's near my apartment, and I'm wearing the nicest shirt that I own. I'm wearing this shirt because I am currently on a blind date. Although, technically, I'm not sure I'm allowed to say that, since the girl hasn't shown up. And because the world has this uncanny knack for kicking people while they're down, every forty-five seconds or so someone asks me if the bar stool next to me is taken.

"I'm waiting for someone," I say.

The first few times I said this, people seemed to believe me. They nodded and moved along. However, they've started growing increasingly skeptical. In their defense, I've been saying this for more than an hour.

"Here you go, man."

It's the bartender. He slides a new drink in front of me. Short of a tail or maybe horns, it's probably the last thing I need.

"Maybe she's caught in traffic," he says. "The subway could be messed up, too. That happens all the time." He walks away, off to pour some shots. There wasn't a ton of conviction in his voice, but I appreciate the effort. I take a sip of my new drink, which is painfully strong. I'm a bartender, too, at a place a few blocks over called the Underground. In the bartending business, we call this a "sympathy pour."

The subway is a possibility, I guess, along with any number of traffic-related Armageddons that can happen here. However, what's equally possible is that she arrived, took one look at me sitting here, and bolted. *I can talk to this guy for the next few hours,* she could very well have thought. *Or I can go home and put on some Crest Whitestrips and watch* The Bachelorette.

"The worst part is, I didn't even *want* to go on a stupid blind date!"

I'm pretty sure I meant to say this to myself—a soliloquy or maybe an inner monologue. But it ended up being more of an announcement, like something you might shout at a crowd of ill-behaved toddlers, and now everyone at the bar is looking at me. "Sorry," I say. "But it's true."

The bartender reappears. "You good, man?" he says. "Everything all right?"

I recognize his tone—it's the one bartenders use when someone is on the verge of being stupid. I could point out that I'm not the one who's been pouring me drinks strong enough to send a DeLorean back in time. Instead I say, "Can I ask you something?"

He glances over at some guys holding twenties at the other end of the bar. "Yeah, man," he says. "Shoot."

"Objectively speaking—and I want you to be totally honest with me here, OK?"

"All righty."

"If you were a woman . . . Would you sleep with me?"

He laughs, which is borderline hurtful, and then, just like that, my drink is gone, replaced with a cup of coffee. There's a sweaty little creamer beside it and everything. Professionally speaking, it's impressive.

I watch the mirror across from me for a while, and in the reflection I see that the place has filled up. People are laughing. Groups are mingling. People are meeting, looking interested and interesting. People are wearing shirts that are way nicer than mine, if I'm being totally honest with myself. I picked this place because it seemed fun—cool, trendy, but not too trendy. I thought maybe she'd like it, which is funny, because I have no idea who she is or what she likes. In fact, it dawns on me that I can't even remember her name.

"Is this seat taken?"

I turn, and it's a guy. He's good-looking. He's wearing a black suit jacket with jeans, which makes it tough not to hate him a little because it's a look I could never pull off. I almost tell him that it is—thank you very much, for Christ's sake—but I notice that he's with a girl. She's in a nice dress and she's pretty, and I'm not prepared yet to be the type of person who snaps at innocent, perfectly pleasant-seeming people in bars.

For a while now, I've had to keep reminding myself that I'm a nice person. Like, nice-nice. Midwestern nice. Half the people who signed my high school yearbook told me so—it's documented. A few of them even mentioned that I should never change, never ever. I once helped a blind lady walk across a grocery store parking lot in the rain. I used to run 5Ks on Saturday mornings to fight cancer and juvenile diabetes and all of that horrible shit.

"No, not anymore," I say. "All yours, man."

He smiles and thanks me because it's the last seat in the whole place. He tells his date to sit, and when she does, she's right next to me, and I see that she's not his date or even his girlfriend but his fiancée. Her ring catches the light. A princess cut, not terribly big, but just right for her small hand. Cut, color, clarity, carat. The four Cs of engagement ring shopping. For some reason, that all stuck with me.

"Is this good?" the guy asks the girl. He's eager, happy to be making her happy.

"Yeah, yeah it's great, babe," she says. They kiss, but when their lips meet, she's looking at the list of wines written on the chalkboard above the bar, and I wonder if this is a sign that she will eventually fall out of love with him.

When she looks at me and smiles, I'm startled. "Is that your phone?" she says.

"Excuse me?"

"Your phone? That. It's . . . ringing. Well, vibrating."

She's right.

My iPhone is buzzing away on the bar top. I forgot it was even there. Maybe it's my blind date. Maybe she's calling to tell me about the traffic or the subway or the mugging or the locusts or the zombies or whatever else has happened. But that's impossible, because she doesn't even have my number. My screen is cracked and a little damp. My phone buzzes one last time and says "Missed Call."

"Shit," I say.

The girl who will almost certainly hurt the poor, unsuspecting bastard in the cool jacket someday looks concerned for me.

"It's my mother," I say, as if that explains everything.

It's barely after 11:00 p.m., early by New York standards, so the street is busy.

I'm still not used to living here. I'm not used to the crowds and the constant noise and the weird hours. I'm not sure exactly what it feels like, but it doesn't feel like home—more like a strange, wildly expensive sleepaway camp for pseudoadults. I step across the street and am nearly run down by a pack of skinny men on bicycles.

"Heads up, bro!" one of them shouts. I hop back onto the sidewalk. They pass in shimmering skin-tight Lycra suits.

My phone makes its voice mail sound. There's no need to listen, though. I know why she's calling, which is why I'm taking my time calling her back. I lean against a pole and watch the city. A line of girls walks by on the other side of the street. They're in heels and dresses, laughing on their way to the subway. God bless their optimism.

When I finally hit "Nancy" on my screen, I hear my name from halfway across the country. "Andy."

"Hey, Mom."

She starts to say something, but stops. "Where are you? It's loud."

"Outside. This is what outside sounds like here." I look at the bar across the street, the one I just left. A few more people wander in.

"It's Grandpa," she says. "It's time."

Even when something is inevitable, you still feel it, and for a while, I don't say anything.

"Are you still there?" she says. "Andy?"

"Are they sure?" I say. "Is there anything . . . they can do?"

"No. There's nothing they can *do*. That's not how this works. You know that."

"Oh," I say. My grandpa has been sick for a long time, so long, in fact, that I struggle briefly to think of a time when he was totally healthy.

"He asked about you. I told him you're coming. He's in and out of it, but he wants to see you. I've got you on an 11:50 a.m. flight tomorrow out of LaGuardia. I'll text you the details. You have a layover in

Chicago. From the way you sound right now, it's probably good I didn't put you on the 8:00 a.m."

"Mom, I'm fine."

"Anyway," she says. "Your brother's picking you up. He has all the information he needs."

"I don't know, Mom," I say.

"What do you mean you don't know? There's nothing to know. It's all been arranged. You just have to get to the airport."

"I don't know if I'm ready to come back yet," I say.

My mother is the type of woman who's prepared for things—a no-nonsense type of woman, a take-no-prisoners type of woman, et cetera. She takes a long breath, gathering herself. "Andrew. Your grandpa is about to die. *My father* is about to die, and he wants to see you. You're not a teenager. You're a thirty-one-year-old man. You're getting on that plane, and you're coming back to Omaha. Do you understand me?"

I'm a kid again—a skinny teenager with bad skin and an enormous Adam's apple—totally powerless. "I'll think about it."

"You'll think about it? Your plane takes off in . . . twelve hours. There is no thinking."

"Just . . . I'll call you, OK."

"So help me God, Andy, if you're not on—"

I slide my phone into my back pocket and wish I'd actually said the word *good-bye*. It would have felt much less like I was hanging up on my mother. And now I'm thinking about my grandpa laughing. It was years ago, over Thanksgiving break. My brother and I were watching *Austin Powers* in the basement in our pajamas. "What's this stupid thing?" my grandpa asked. He sat down between us on the couch with his coffee mug. "Holy Christ, is that Robert Wagner?" Within minutes, despite himself, he was cackling like a little kid. All three of us were. He spilled some of his coffee on his pants, which made it even funnier.

I step off the curb and back into the street, headed toward my apartment. There's a shape in the corner of my eye. It's blurred out and silent, and it's on top of me in seconds. There's another flash of reflective Lycra, of skinny arms and legs, of a bicycle gliding and then weaving and then striking. *Dude!* And now I'm tumbling to the ground.

3

I'm walking up the four flights of stairs to my apartment.
I've got a half-pint of mint chocolate chip ice cream pressed to
my face. I bought it a few minutes ago, along with some gum, a six-pack
of weird-looking Japanese beer, and a box of Nerds.

The checkout guy at the all-night corner store stared at me as he
rang me up. "My friend," he said. "Your face, it is very much fucked."
His accent was so thick, and so completely unidentifiable, that I wondered if these were the only words of English he knew and this was his
one-in-a-million chance to finally use them.

I tossed back some Nerds. "You should see the other guy," I said.

The bicyclist's bony shoulder hit me square in the side of the face,
at the corner of my left eye, like a punch. He was riding alone, flying
through the night, trying to catch up with his friends. He was really
sorry. I know this because he said so as he rode away, right before he
suggested that I look where the fuck I'm going next time.

When I finally make it up to my floor, there's a cat sitting in front
of my door. His name is Jeter, and he's this mangy, gray-and-black thing
that wanders my building all the time. He stands up and thumps his

tail against the door. Little particles of dander float all around him like a solar system.

"It's really not a good time," I tell him.

He doesn't care, though, because he's a cat. When I open the door, he darts inside and parks himself right in the middle of everything. I pour him a bowl of Cap'n Crunch and he goes crazy for it. Like pretty much every cat I've ever met, Jeter swings back and forth between loving me and trying to murder me, so I never know exactly what I'm getting. He started showing up right when I moved in. His tag just said "Jeter," no number or address.

I open my top drawer and look for a while at my underwear, stacked and wrinkled in a pile. This will be my second attempt at returning to Omaha. Five months ago, I was supposed to go back and sign the divorce papers, but I didn't make it past security. I chickened out and bolted from the line in my socks. Consequently, my divorce was made official at a UPS store on 8th Avenue a week later. A notary public named LaShandra stamped the pages with her special little stamper. "Done and done, baby," she said. And then she gave me a free New York Knicks pen.

I take out my phone and dial Byron. He's my boss at the Underground and, technically speaking, he's the only friend I've made in New York. "Yo!" he shouts over bar noise. "How was the date?"

"Not great," I say. I can't bring myself to yell back.

"What? Shit, wait up! Hold on! Let me go outside!" There's rustling, and a girl shouts about a 7 and 7, and then he says, "Hey, you there? I'm back."

"Why don't you just turn the music down?" I say.

"I tried that once. Didn't work. People ran out of stuff to say to each other, I guess. Anyway, the date. Good? Did you guys make out? First base?"

"She didn't show up."

"What? No. Shit, man."

"Stood up."

"She totally seemed into it. I thought you'd hit it off."

"Why, exactly, did you think that, again?"

He pauses. I can hear New York City behind him. A police siren and some talking. "I don't know. You're both kinda short. You like white-people music." Byron is black—and very big and very tall. He was a linebacker at Rutgers once, and now he manages the Underground and makes broad, sweeping generalizations about Caucasians. He apologizes, like it's his fault that she didn't show, which it is, of course. I didn't want to go on a blind date with his sister's new roommate. Not even a little bit. But he kept badgering me, and you can only tell your boss to shut up so many times before he's bound to get pissed. "How is it over there tonight?" I ask. "Busy?"

"Apparently it's National Bachelorette Party Night. I'm up to my ears in appletinis and dick straws. Summer in the city, yo."

"Sorry I'm missing that," I say.

"Don't be. Save yourself."

I watch Jeter gorge on cereal. His tail sways back and forth. "So listen," I say.

"No," he says. "You're not quitting, are you? Shit. Are you that pissed about the date thing? You can't quit. You're, like, my third-best bartender."

"I'm not quitting. I'm— Wait, third? Really?"

This is a shocking revelation considering how many free drinks I pour myself on a nightly basis—not to mention the fact that I'm unable to do even the simplest math in my head.

"Yeah," he says. "Number three. I like that you're *just* a bartender, you know. Too many wannabe actors and models in this town. Singer-songwriters and shit. You're a bartender. I respect that."

"Actually, I used to sell insurance," I say.

There's a long silence. "You mean, like that little lizard on TV with the English accent?"

"No. Not that kind of . . . It doesn't matter. Anyway, I'm not quit-ting, but I have to go back home for a while."

"Ohio?"

"Omaha."

"Right. Omaha. Why? You kill someone? Gotta lay low until the heat dies down?"

I look at my reflection in my microwave. The foreign guy was right. My face . . . It really is very much fucked. "My grandpa's dying," I say.

Another silence. "Well, now I feel like an asshole."

Jeter is done eating. I know this because he flips the bowl over and hisses at me. I open the door and he takes off. "Sorry," I say. "You're right. I should have led with that. But I have to go. I don't really know how long I'll be. Is that OK?"

"Dude, we're not splitting the atom over here. I got it. We'll cover you. Go home, be with your family. But I do need you to promise me something."

"What?"

"It's simple."

"OK."

"You gotta stay away from the girl."

"What?"

"What what?" Byron says this in his white-person voice, which sounds nothing like me or any other white person in the history of Caucasiankind. "The ex, Andy. *Theeee* ex. She's dead to you. Dead."

"Fine. Deal. I don't want to see her anyway."

"I wanna hear you say it."

"Say what?"

"This is what I want you to say. I want you to say, *Byron, the bitch is dead to me.*" It's his white-person voice again, and I wonder if white people are allowed to be offended by this sort of thing. Seems doubtful.

"I'm not gonna say—"

"Say it. I'm not letting you off this phone 'til you do."

"I could just hang up on you," I say.

"What are we, savages?"

I lean against my sink, which is about three feet from my couch/bed. I'm tired, and half of my face is pulsating, which probably isn't a good sign. Stupid Jeter is outside my door again, scratching like a tiny third world refugee. "Fine," I say. "Byron, the bitch is dead to me."

"Damn right she is. You fuck a fireman behind your husband's back, you go to the top of the dead-to-me list. Bolded and underlined."

"Paramedic, actually," I say, for some dumb reason.

"What? Like a . . . a fucking ambulance driver? I thought you said a fireman."

"No. A . . . a fucking ambulance driver."

He's quiet again. "Well, shit, man. That's even worse."

Not sure why, but he's right, it is worse. I grab a handful of underwear and drop it into my duffle bag. Some T-shirts, too, and a pair of jeans. And then, apropos of God knows what, Byron asks me if there are any black people in Ohio.

"You mean Omaha?"

"Shit. Yeah, that's what I meant. Omaha. Any of my folks out there getting it done in the heartland, eating corn and steak?"

I'm actually used to questions like this. A few weeks ago, a girl from Jersey asked me if we have Bon Jovi in Nebraska.

"I met one once," I say. "He was from Chicago, though . . . just passing through. I'll call you when I get back to New York. Cool?"

"Wait, wait," he says. "What's he like, anyway?"

"Who?" I say. "The black guy? I was ki—"

"No. Your grandpa. You guys close? He a cool guy or what?"

This question cuts through something—something the conversation with my mom didn't. I sit down on my coffee table/kitchen table/nightstand. "He gave me my first beer when I was twelve," I say.

"I'll drink to that," says Byron. "Respect to your pops, cracker."

For a while, after I hang up, I pack more random crap and try to ignore Jeter. I throw in some sneakers, a belt, and more socks. I grab the Cap'n Crunch box off the counter and take a few handfuls. I open one of the Japanese beers. The scratching gets louder, though, so I finally open the door.

"What?" I say. "Jesus. What do you want?"

Jeter is sitting on my shredded welcome mat, staring up at me. He's purring and his eyes are big and dewy and vulnerable, and it actually looks like he's smiling. Beside him, in a tangle of blood-matted fur, sits one expertly decapitated mouse.

"That's sweet," I say.

And then he hisses at me and vanishes into the lonesome night.

4

I'm on a stone bench outside of Eppley Airfield in Omaha.

For the sake of ambiance, I imagined it'd be raining when I got here. It's not, though. It's a beautiful Midwestern summer day—warm, breezy, and sunny.

A guy in a big silver Range Rover is honking his horn in the loading and unloading zone, and I'm watching a YouTube video on my phone. It's grainy and the sound is shitty, but you can see a guy in a tuxedo standing in front of a bunch of people. He says something and then pauses. And then, with no warning whatsoever, he throws up all over the stage.

More honking—three long, loud bursts.

Worst Best Man . . . Ever!!!! is the video's title, and I'm the nine hundred and seventy three thousand four hundred and twelfth person to watch it.

"Hey there, young man."

I look up, and a traffic cop smiles down at me, an old guy with a white mustache and an orange police sash. "I believe that fella over there is trying to get your attention."

I look up and see the man sitting in the Range Rover. He throws up his hands.

"Jesus," I whisper.

"Welcome to Omaha," the cop says.

He's just being friendly, of course. But as my brother inexplicably honks at me three more times, it is, without question, the most ominous thing anyone's ever said to me.

Jim holds up a finger when I get in. "Shut up," he whispers.

He's wearing a Bluetooth earpiece, and when he hits the gas, I very seriously consider grabbing the door handle and flinging myself onto the pavement like a stuntman.

"Oh, come on, George," he says. "You know how short-sighted you sound? You and Judy are in this for the long haul, right? That means not obsessing over the Dow, like some overleveraged day-trading poser." Jim rolls his eyes at me and makes a blah-blah hand puppet. "No, George. You're insulated from that. We're golden."

He goes on like this, and I feel sorry for poor George, whoever he is. I turn around and check out my niece and nephew in the backseat. Bryce is playing a handheld video game and wearing full-on karate gear. "Hey, Uncle Andy," he says.

"Sweet robe, dude." I say this quietly so as not to distract my brother's rampage.

"It's not a robe . . . it's a karate *gi*." I can't remember exactly how old he is, but seven sounds about right. "It gives me one hundred percent mobility for my fighting moves."

"That's pretty cool," I say.

"That's what I've been saying," Jim says. He gesticulates with both hands, so the car is briefly steering itself. "Let's ride the wave. Gas prices are down, interest rates are low. Everyone wins."

"Your dad's really getting after it, huh?" I say.

"Yeah. That's his butt-kicking voice. He uses it when he kicks butt."

"I recognize it."

"What happened to your face?" he asks.

"A ninja got me," I say. "I didn't have one of those robes—my mobility was compromised."

"Gi," he says. "Karate gi."

"Exactly."

There's a little girl in the seat next to him with frizzy blonde hair, and she's staring at me, wild-eyed. She was an infant when I left town, so she has no idea who I am. "Hey, Emma," I say.

Her eyes go even wider. There's a Cheerio stuck to the side of her face, and she's clutching a Dora the Explorer doll. "Blare," she says.

Bryce sighs. "She's terrible at talking. She just says *blarg* and *bling* and junk like that. It's superannoying."

Emma takes the Cheerio off her face and puts it in her mouth. After a few good chews, she pulls it out and offers it to me in a glob.

"No, thanks," I say. "You should eat it."

Bryce pauses his game and gives me a long assessing look. "Uncle Andy," he says. "Are you drunk?"

"Am I what?"

"Drunk? Like . . . *wasted*?"

"Do you even know what that means?"

"Uh, yeaaaaahhhhh," he says. "Dad bet Mom you'd be drunk when we picked you up."

"Seriously?" I say.

"Seeeeriiiiiaaaa!" shouts Emma. She wants in on this, too.

"Yep. Twenty bucks. I just got *Urban Death Fight III* for my PS2, and that cost thirty-five dollars. That's more than twenty."

I look at Jim, who's still quoting lines from *Wall Street*. "And there's no way we're chasing after some stupid IPO again," he says. "Diversity. That's the play. Less exposure, slow and steady."

"Tell him to buy low and sell high," I say, which he totally ignores.

"So, are you?" Bryce says.

"Am I what?"

"Drunk?"

"Oh, right." I tell him no, which is only partially true, but I like the idea of my brother being out twenty bucks. Emma has even more Cheerios on her face now, four by my count. She removes and eats each one systematically while continuing to stare at me.

"What about crazy?" Bryce says. "Are you still crazy? You know, from your *breakdown*?"

"Did your dad say that, too?"

He nods. "He said you went off the reservation. Did you live on a reservation, like with Indians?"

Jim's just sitting there in his suit, weaving through traffic, yammering away, and I imagine seizing the wheel and crashing us all into a Taco Bell. "I'm all better now, Bryce," I say. "Perfectly sane. Nothing to worry about."

Bryce accepts this and goes back to his very violent-sounding video game. Up ahead, Omaha's small skyline appears. It looks like someone took a sliver of New York City and airbrushed it.

When Jim is finally done emasculating George, he touches his ear and slaps me on the thigh. We're not huggers, the Brothers Carter. Whenever we try, it turns into one of those embarrassing hug-handshake hybrids that make white people look so stupid, so we usually just resort to hitting. "What's up, NYC?" he says.

"New car?" I say.

He rubs the steering wheel. "Few months now. Traded up."

"White-collar crime is still paying well, then?"

He smiles. "I'd be offended if I thought you had any idea what that even means. How's the big city treating you?"

One of the odd consequences of spending so much time alone in the last year is that I've started thinking in movie montages. So, in lieu of answering Jim's question, I splice a few New York scenes together in my head. There's me being yelled at by a homeless lady who looks kind of like Madonna. There's me screaming when I find a rat the size of a Muppet in the dumpster outside of my building. There's the guitarist from a mariachi band falling on me in the subway. There's Jeter leaping out of the shadows and slashing my Achilles tendon. And finally, there's me, shamefully masturbating to one of the Victoria's Secret catalogs that keep arriving in my mailbox for the former tenant.

"I saw Liam Neeson the other day," I say.

"Oh, yeah? Where?"

"Rite Aid. He was buying Greek yogurt."

"Well, sounds like the move was worth it, then."

"I killed Zeus, Dad," says Bryce.

"Right on, buddy. How?"

"Pulled his spine out and then beat him with it."

"Yeah you did!"

We turn onto Dodge Street, and Jim punches it around a minivan with Iowa plates. The Range Rover sounds like a speedboat.

"Dad, Uncle Andy says he's not drunk," says Bryce.

Jim lifts his eyebrows. "That's interesting, Brycie. Then maybe you should ask your Uncle Andy why he smells like the floor of a Mexican Hooters."

Bryce *doesn't* ask me this, but I answer anyway. "Little airplane bottles of tequila, Bryce," I say. "Best part of flying. Drinking is awesome. Tell your friends."

"OK," he says.

"Correction, Bryce," says Jim. "It's awesome until you cash in your 401(k) and move to the most expensive city in America to become the world's least charismatic bartender."

I'm pretty sure we lost Bryce somewhere around 401(k). Emma is entranced, though, watching us. She looks just like my brother—fair skin and blue eyes, tall. Aside from me, my whole family basically looks like that. In all our family portraits growing up, I looked like a short, half-Jewish kid being held captive by a family of Vikings.

"So, the shiner?" Jim says. "You gonna tell me what that's about?"

"First rule of Fight Club," I say.

He smiles. "I kinda like it, actually. The whole look. Black eye, messy hair, dressed like an eighth-grade alcoholic. You're doing us proud, Andy."

Sometime in the last forty-five seconds, Emma has passed out cold. Her head lolls back and forth with the motion of the car. Jim turns the stereo on, and we slip into cool, brotherly silence for a while and listen to '80s music on satellite radio. In the time it takes to get through "Hungry Like the Wolf" and "Never Gonna Give You Up," we're out of the city and into the suburbs. We cross 72nd Street, and then 90th, near where Jim and I grew up. Bryce plays his game, and Emma murmurs a few half words. And then I see an enormous picture of our mother's head rolling along beside us.

"What the fuck?" I say.

Jim swerves. "Jesus . . . what?"

"Dad! Uncle Andy said f-u-c—"

"Uck!" shouts Emma, wide awake.

"Dad! Did you hear what—"

"Your Uncle Andy's a degenerate, Bryce. Don't listen to him." He leans into me. "Hey, Scorsese, you can't talk like that in front of kids."

"The f-word is the worst word you can say," says Bryce.

"Uck!" says Emma. She seems to be enjoying herself.

"Great," says Jim.

"Sorry, but are you not seeing . . . this?" I point to our mother's head, which is plastered to the side of a bus. "Dr. Nancy Knows. Always Right. Always Right. Weekdays."

"Yeah, I probably should've warned you about that. I hardly even notice them anymore. They're all over town. The station's finally putting some money behind her."

"Always right, always right?" I say.

"That's her tagline."

"She has a tagline?"

"Yes, sir. Bus signs. Newspaper ads. Billboards. Bumper stickers. Oh, and urinal pads. Found that out the hard way. I'd avoid the restroom at The Cheesecake Factory if I were you."

"Jesus," I say.

"Dad, Uncle Andy sa—"

"Hush it, Bryce," says Jim

"Really?" I say. "We can't say *Jesus*?"

He shrugs. "Gina runs a tight ship."

We roll to a stop at a red light and idle directly beside our mom's head for a while. I roll the window down and get a good look. "Why is she so . . . blonde?"

"That's also new. Makeover. They got her a trainer, too. It's a little jarring at first, but you'll get used to it. Think of it as Mom 2.0."

I wonder what people who aren't allowed to swear say when they see five-foot-tall cutouts of their mother's head on the side of public transportation. The light turns green. We go straight and the bus goes right. The children wave good-bye to their grandmother.

We drive farther and farther west. Eventually, Jim makes a show of checking his watch. "You know, speaking of Nancy," he says. "Hey kids, who wants to listen to Gam-Gam on the radio?"

Bryce says yes, and then Emma says a word that might mean yes, and I say a word that's less of a word and more of a groan. "Come on, Jim. Maybe let me get settled before—"

"Seriously, man," he says. "Her ratings are up big-time. Syndication is up, too. Like ten new markets picked her up last month. Apparently, Fox is in the mix now. Like, *the* Fox. The big one."

"Fox?" I say. "News?"

Jim mouths *fuck yeah* and hits the "AM/FM" button, cutting "Jessie's Girl" right in the middle of the chorus. There's a quick hit of static, and then Nancy's voice fills the car.

". . . on't misunderstand me. I've said this before. Let me reiterate. I'm not saying gay people are bad people. This isn't about that. What this is about is a tiny minority of people getting to turn things completely upside down for the rest of us. That's just not right—plain and simple. This is how civilized society has been operating for thousands of years. One man, one woman, the true definition of marriage. And you know who's going to agree with me on this? The Supreme Court, that's who. Don't let the liberal media lovefest fool you. Mark my words. Later this month, when the justices get behind closed doors and start hashing this thing out, and when they look at the letter of the law and what this country stands for, they're going to come down on our side. The right side. The side of history. Sorry, liberals. Not this time."

We hear a low chime and a burst of the same theme music she's had since I was in high school. Jim is laughing. "Classic," he says.

"This is Nancy Knows . . . always right, always right . . . and back after this."

"Jim," I say. "Do you think we're too old to be scarred by our parents?"

He actually seems to be giving this some thought. But then he tells me to shut up again. His Bluetooth is ringing.

5

We turn into a big, sprawling neighborhood called Prairie West Village. We take a left turn, then a right, and then we wind around for a while. The farther we go, the bigger the houses get. Each one is slightly more elaborate than the last.

"This is their neighborhood?" I say. "This is where they live?"

Jim thinks this is funny. A giant poodle watches us from the middle of an enormous yard as we roll past. "Told you her ratings were up."

Two roundabouts and a little bridge later, Jim turns into a long driveway, stopping at a big brick mailbox. He puts the car in park, and for a while we just stare. A few months after I left town, my dad retired from his accounting job, my mom renewed her contract at the station, and they moved here.

"Seriously?" I say.

"Home sweet home."

My mom sent me pictures when they moved in, but they didn't do the place justice. It's huge—two stories, a three-car garage, an enormous green yard. And in the corner of the driveway sits one very long, very beige car. "Is that Grandpa's Caddie?" I say.

"Yep," he says. "They've had it since Grandpa went to hospice."

I step down out of the Range Rover and onto the driveway. I've hardly got both feet on the ground before a golf cart comes to a screeching halt in the middle of the street behind us. The guy behind the wheel is about our dad's age. He pulls a pair of sunglasses down and glares at me.

"Afternoon, gentlemen," the guy says.

"Oh, jeez," says Jim.

"Music's a little loud, don't you think? This is a residential neighborhood."

Jim rolls his eyes. "Oh, relax, Don," he says. He reaches for the volume knob. But instead of turning it down, he actually turns it up. It'd be a pretty rebellious little statement if the song playing were anything other than "The Safety Dance" by Men Without Hats.

"Consider this a warning," the guy says, and then he speeds off. There's a decal on the back of the cart: "Prairie West Security." When he's gone, I pull my duffle bag out of the front seat.

"Did I just hallucinate that?" I say.

"Unfortunately, no," says Jim. "That's Don."

"Don?"

"Officer D-o-u-c-h-e-b—"

"I know what that spells, Dad," says Bryce.

My brother sighs. "Play your game, Bryce," he says. "Neighborhood security guard. Total DB." He puts the car in reverse and says good-bye, which seems a little abrupt.

"Wait, you're not coming in?" I say.

"No. I gotta get Bryce to karate . . . I think. Bryce, it's karate, right?"

"I'm wearing my karate gi aren't I? Duh."

Jim looks at me, tired. When he notices my duffle bag, he says, "Wait a minute. Is that all you brought?"

"What do you mean?" I say.

"That's all you've got? Didn't you bring a suit?"

"Like . . . a dress suit?"

"No, Andy, a scuba suit. I thought maybe we'd go for a dive this week. Yeah, a dress suit. Forget it. Who am I talking to here? Did you even bring pants?"

I look down at my jeans and wonder what exactly constitutes Jim's legal definition of pants.

"You're gonna need a suit," he says.

I nearly ask why, but then I remember why I'm here, and I feel a wave of encroaching dread.

"Yeah," Jim says. "Grown-ups wear suits to funerals."

I must look helpless standing here in this perfect driveway, because my brother's expression softens and he puts the car back in park. "When was your birthday?" he says. "Like last month or something, right?"

"Yeah. Well, two months ago."

"Did we send you anything? Like a present?"

"Gift certificate to iTunes," I say. "Gina wrote the card. It was nice."

He nods. "Fine. Go get yourself a suit. I've still got an account open over at the Gentleman's Closet. Happy effing birthday."

"Really?" I say.

"Effing is just the same as saying f-u—"

"Bryce!"

He starts rolling up the window, but he stops halfway, and I wonder if he's about to say something nice, like how it's good to see me or how maybe we should go get a beer or play catch or give each other buzz cuts in the backyard or whatever the hell it is that brothers do. "Oh, yeah," he says. "The suit . . . Get gray or black. Something legit. Otherwise you're gonna look like an idiot."

As the Range Rover backs out, Emma waves at me. And then she presses Dora the Explorer against the window, offering it to me, I think, like she did with her chewed-up Cheerio. It's a sweet gesture—a little girl offering me her toy. All things considered, though, it's probably a bad sign that even a toddler can tell that I'm in way over my head.

6

For a while, I stand looking in the window of my grandpa's Cadillac. The Caddie. That's what Jim and I have always called it. He got it when we were kids. It looked big back then, and it still does, like something that should be floating down the Missouri River.

I check the door, and it's open. The leather seats are wrinkled, the dash has a faint crack, and it smells like the stuff my grandpa puts in his hair to make it look shiny.

He let me drive it once when I was thirteen. He took me to the enormous parking lot at the Nebraska Furniture Mart on a Sunday morning, and I drove in long, slow circles. "Look at you, kid," he said. "You're a certified natural."

Eventually, I head up to the house. I climb the steps to the porch and stop at a welcome mat that I've never seen before. "The Carters," it says, and I find myself asking an odd question. I say it aloud, to no one, which just makes it odder.

"Do I knock?"

When I don't immediately have an answer, I set my bag down and step out into the yard. There's a birdbath and an old antique bench out there next to some very pretty flowers beside a red-white-and-blue political sign. "Protect Marriage," it says.

The lawn is freshly mowed, like an outfield at a baseball stadium. It's so perfect, in fact, that I see something out of place lying in it. I wade out there, my sneakers sinking into the plush grass, and I find two Ken Dolls. They're in tuxedos, facedown, and their hands have been glued together. They smile at me blandly.

Up the street, Don—or Officer D-o-u-c-h-e-b-a-g—is on the move again. He eyes me from two blocks away. For some reason, my immediate reaction is to wave. He pretends not to see me, though, and then disappears into a cul-de-sac.

And then I hear something.

I'm not sure what it is, but it's loud, like screaming. I toss Ken and Ken up onto the driveway and start following the noise. I step down a stone walkway and around the side of the house. There are more flowers back here, tons of them in big, bright bursts of color, and the noise gets louder. When I make it to the back of the house, I find the source. It's the biggest bird feeder I've ever seen—three, actually, woven together like a bird skyscraper. There are no birds on it, though. They're all in the surrounding trees, screeching their bird asses off, because a single rogue squirrel the size of a lapdog is dangling from the feeder, gorging himself.

Cardinals swoop, and a few brave sparrows dive. Other birds take their turns, too, attacking, but the squirrel ignores them. He actually seems to be enjoying himself. And then there's a soft pop. The sound echoes off the side of the house, and a hiss follows it. And then the squirrel explodes.

It happens that suddenly. There's a violent red burst, like a water balloon breaking. Birds launch in every direction, and the little animal's body hangs in suspended animation before splattering into the grass.

"Shit!" I say.

"Gotcha, you bastard!"

There's a man hanging from the second-story window. He's tan with a full beard, and he's waving a gun around the yard like the Rock. This man is my father. He wheels, wide eyed, when he sees me, and I throw my hands in the air. "Dad!" I say. "Shit! It's me."

He squints. "Andy?" he says.

"Yeah."

"How was your flight?" He asks me this smiling, as if none of what I've just witnessed requires any sort of explanation.

"Pretty good," I yell. "But maybe you could not point that at me?"

He looks at the rifle in his hands and aims it out toward a big white gazebo in the yard. The mutilated squirrel is lying still in the grass. A gust of wind blows, and its tail flutters.

"You changed your hair," he says. "It's longer. I like it."

"You grew a beard," I say. "And you totally just wasted that squirrel."

"They've been stealing the bird food," he says. "I read about this on the Internet. Supposedly they hate these things. If you hit them enough times, they're supposed to . . . Oh, crap. Hold on a second."

Maybe I'm still partially drunk, or maybe I have altitude poisoning, because, somehow, the squirrel is coming back to life in the yard. It rolls over, covered in blood, and starts running like hell.

"Not so fast!" He actually says this, my dad, a retired accountant. Bullets fly and red explodes. Too much red, actually. That's because my dad isn't shooting bullets. He's shooting paintballs. The squirrel jumps onto a tree and scurries straight up. When the shooting stops, everything goes still. The yard looks like the opening scene of *Saving Private Ryan*.

"Did I get him?" he asks.

Hidden up there behind some branches sits one glaring squirrel. "I don't know," I say. "He looks pretty pissed, though."

"Good."

I see now that there are more of them in the tree. There's a whole team of them up there hiding. One squirrel is wearing a yellow Zorro mask. Two others stand stock-still: one green, the other disco-ball silver. Three others have matching gold-covered bellies. Together they look like a creepy family of angry Christmas ornaments.

"So, retirement's good, then?" I say.

"No complaints."

The birds have started returning to their food. We watch them, swooping and squabbling. There's a hot tub back here, and a brand-new grill. Aside from all the splattered paint, it's quite lovely.

"It's just us for dinner," my dad says. "Your mom's got a thing tonight." He pulls the gun back in through the window and strokes his new beard. And just like that, we've run out of things to say. My flight was fine. My hair is slightly longer. He's grown a beard. My mother has a thing.

"So," he says. "You want a drink?"

And the answer is yes. A million times yes.

7

Have you ever stopped and asked yourself, "Where's the worst possible place I could be right now?"

It's 11:36 p.m. (central standard time), and that's exactly where I am.

Here's how the night went. My dad and I grilled steaks and drank Coors Lights from cans like men. While our food hissed on the grill, we took turns shooting at squirrels. I was conflicted about this at first. I'm not really a shooter of animals—with paintballs or otherwise. Turns out I'm a terrible, terrible shot, though, so it didn't really matter. Around ten o'clock, my dad excused himself to bed. As I listened to him thud his way up the stairs in his socks, I was very much aware of the fact that I was alone. I found some M&M's in a cupboard. I looked at pictures of Jim and me on the walls. I opened the fridge and stared at Nancy's Weight Watchers meals stacked there like Tetris pieces. Then I saw the keys to the Caddie in a change dish in the kitchen. I told myself I was just going to Dairy Queen.

But I was lying. Well, half lying.

It's 11:38 p.m. now, and I'm sitting in a cushy new lawn chair drinking a grape Mr. Misty float in Karen's backyard. My former backyard. *Our* former backyard. The worst place I could possibly be.

The light from the TV is flickering in the bedroom, all soft blues and greens. I imagine climbing into bed next to her. Her hair is back, and her moisturizer smells like apricots. Her feet are freezing. The end of another day of perfectly reasonable Midwestern happiness.

I should call Byron. I should tell him where I am and have him yell at me.

Maybe they're reading—Karen and *him*—the two of them in our old bed. Or maybe they're catching up on their DVR. Or maybe she's on top of him, riding him slowly, biting her lower lip and thinking about how much better he is at sex than I was.

His name is Tyler, by the way. Tyler Sullivan. The fucking ambulance driver.

It's a cruel fact that if your wife cheats on you, the guy will have a name like Tyler. Something cool—something your parents never would have had the guts to name you.

The funny thing is, as much as it sucks thinking about Tyler Sullivan watching my old TV or fucking my wife, what's somehow worse is that the house has never looked better. He repainted it. The gutters are all new—the rotting shutters replaced. He resodded the yard and landscaped with flowers and bought all this classy lawn furniture. A garden gnome in a Nebraska football jersey is looking at me.

The bedroom window is open just a crack, and through it I can hear laughter. It stops, and then it starts again. It's not really laughter, though. It's *Friends*.

This is Karen's nightly routine. She falls asleep to *Friends* reruns on basic cable. I close my eyes and listen. The words are muffled, so it's just voices. Chandler's, then Phoebe's, then Monica's, then a big laugh. I think about hundreds and hundreds of nights lying beside her, me in boxers, her in sweatpants.

Jesus. Fucking. Christ.

I miss her.

"Hey!"

I open my eyes, and he's standing at the window. Tyler.

"Who's out there?"

He yanks the window open wider and sticks his head out, all square-jawed and broad-shouldered. I'm hidden in the shadows of my old house, motionless. There's canned laughter behind him, and he's not wearing a shirt, of course. Fuck him for that, for not wearing a shirt. Fuck him for protecting the house he stole from me and for trimming his chest hair. Fuck him for this creepy Nebraska garden gnome and for making everything look so much nicer than it was before and for erasing me from existence with a new coat of weather-resistant paint and some mulch.

I stand up and step forward into the moonlight, and for three unbroken seconds Tyler and I stare at each other. My hands are shaking. He takes a breath, like he might yell at me, but then he doesn't. Instead he just shakes his head.

The melted remains of my Mr. Misty float are airborne before I even realize that I've thrown them, and now I'm just an observer, watching the extralarge plastic cup tumble through time and space. When it finally hits the siding, it's louder than I thought it'd be.

"Hey! Jesus Christ!"

And then I kick the stupid lawn gnome. Its body stays anchored in the grass, but its smiling head pops clean off and sails into the night. I don't hear it land, though. A dog barks from across the street, and Tyler swears some more. Maybe he's still up in the window, or maybe he's coming after me. I don't know because I am running away.

8

"Turn left onto Meadow Lane Park Road."

It's Siri on my iPhone, which is helpful, because I have no idea where I am. It's hard not to detect the judgment in her terse robot-lady voice, though, like she's been programmed to make me feel like an even bigger dipshit than I already do.

Have you been drinking, Andy?

I'm fine, Siri.

You don't seem fine, Andy. Would you like me to search for the definition of fine? Or maybe the definition of psycho instead. There it is. Psycho is defined as a person who sits quietly outside of homes that aren't his anymore and then—

Siri!

I'm not sure how I wanted all that to go down, exactly, but I definitely didn't want it to go down like that. I'd look, I'd take it all in, and then I'd drive away. Simple. Because, as crazy as it sounds, I needed to see it. I needed to see everything—the house, Tyler's SUV in the driveway with its shiny wheels, the home improvements, and the new grass. I needed to see her new life. It's like slowing down to stare at a car accident or picking at a bug bite until it looks like a stab wound. You just have to do it.

Siri guides me through a few more turns, and as I pull onto my parents' street, things start looking familiar. When she tells me that I am less than a quarter of a mile from my final destination, I see the house in the middle of a dark line of other houses, and I see that it's lit up like an airport runway. The lights in the yard are on. The front porch, too, and the bedroom lights and the floodlights. It's a strange thing to see at this time of night. Even stranger is the blonde woman in the black dress standing at the end of the driveway in heels, screaming at a VW Bug.

It's my mother.

I pull over, running the Caddie up onto the curb.

"I'm calling the police!" she shouts.

Three guys are in the VW, the windows are all rolled down, and they're laughing.

"Go right ahead, Nancy, call 'em up!" one says.

"Be our guest," says another.

"Tell 'em hi for us."

Their voices are over-the-top gay, like characters in a late-night skit. The VW pulls away, and they toss handfuls of glitter out the window. It hangs in the air like swarms of sparkling fireflies. I'm out of the car now, watching this from the curb. My mom kicks her shoes off and starts running after them barefoot. This just makes them laugh more.

"I see your license plate! I'm reporting you to the authorities!"

"Fuck off!" one of them says.

"We're here, we're queer . . ." One of them sings this—shouts it, really—then they all yell, "Deal with it, bitch!" in unison.

My mom winds up like a Little League outfielder and throws something. It looks like a shoe, but it can't be, because it's flapping and fluttering. It's a Ken Doll. It misses its mark and skitters across the pavement in its little tuxedo. The sound of their laughter trails off slowly, and when they're gone, it's quiet.

The yard is a mess. There are more Ken Dolls than I've ever seen—I'd guess a hundred—strewn everywhere. My mom's "Defend Marriage" sign has been mangled and pulled from the ground, replaced with a new sign, written on pink glossy paper. "Always Wrong! Always Wrong!"

Nancy is leaning against the mailbox, tanner and blonder and skinnier than I've ever seen her. She raises her arms up from her sides and they sparkle. Her hair does, too. My mother is glowing in the streetlights. "They glitter-bombed me," she says.

I walk around the Caddie, stepping over a few random rainbow flags and a cutout photograph of the actor Neil Patrick Harris. "They what?" I say.

"They glitter-bombed me. And they put that . . . that *thing* in your father's favorite tree."

I follow her eyes. It looks like a man up there, a naked man, clinging desperately to a branch. It's not, though. It's a sex doll—a life-size, blow-up male sex doll.

I meet her at the mailbox, and she hugs me. And after I get my bearings, I hug her, too. Her hair smells like chemicals.

"Your eye," she says. "Did . . . did someone hit you?"

I've forgotten about the cyclist and the black eye.

"Why is there a sex doll in that tree?"

"Why did somebody hit you? And why is there purple all over your shirt?"

"It's Mr. Misty," I say. "Who were those guys?"

"Why is there Mr. Misty on your shirt?"

The questions come quickly to a halt when we realize that my dad is standing on the front porch. He's in plaid pajamas and a pair of dad sneakers. His hair is sticking up, and he's holding a handful of garbage bags.

"I caught them in the act, Bradley," Nancy says. "They've gone too far this time."

He surveys the yard and then his wife, and then me, and then the Caddie, which I've crash-landed at the foot of the driveway. I left the headlights on. And then four small golf cart tires squeal to a stop.

"Did you see 'em?" It's the security guy from earlier today, Don. He jumps out of his cart. He's in pajama pants, too, and a Prairie West Security windbreaker.

"Just in time again, you idiot," my dad says.

"I missed them?"

"Yeah. Big surprise. How about you turn around and get the hell out of here before I jam that RadioShack siren up your a—"

"Mr. Johnson," my mom says. "I think it'd be best if we all deal with this tomorrow morning, OK?"

"I wanna file my report right away, Nancy. The sooner I get—"

"Report?" My dad hacks this word out like phlegm. "Report . . . Are you kidding me? You're an entirely made-up—"

She stops him with a look, and then she gives Don the same look, and he stands down, too. Apparently my mother is in charge here.

"Fine," says Don. "Suit yourself, if that's how you want to play it."

"Thank you, Mr. Johnson," Nancy says.

The three of us Carters watch him as he goes. The streetlights reflect off his bald spot like a beacon. "Asshole," my dad says.

Wind scatters some of the mess in the yard. A rainbow flag blows across the lawn and sticks to the base of a tree.

"Wait a minute," I say. "Is that guy's name really Don Johnson?"

"Andy," my dad says. "Go in the garage and get the ladder."

The garage is clean and new-looking, and everything is orderly and well kempt. I spot the ladder up on the wall, hanging from some pegs directly behind a vintage motorcycle that I've never seen before. It's red and a little rusty. I touch the handlebars. It smells like gasoline.

The ladder is heavier than I thought it'd be. And in my struggle to take it down without crashing into the bike, I manage to knock into a line of green plastic garbage cans. A lid pops off, clattering to the cement floor, and what I see staring at me from inside is enough to make me nearly drop everything. Eyes. Little blue eyes. A shitload of them. Mouths, too. Smiling mouths. The entire bin is full of Ken Dolls, and they're all wearing tuxedos. There's stuff in the other bins, too. I look inside each one. There are Teletubbies—the gay one, I guess. There are more pictures of famous gay people, a few dildos, some stretched-out, colorful condoms, dirty magazines, and naked photos of men printed onto 8½ x 11 computer paper.

"Oh, Nancy," I say.

I drag the ladder out of the garage and haul it across the driveway. I need an explanation. I need them to tell me why all this has happened and who those guys are. At the front of the house, though, the sight of my parents stops me. They're just standing there next to each other, their arms at their sides, my mom barefoot in an aggressively tight dress and my dad in pajamas that are too small for him. I can see his thin, hairless ankles, exposed and vulnerable.

Something is wrong here. And not just the obvious stuff, like the dildos, the trashed yard, and the fact that my mother is covered in glitter. It's something worse.

There's more wind now, and the sex doll catches a gust. Its plastic arm bobs up and down, and it's smiling, and for a moment it appears to be waving at me.

Welcome to Omaha.

9

The next morning, my dad and I are at a place called New Beginnings.

I imagined some cold, institutional thing, but set against a big wall of trees, it looks like it could be a resort and not an old folks' home. If it weren't for the Starbucks and Bed Bath & Beyond directly across the street, it'd be picturesque, complete with an enormous green space, walking paths, and bocce ball court. Even the sign is classy—a yellow sun over an orange horizon. "New Beginnings: Where Every Day Is Something Special."

We're in the parking lot. The engine is running. We just pulled in, but neither of us has made a move to do anything.

"You want me to come in with you?" he says. "I have a few minutes."

"I'll be OK," I say, which probably isn't true.

I'm nervous to see my grandpa, and I'm moderately hungover, and the toe of my right foot hurts from placekicking that garden gnome.

"Where'd you go last night?" he asks.

"Dairy Queen," I say.

"It was pretty late." He fiddles with his beard. His concern for me is like a fog in the car, this actual tangible thing I can see. He looks less like a mental patient today than he did yesterday when I found him shooting at vermin. He's in gray pants and a crisp button-up shirt—business casual, even in retirement. I can tell he's tired, though. We were up until after two gathering Ken Dolls and fishing pornography out of the shrubs.

"So," I say. "Dad . . . are we maybe gonna talk about last night?"

"What do you want to talk about?"

"Well, late last night, I held a ladder for you while you pulled a sex doll out of a tree. We could start there."

An old woman is making her way across the green space near the bocce ball game. She's in a baby blue robe and slippers even though it's already hot out. We watch her for a moment.

"They hate your mother, Andy," he says. "You know that. Don't be naïve."

"Who does?" He gives me a look, like this is a dumb question, which it is. "Fine," I say. "She's got enemies. But what's with the escalation? We got TP'd every few months when I was in high school. Prank calls sometimes. It was nothing li—"

"They didn't *hate* her when you were in high school. They made fun of her. She was the butt of jokes. But they didn't *hate* her. That's what people do now. They don't disagree, they hate."

"Well, it's not like she's bringing some of it on herself, right?"

He doesn't look at me—his eyes are still on the old lady—and I'm pretty sure I'm a shitty son because I just inadvertently sided with three strange men who called my mother a bitch and vandalized our yard.

"You think the other side doesn't say things like that?" he says. "Watch MSNBC for more than thirty seconds. You'll see what I mean. There's plenty of it to go around."

Across the street, a car honks in the Bed Bath & Beyond parking lot, and I notice a girl standing outside of Starbucks. She's skinny in a black T-shirt and jeans. Her hair is dark, and she has a sleeve of tattoos running up her right arm.

"I should get going," he says. "Are you sure you're going to be OK by yourself?"

I look away from the girl and tell him again that I'll be fine, but it's just dawned on me that I've arrived empty-handed. I have no idea what I should have brought with me, but surely I should have brought something. I don't know what I'm doing, and I don't know how to behave. My dad's parents died when I was little, and Grandma Dot died suddenly watching one of the *CSI*s when I was away at college. This is all completely new to me.

"One thing," he says.

"I don't know what Mom has told you, but there's a chance he's not gonna know who you are."

"Really?"

"And don't be thrown if he asks about Grandma, OK? He gets confused sometimes."

I try to remember the last time I talked to my grandpa. He called me a few months ago. I didn't answer because I was at work. I could barely hear his voice mail.

I really hope I called him back.

"But just remember, whatever happens, it's still just him. Grandpa Henry. You've known him your whole life."

For some reason, I look back at Starbucks. Maybe I'm looking for the girl again, the girl in the T-shirt, I don't know. Either way, she's not there anymore.

"Now get out of here," he says. "I'll pick you up in two hours."

10

A nurse about Nancy's age named Nurse Sandy leads me from the main registration desk down a long corridor to the hospice center. Each door has a suite number and a person's name.

We stop at a sign stenciled on a little card slid through a clear plastic sleeve, temporary. "Suite #5, Henry Allen."

Nurse Sandy gives me the once-over, acknowledging the general state of me. I half expect her to lick her thumb and try to wipe away my black eye. When she opens the door, the smell hits me before anything else, like a slap across the face. It's raw and sick, and it actually stops me there like a force field.

"And here we are," she says, announcing us. "Hello, hello, hello." Her voice is so cheery that she's practically singing. "How we doing, Henry? Someone special is here to see you."

There are a bunch of machines beeping, wires and tubes and blankets and pillows and a big, crooked bed with metal rails. Somewhere in the middle of it all is my grandpa.

"Henry? The Cubbies playing today?" She checks some of the machines and jots something down. There's a baseball game on a flatscreen mounted to the wall. It's not the Cubs, though. It's some college game on ESPN2.

She touches his forehead and lifts a strand of errant white hair off his brow.

"You look older," she says.

I assume she's talking to him, which is pretty rude. But she's actually talking to me. "Um, pardon me?" I say.

"The picture. See?" She nods to a shelf on the wall opposite from the TV. There are bouquets of flowers lined up and a bunch of photos tacked to a corkboard—yellowed Polaroids of kids, some old family shots, a few printouts. I find what she's talking about. Jim and I are wearing hideous sweaters, a Carter Family Christmas Eve tradition.

"When was it taken?" she asks.

"A year and a half ago," I say.

She's surprised, I can tell. She thought I was going to say it'd been much longer than that.

"See the remote on the end table over there?" she says. "It works. Just about any channel you can think of. There's a little fridge against the wall. All the free ginger ale you can drink. Not a bad perk. That button over the bed? The red one? Hit that if you need me. But I think you two will be just fine. Isn't that right, Henry?"

"Can he hear us?" I say.

She smiles and touches my arm. "He's just sleeping, sweetie. He does that a lot. It's all part of it."

When she closes the door behind her, I watch his chest move in time with the loudest of the machines. His room is nice, less like a hospital room and more like a hotel room. There's a couch about the size of a loveseat and also an easy chair. I go over to the window and look at all the flowers. There are random vases with lovely bouquets. The biggest one is full of sunflowers. There's a card attached that says simply, *Love D*. I recognize most of the names on the other cards—old family friends, a few distant relatives, Nancy's radio station.

It's way too dark in here, I decide, suddenly and wholeheartedly. I slide one of the blinds open, and as I do, I nearly knock a coffee mug off the windowsill. I recognize it. "I ♥ NY." I mailed it to him a few weeks after I left Omaha. I thought he'd like it. I wanted him to think I was doing well.

When I turn around to look at him again, his eyes are wide open and I fight back what would have come out as a frightened yell.

"Grandpa?" I say. I say it again, and he just watches me. His eyes blink, and I try to remember what button Nurse Sandy told me to push. But then he holds his hand out, and I take it. And then he holds his other hand out, and I take that, too. His skin is warm, like anyone else's skin, and I'm doing my best not to look at the tube in his throat. He touches the bed beside him, and I sit. He finds a wrinkled legal pad and a pencil, and I watch as he slowly writes.

Can't talk.

"I know," I say. "It's OK."

Glad u r here.

He underlines it for emphasis.

"Me, too," I say, and I feel a lightning bolt of shame about how close I came to not coming. When the cab showed up out in front of my building to take me to LaGuardia yesterday morning, I let it sit there until the driver got pissed and started honking. If he'd just left, I probably wouldn't be here.

How r u?

"Good," I say. It sounds so upbeat the way I say it, like I'm a high school cheerleader. He shrugs. If he had more energy, he'd write "Liar," but he's tired now, so we just sit and look at some of the drawings and cards tacked to the wall above the flowers. Bryce has drawn some baseball players and ninjas and what appears to be an exploding car. Emma has done her best, but her cards are mostly just princess stickers and slashes of crayon on construction paper. There's a "Get Well" balloon swaying next to the air conditioning vent, and a yellow petal detaches from one of the sunflowers and flutters to the ground.

Eventually, I say, "Does it hurt?"

He touches the tube at his throat and nods.

When he dozes off, I watch the game for a few innings. Sometimes he wakes up and watches it with me, but whenever he does he drifts off again after a few pitches. In the eighth inning, a chubby player from the red team launches a home run into the empty left field bleachers. My grandpa reaches for his pencil and starts writing. It takes him forever as he scratches and scratches away. When he finally hands me his pad, he looks exhausted.

Poor kid can't throw a curve to save his life.

11

I'm trying to find my way out of the hospice wing and back to the parking lot.

I'm lost, a little dazed. I walk down a hallway and pass a yoga studio of all things, and now I'm in a big lobby that looks like a ski lodge. A TV on the wall plays *Cocoon*, which seems a little obvious. Some old people in matching burgundy tracksuits play chess. Two ladies are sewing pink sweaters. Conservatively speaking, I'd say it's about 115 degrees in here, so when I finally see the front doors, it's like a prison break.

Two hours with my grandpa felt like eternity, but also like not long enough. I should have come sooner. I should have called him more this past year. I should have watched more Cubs games with him, and I should have been better at being his grandson.

I stop where the sidewalk meets the parking lot and look for my dad. There's no sign of him. I look at my watch and then over at Starbucks and Bed Bath & Beyond. He's not over there, either. And then I hear my name.

"Andy! Andy, over here!"

It's the robe lady, from earlier. She's shuffling toward me from the entrance. For some reason she's waving at me. I turn and look around, just in case there's another Andy standing here in this parking lot. Her hair is a little wild atop her head, and her matching blue slippers are damp and matted. "You made it," she says.

"Hi there," I say.

"Was afraid I missed you. I was waiting for you in the lobby. You must've snuck by. They wanted me to do a yoga class, if you can believe that, but I told them I needed yoga about as much as I needed them to hit me across the head with a frying pan."

I resist the urge to look for the other Andy again.

She tries to press her hair down, but it springs back up, uncontrollable. "You're shorter than I thought you'd be," she says. "They're all so tall, your family. Even your mom. I've never been entirely comfortable around tall women. They make me nervous."

"Are you supposed to be out here, miss?" I ask.

"It's *missus*," she says. "Mrs. DiGiacomo. And of course I'm supposed to be out here. I live here. Your grandpa and I are friends."

"OK. Well, Mrs. DiGiacomo, it's nice to meet you. Are you . . . all right? Do you need me to call som—"

"Nah, don't worry about it," she says. "I'm fine. I have the run of the place, for the most part. Let me ask you something. Do you like *The Young and the Restless*?"

"The what?"

"It's a soap . . . but one of the good ones. I tape it every day on my DVR machine. It's connected to my TV. The nurses helped me set it up. I can tape all my programs and then watch them whenever I want. It's like a VCR, but more organized, like a computer."

"I have one of those, too," I say. I look up toward the entrance. I assume there are people looking for this woman, men in white coats. They're scrambling around as we speak, looking behind curtains and inside closets, cursing at each other.

"Maybe you'd like to watch with me sometime," she says. "I have seven episodes saved. I could explain the characters and stories to you.

It wouldn't take you long to catch up. Everyone is trying to have sex with everyone else. That's the gist. And Victor Newman is suspected of murder. He's very handsome. Probably the most handsome man on the show. Do you want to watch it with me?"

"Like . . . right now?" I say.

"Well, not *right* now. Maybe next time you're here? You could take a little break and join me."

I say yes, because I can't imagine how someone could possibly say anything other than yes in this situation. I don't think it really matters, though, because she's staring over my shoulder now, off into the sky.

"Would you like me to take you back inside, Mrs. DiGiacomo?"

"Hold on," she says. "There was something I was supposed to tell you, and I'm trying to remember." After what feels like ten unbroken minutes of her thinking, she snaps her fingers. "Yes! Of course. Your sister left a note for me to give you."

"My sister?"

"She was just here. Earlier, before you got here. She brought the prettiest sunflowers. I don't really know flowers—I mean, their names and all. But I know sunflowers. Tough to miss those things."

"Oh, right," I say. "I think I saw those. But who are—"

"You look even less like her than you do the rest of them, you know," she says.

"I don't . . . I don't actually have a sister, Mrs. DiGiacomo."

"I don't understand why such a pretty girl like that would want to have all those ta . . . Wait, what'd you say?"

I say it more slowly this time, like I'm talking to a foreigner.

"Of course you do. She gave me this note. See?" She takes a piece of paper out of the pocket of her robe and hands it to me. It's a receipt—venti iced latte and triple espresso, which is a pretty startling amount of caffeine.

"This is from Starbucks," I say.

"Yeah, I know that. I'm not blind. Turn it over."

There's writing there on the other side—blue pen, loopy and smeared, written in a rush.

TONIGHT! 8 pm. Go to the Bookworm on Pacific Street. It's important. It's about your grandpa. But don't tell Mom & Dad.
-D

D?

I look over at Starbucks. A construction worker walks out eating a muffin. "Someone gave this to you?" I ask.

Mrs. DiGiacomo is beginning to lose patience with me. "Have you not been listening to me at all, Andy?" she says. "Did you get into the morphine up there?"

"Was it a gir—"

"Oh, look," she says. "Your ride's here."

My dad is in the parking lot now. He's stopped, giving me an apologetic look through the windshield as he waits for four old people making their way to the bocce ball court like a family of meandering ducks. I jam the receipt into my pocket—*But don't tell Mom & Dad.*

When he pulls up, I tell Mrs. DiGiacomo good-bye. She says she's sure she'll be seeing me around, because she's always here. "And God knows I won't be doing yoga." She smiles and watches me climb into the car.

"You know this lady?" I whisper.

My dad gives her a neighborly little wave.

"Hi, Bradley," she says.

Behind us, stacked in the backseat, sit three enormous bags of birdseed. "Here's some advice," he says. "Don't ever, ever watch *The Young and the Restless* with that woman."

12

The Bookworm is an indie bookstore in Midtown.

It's well lit and airy, a nice little store, and I totally shouldn't be here. I spent most of the afternoon debating whether or not to come. The case against seems solid. An old woman I don't know who was wearing a bathrobe in a parking lot handed me a message she claimed came from my sister who doesn't exist. There are some potential red flags there. However, D, whoever that is, said it's important, and it's about my grandpa. And even though I know that it's stupid and far-fetched, the pathetic glutton for punishment lurking inside of me wonders if it has something to do with Karen.

So, at a quarter to eight, I told my parents something vague, and I hopped in the Caddie. This must be how all those teenage girls get lured into sex trafficking.

"Are you looking for anything special tonight?"

I look up, and the lady in the Shakespeare sweater is smiling at me. Her name tag says "Gayle," and this is the third time she's asked me this question.

"Doing great," I say. "Still."

"You sure?"

She doesn't seem to believe me, which I guess makes sense. After all, I'm an adult male with a black eye standing alone in the Self-Help section reading a book called *Light Your Own Fire: Why Feeling Better Is Up to You.*

"Aces," I say.

She tells me to help myself to some free coffee even though it might be a little cold by now. When she's gone, I look at my watch. It's 8:42 p.m., and I'm clearly here to see no one. I have now been stood up twice this week in two separate time zones. So I read on.

> *Imagine watching the saddest scene of the saddest movie you can think of. A real tearjerker.* Old Yeller. Terms of Endearment. Steel Magnolias. Schindler's List. *Now, imagine watching that scene over and over again—day and night. How do you think that would make you feel? Probably pretty darn sad, right?*
>
> *Well, when you're struggling to move on from something painful, like a divorce or a death in the family, that's exactly what you do.*
>
> *We all have a movie screen in our head, and we run depressing memories, flashbacks, and anecdotes on that screen repeatedly. Double features. Triple features. I call them Feel Sorry Flicks. And until you make an <u>ACTIVE</u> decision to turn those flicks off, they're going to keep playing and playing on a loop. And you're going to keep . . . feeling . . . sad.*

I turn the book over and look at the author's picture. Her name is Janice Perkins, and she's holding a grim-faced little dog.

"I really wouldn't waste my time with that one, if I was you."

I look up again, ready to be fully annoyed with Gayle, but it's not Gayle. It's . . . a girl. A woman. I'm not sure which. I blink.

"It's mostly bullshit," she says. "Emotionally manipulative, overly simplistic, poorly edited, you name it." Her nose is pierced—a little silver stud catches the overhead light—and tattoos peek out from under her pushed-up sleeve. "Starbucks girl?" I say.

"I've been called worse. I'm Daisy. Sorry I'm late."

D. Daisy.

We shake hands. Hers is small, but her grip is weirdly firm, and five seconds pass during which I say absolutely nothing. "I'm An—"

"I know who you are, dummy," she says. "You got my note, huh? Mrs. DiGiacomo . . . coming through in the clutch. I'll be honest, I had my doubts. Oh, by the way, spoiler alert. I'm not your sister."

"That's a relief," I say.

"It's easier letting Mrs. DiGiacomo think I'm part of the family. Less complicated."

She looked young from across the parking lot at New Beginnings, like a teenager, but, up close, I see the creases framing her eyes, the same kind I have, the ones you get when you're at least thirty. The few people here in the bookstore are looking at us. I was invisible a minute ago, but I guess she's made me more interesting. A guy in a Members Only jacket with an unfortunate comb-over watches us from the Arts & Crafts section. He's holding a giant book about Eastern European woodworking.

"You're allowed to talk, you know," she says.

"Do you work at the . . . the home? New Beginnings?"

"They call it a *facility*, actually. *Home* makes it sounds like where you put lunatics. And no, I don't work there. I'm Henry's friend."

"Henry?" I say.

She smiles, kind of. "Your grandpa. It's weird that they have names, right? Grandparents? You never think of them like that, as people with real names. My grandma was named Colleen. She was addicted to keno, but we never talked about it."

"Friends? With my grandpa?"

"Yep. Henry."

"He's never mentioned you before," I say.

"Well, we have a unique relationship. You didn't tell your mom you were coming, did you?"

I say no.

"Good. Snitches get stitches, right?"

"You know my mom?"

"Everyone knows your mom. She's not really a doctor, is she?"

"Sort of," I say. "The same way Dr. Dre is a doctor."

I've heard this question a lot over the years, and this is my practiced response. She kind of smiles again—kind of laughs, too. "Henry told me you were funny."

"He did?"

"Well, not exactly. He said funny *sometimes*. Jim is the hyper-achiever. You're the moody one. That's not a bad thing, by the way. Never trust someone who isn't miserable at least half of the time. That's my motto."

"Why did you ask me here?" I say. I look around the little store. "And why did you ask me . . . *here?*"

"*Here* because reading is fundamental, Andy. And I asked you here because I wanted to meet you."

"Why?"

"Did someone punch you?" she asks.

I touch my face. "I got run over by a bike."

"Drag," she says. She takes a step away and then touches my elbow, giving me a tug. "We should browse," she says. "Maybe, you know, walk around a little. People get suspicious in bookstores if you're not looking at books."

And so that's what we do, the Starbucks girl and me. Honestly, though, I'm too confused by all this to actually look at books, so I really just follow her around while she touches book spines and picks up random paperbacks. She smells a few along the way. She opens them in the middle and gets a quick whiff. She tells me she's a certified smeller of books and that that is probably her best quality. "So It Goes." is tattooed on the inside of her left forearm. The words are puffy and raw-looking. "Read." is tattooed on her opposite wrist. The period makes it look like an order.

"You said it was important," I say.

"What?"

"Your note. You said it was important."

"Well, if I hadn't said that, would you have come?"

"I don't know," I say. "Maybe."

"Definitely is better than maybe."

"Is there something going on with my grandpa?" I say.

"Yeah. Something really terrible. He has cancer."

"Is that a . . . a joke?"

She sighs. We're standing over a table of fanned-out paperbacks. There's a black-and-white photo of the writer Curtis Violet next to a droopy purple flower in a vase. She picks up one of his books, *The Son of Hollywood*, and holds it to her chest. "Have you read him?" she says.

"Curtis Violet? Yeah."

She seems to like this answer. "I'm making my students read this one. I actually haven't read it yet. I know it's been like six years, but I've been scared to. You know, since it's his last one."

"Students? You're a teacher?"

"I'm *kind of* a teacher. I lead a creative writing workshop for adults who wake up one day and decide they want to be writers."

"Do people do that?" I say.

"All the time. Mostly housewives. There's an entire genre of writing now that's empowered women to type out their sex fantasies and publish them on the Internet. If you knew how many euphemisms for *vagina* I endure on a weekly basis, your little heart would break."

I wasn't prepared to hear the word *vagina* this evening. Up front at the register, Gayle, apparently, wasn't, either. She clears her throat and gives us a librarian look. That's the thing about the word *vagina*: it really carries in a quiet place.

"I keep a list of my favorites on a corkboard in my bedroom," she says. "*Tunnel* is getting a lot of play lately. Like *love* tunnel. No idea why. It can get pretty bad. I actually had to put a story down the other night when I came across *dewy, hollowed-out meadow*."

"Whoa," I say.

"I know, right?"

She opens *The Son of Hollywood*, carefully, like she's trying not to crease anything. She leafs through the first few pages and starts to read. And for a moment, it's as if I'm not there at all.

"So," I say. "About my grandp—"

She snaps the book closed. "You have questions," she says.

"Yeah."

"And perhaps I'll answer some of them. But first I want to pay for this." She tells me to grab two coffees and to go sit down while she buys her Curtis Violet book.

There's an old leather sofa at the back of the store, and it feels nice to sit and hold the lukewarm Styrofoam. At the register, Daisy unclips her brown hair and it falls over her shoulder in a messy heap before she sweeps it back up again. I notice the comb-over guy again. He's watching me watch her. "How's it going, man?" I say, but he immediately vanishes behind a shelf of World War II books.

When she's done paying, she joins me at the back of the store. She steps out of a pair of laceless Chuck Taylors and sinks barefoot into the couch next to me. There's a bold star tattooed on the top of one thin foot.

"Fifteen," she says.

"What?"

"That's how many tattoos I have. You looked like you were wondering. It's the first question most people ask me."

"Did they hurt?" I say.

"And that's the second question most people ask me." She holds out her star foot. "This one did. Like a motherfucker. I had to bite a little rubber stick, like a chew toy. Not this one, though." She shows me her wrist. "Just got it. I hardly even feel them anymore. Like kitten bites."

"So it goes," I say. "Vonnegut."

Her eyes go bright, like match flames. "Look at you, professor."

She's a stranger, but I think my face is getting hot anyway. In my defense, it's been a long time since I talked to a girl who wasn't ordering a drink from me.

"There are two types of guys in this world," she says. "Guys who know that 'So It Goes' is a Kurt Vonnegut reference, and guys who I want absolutely nothing to do with. I'm glad you're one of the first ones."

I feel like I've walked into a movie fifteen minutes late. The previews are over, I've missed the first two scenes, and I don't know who the hell anyone is. I take a sip of my coffee, and it tastes very much like free bookstore coffee.

"I have a proposition for you," she says.

"OK."

"You know when you first meet someone? You know how it's all awkward, and you feel self-conscious, and you wonder if you've got something in your teeth, and you don't know what you're supposed to say?"

"Do I have something in my teeth?" I say.

"No. Shut up."

"OK."

"Let's skip it. Just skip over all that awkward stuff."

"Skip it?"

"Yeah. Let's jump ahead and go right to feeling comfortable and being friends."

"I don't think people can just do that," I say.

"Sure they can. People can do whatever they want. I tell my students that. They're always like, 'Would my character *really* do this or *really* do that?' And I'm like, 'Who gives a shit? Just make them do it, you coward. Don't be so passive.' You and I, we're in charge of what we *can* do and what we *can't* do. And we're allowed to immediately be friends if that's what we want to do. Sound good?"

"OK," I say.

"And as long as we're talking about writing, let's discuss your motivation."

"My what?"

"Your motivation. What do you want? Do you want her back?"

This catches me off guard. There is, of course, only one *her* she could be talking about. "Um," I say.

"Do you want to kill the new guy and make it look like a suicide? I assume there's another guy, because—well, there's always another guy, right? You need to answer these questions, Andy. It's important."

"Jesus, who . . . *are* you?" I say.

This turns some more heads. I've said it louder than I meant to, but I probably should have asked this earlier, like maybe sometime around *dewy, hollowed-out meadow*, for example.

She smiles. One of her front teeth is crooked, just barely. "I told you, Andy. I'm Daisy, and I'm friends with Henry. And I teach Vagina Fiction."

"Why didn't you want me to tell my mom and dad I was coming here?"

"Your mother doesn't like me very much."

"Why?"

She bats her eyes. "Do I look like the kinda girl *your* mother would like?"

"Fair point," I say.

"So you're a bartender, right?" she says.

"How do you know that? And how do you know . . . about . . . my ex-wife?"

She doesn't answer. Instead she pulls a silver Hello Kitty flask out of the waistband of her jeans and then proceeds to spike our coffees without comment.

"I don't think that's legal," I say.

"Are you a cop?" she says.

She settles back into the couch, tucking her legs up under herself like a bird.

At the front of the store, a few employees are pushing carts of books and magazines, putting things back where they belong. "Henry was right," she says.

"About what?"

She nods at the book sitting in my lap. *Light Your Own Fire.* I didn't even realize I still had it. There's a drawing on the cover of a big cartoon heart with a Band-Aid over it. "You," she says. "You're a mess."

"I wouldn't say I'm a m—"

"Henry told me everything," she says. "The whole story. The other guy, losing your job, your friend's wedding, the spur-of-the-moment moving-to-New York thing. I know about you, and I know about *her.* I won't say her name. It sucks when people say her name, doesn't it? It's like it physically hurts to hear it. Why does nobody get that?"

"Why is Henry . . . Why is my grandpa—"

"Henry and I talk a lot. Talked. He's worried about you."

A head pokes up from behind a shelf about ten feet away—the guy again. He's taken his Members Only jacket off and he's wearing an X-Men T-shirt.

"That guy keeps looking at you," I whisper.

"He's harmless," she says.

"How do you know?"

"Kenny, you're harmless, right?" She pitches her voice so the guy can hear. "You're not gonna murder me or kidnap me or anything, are you?"

The head vanishes, a man-size whack-a-mole.

"The jig is up, sweetie. Did you really think I wasn't going to see you? You're like seven feet tall."

The guy, Kenny, reveals himself again. He looks ashamed. "Hi, Daisy."

"A hundred yards, right? That's the rule."

"Yeah."

"This is a lot less than a hundred yards. This is, like, three yards."

"I know. Sorry, Daisy. I like your jeans. They're really cool."

"That's sweet, Kenny. But maybe it's time to go, OK?"

He sets a few comic books down on a shelf and slinks away. The door chimes behind him when he's gone, and Daisy and I are now officially the last two customers here.

"Friend of yours?" I say.

"Not a friend, exactly."

"That's ominous."

"People like Kenny find me sometimes. Occupational hazard."

"He doesn't look like a housewife."

"I have a couple of jobs. Gotta eat, right?" And then, without even taking a breath, she asks me how long it's been since I kissed someone.

"Excuse me?" I say.

She just stares at me, picking her chipped toenail polish.

"Seems a little personal, doesn't it?"

"Man," she says. "We've got a lot of work to do on you, huh?"

"Work?"

"It's official . . . You, Andy, are now *my* motivation."

"What does that mean?"

"You've had a tough year," she says. "And I think I can help you."

"Help me what?"

"Come back to life."

"But why would you want to do that? You don't even know me."

"You're right. I don't. But Henry loves you. And he's worried about you. And there's nothing I can do for Henry right now. And that's not easy for me, because he's a very good friend of mine. So I'm going to do this for you. And frankly, there's nothing you can do about it." She hands me her new book and then gives me a pen. "Write your number in this," she says.

"Where? Like, in the book?"

"Don't worry. I'm a smeller of books *and* a marker-upper of books."

I do as I'm told, writing my phone number over Curtis Violet's name, and she writes her number on the title page of *Light Your Own Fire*, which I guess means I'm going to have to buy it now.

"See, and just like that, we're friends," she says. "Besties."

When she stands up, I do, too. She steps into her Chucks and, before I even know what's happening, she's touching me. Her palm rests against my chest, over my heart, warm through my T-shirt.

"This is where it hurts, isn't it?" she says.

I don't say anything, but, of course, she's right. That's exactly where it hurts, like this constant, low-level heart attack that won't stop. She leaves without saying good-bye. The door chimes, and Gayle pulls a little cord that cuts off the "Open" sign. It's 9:15, and the place is now closed. I'm not in New York anymore.

It's full-on nighttime outside now.

I feel wired from the caffeine-and-alcohol combo, and I think about Daisy's hand on my chest.

It does suck when people say Karen's name, even just casually. One of the local newscasters in New York is named Karen. Karen Yau. She's a pretty Chinese-American lady. She looks nothing like Karen, but I don't watch that channel simply because I hate seeing the name at the bottom of the screen.

Karen.

I'm digging in my pocket for the Caddie keys, but then I stop in the middle of the parking lot because something is weird. The car is off, the color is different—sparkly somehow under the streetlights. It's completely covered in glitter.

"What . . . the fuck?" I say.

An engine starts at the other end of the parking lot, and then a VW Bug pulls onto Pacific Street. It's the VW from last night. It runs a light and speeds away.

"It was those guys!"

I turn around, and Kenny from the bookstore is standing next to a dumpster, pointing up the street. "It was them! It wasn't me! It wasn't my fault. Don't tell anyone I was here." And then he runs away, clomping in a frantic zigzag down the street.

There's a Ken Doll on the hood, sitting in a lake of sparkles. He's alone in his tuxedo, vacant and smiling.

13

When I get home, my options are pretty limited.

My mom is watching Fox News in the TV room. I think about joining her, maybe hanging out in there for a while, but then I imagine that going bad quickly. In my experience, Fox News isn't something you can tune out, like a game show or a cable movie you've seen a dozen times. The colors, the moving logos, the giant fonts, the . . . well . . . the things they actually say. It's like the television equivalent of one of those cymbal-banging monkey toys being duct-taped to your forehead. So this is how it'd go. I'd hear something ridiculous, and I'd scoff or make some smart-ass comment, and then it'd be straight downhill from there.

My dad, apparently, has gone to bed, so I can't hang out with him, either.

I raid the cupboards and find some more M&M's and consider curling up in one of the random rooms in this big place and reading a little *Light Your Own Fire*, but that seems like an even slipperier slope than Fox News. I open to the cover page again and see "For a good time, call Daisy." She added cartoon lips next to her phone number to make it even sillier.

With nothing left to do, I head upstairs to the second extra bedroom on the left, which, henceforth, I will be referring to as the Bizarro Room. The reason: in an odd twist of parental eccentricity, my parents have used two of their three extra bedrooms to re-create the rooms my brother and I had when we were teenagers at the old house. The furniture is the same. My twin bed, my old desk, and my bookcase are all there. The walls are the same color, too, light blue, and they've added an edited assortment of my old posters, like the naked baby from the *Nevermind* album cover, the movie poster from *Swingers*, and a panoramic shot of Memorial Stadium in Lincoln. They even brought my *Star Wars* Legos over. The *Millennium Falcon* is intact, just as I left it, its awesomeness on full display by the window. About half of my Lego Ewok Village has been destroyed. The loose contents are in a Ziploc bag beside it. It's like someone has painstakingly built a museum dedicated to the study and analysis of teenage virginity.

I grab my duffle bag off the floor. I didn't unpack last night after the lawn gnome fiasco, so I start pulling things out. I open the closet door, expecting to find it empty, but it's packed with more things. My old flannels from the '90s, hung in a row. My broken-down New Balance running shoes. The archaic CD boom box along with stacks and stacks of CD jewel cases. It's mostly obvious stuff, Nirvana and Pearl Jam, U2 and some Green Day. But there's the Parental Advisory stuff, too. Dre, Snoop, Eazy-E, N.W.A., more rap and hip-hop than is and ever was reasonable for a teenage white kid from the suburbs of Omaha, Nebraska, to own.

And then I see the box on the floor. The one that I forgot I even had. The one that ended up with me, somehow, on that ugly day when Karen and I divided everything up and I drove off with my dad in a U-Haul that was less full than I imagined it would be. It's purple and plastic, about the size of two shoe boxes put together. Karen bought it when we got back from our honeymoon. "Just for stuff," she said. "You know, stuff about us."

There's a sticker label on the lid, and her writing, perfect and cursive. "Andy & Karen."

Fuck. This is gonna be bad.

14

I open my eyes, and then I immediately close them again because my brain and all the things inside of it are wrecked.

I'm not an alcoholic—I don't have the discipline to become one—but, generally speaking, I've been drinking too much since Karen left. Consequently, I have some experience with this feeling, those first few nasty seconds of consciousness when you're hungover. I'm also familiar with what's worse, which is the relentless and rapid formation of memories the morning after of doing something stupid. That's what's happening now.

I saw the goddamn box—"Andy & Karen." And then I made a conscious decision to go back downstairs and get the bottle of Jack Daniel's from my parents' liquor cabinet. It seemed like a really good idea at the time.

I open my eyes again. I'm lying on my side, and the first thing I see is the *Nevermind* baby floating there on my wall. He looks innocent and pure, his whole life ahead of him. He's in his twenties now. Even though that can't possibly be right, it is.

As I begin to drift back to sleep, I wonder what he looks like now as a young adult. I wonder if it ever bothers him that millions and millions of us have seen his tiny penis? Did he go to college? Did he get a degree in business administration like I did or some other dreadful thing? Does he have a cubicle and a five-year plan and pretty decent health coverage?

My career, if that's what you want to call it, is currently on pause.

On a random Tuesday afternoon at around three p.m., I started crying in a staff meeting. That's what finally did me in. It was the beginning of my quote-unquote "breakdown." It wasn't even an important meeting—just one of those recurring weekly things where you sit and listen to your six or seven bosses hash things out while you doodle pictures of Yoda on a legal pad. I don't know why, exactly, but as I sat there that afternoon, I started thinking about Karen. More specifically, I started thinking about a blizzard from a few years ago. Two solid feet of snow. The city shut down. Karen and I couldn't go to work. My office closed. The ad agency where Karen was an account executive closed, too. We did nothing but lie around on the couch in our sweatpants for three days, and it was wonderful.

I wasn't full-on sobbing or anything. I was just sniffling, but then, when everyone was looking at me, my shoulders shook and the air got caught in my throat. My boss, Dale, stopped midsentence. "I don't see the value in throwing good money after—" He sighed and shook his head. "All right, Andy. That's enough."

They referred to it, officially, as a "sabbatical," which sounded like I was being sent off into the woods to find higher meaning. I signed some paperwork, and a lady from HR handed me a cardboard box. I had to watch her struggle to construct it, which took so long that I actually offered to help her. "Let me know if everything fits," she said.

"Andy. Andy, it's time to wake up."

I roll over and find Nancy sitting on the end of my bed and it scares the hell out of me. "Mom! Shit!" I pull the covers up. I'm in boxers, and God only knows what my penis has been doing while I was asleep.

"I knocked, but you . . ." She looks at the bottle of Jack Daniel's on my nightstand. "You were sleeping pretty deeply. One could even suggest that perhaps you were passed out."

"It's not . . . ," I say.

"It's not what?"

"I had a few drinks," I say. I've found with mothers like mine it's often best to go with understatement.

"I'll say."

"I was looking through my old . . . stuff." As I say this, the full destruction of my room comes into focus, like news footage of some devastating storm in Kansas. The contents of the closet are now mostly on the floor, strewn there—everything, from the CDs to the flannels to the "Andy & Karen" box. I notice that there's an N.W.A. poster on the wall now, too, hung crookedly.

"Oh, well, that's a nice touch," Nancy says. "Where did you even find that thing?"

I close my eyes and roll a quick montage from last night. There's me finding the poster on my rampage through the closet. There's me drunkenly unrolling it and saying "Fuck yeah!" There's me standing on a swivel chair trying to hang it up with four mismatched thumbtacks found God knows where. There's me falling onto the floor as the wheels slide out from under me.

"The Most Dangerous Group on Earth" it says across the top.

"I mean, look at this, Andy," she says.

There are pictures of Karen and me on the floor, emptied from the box, and our wedding album is open. Karen is laughing with frosting on her nose, in a dress as expensive as a gently used Hyundai. If Eazy-E were alive today, I suspect he'd think this entire scenario was all pretty wack. And I also suspect he'd have a serious problem with me using the word *wack*.

"This isn't good," she says. "You're not in a good place."

There's a can of Diet Coke next to the Jack Daniel's. I take one tepid sip and clear my throat. "OK," I say. "I'll admit, this might not be my best moment."

"You were drinking last night . . . *alone*. You have a black eye, which you still haven't explained to me. You don't look like you've had a decent meal in a month. You're *wallowing*, Andy. This sort of thing would be charming if you were eighteen. But you're an adult. I mean, you had a 401(k)."

"What is the deal with this family and 401(k)s?"

Outside, an engine fires, and my mother rolls her eyes. "Well, if you can trouble yourself to get up, your father wants you out in the garage. He sent me up here to get you. He needs your help with . . . I don't know . . . Whatever he's doing out there."

"So, Dad bought a motorcycle?" I say.

She bites the inside of her mouth. "Just humor him, OK? He's . . . adjusting."

"His beard is pretty cool," I say.

She looks at me for a moment, lying there, huddled and hungover. She reaches for me, and my first instinct is to pull away, but I'm lying down, so there's nowhere to go. And then she pulls a piece of glitter out of my hair. It's from last night in the bookstore parking lot. She doesn't bother asking about it. She just lets it flutter to the carpet.

"It's clear to me that New York hasn't been good for you. I thought it was a bad idea in the first place. You clearly didn't think it through at all, you just loaded and went. But I held my tongue. There's nothing there for you. You're alone out there."

"I have a cat," I say. "Sort of. And I made a friend. He's black."

"Your little New York experiment is over, Andy," she says. "I think it's time for you to come home."

"Mom, don't do your radio voice, OK? Just talk like a normal person."

"This isn't my—this is how I talk. I don't have a *radio* voice. You should come home. How's that for talking? Home. You need us—your family. You're wallowing in that godforsaken place, bartending . . . with your education? You need to be *here*."

"Here?" I say.

"Not *here*. Not this room. Not this house. Omaha. Maybe you could get your old job back."

I think about my last moments as an insurance salesman. I accidentally left the cardboard box on top of my car as I pulled away. Notebooks and insurance manuals and three-hole punches and pens and coffee mugs scattered across the parking lot. I didn't even bother to stop and pick them up.

"I'm thinking that's not an option," I say.

She sits for a while, thinking. "We have openings at the station," she says.

I laugh, which hurts a bunch of things—head, neck, eyes, face, lower back.

"Well, you need to do *something* different, because what you're doing right now is going exactly nowhere."

I feel like a caller on her show—a caller who's been muted, unable to defend himself. From the wall above us, Eazy-E looks down at me with utter disdain.

Nancy is wearing a gray suit and a bright-blue blouse. It's her work outfit. She looks airbrushed, like she's climbed down out of her bus ad to tell me how disappointing I am.

"You used to wear jeans to work," I say.

She smoothes out her skirt. "That was then. I have a different plan now."

"I'm not used to you like this."

"Like what?"

"The hair. The . . . body. You've lost weight, Mom. Quite a bit."

"You're damn right, I have. I'm working out. I'm eating better. It's called a makeover. It's called taking yourself seriously so others will, too. It's something you could think about trying."

"Why did you need a makeover? You looked fine."

"Because this is what I wanted to look like. I wanted to look different. So I made myself look different—better than just *fine*. If you want to be something, you make a decision, and then you make it happen. It's called personal responsibility."

There's more revving, and then the motorcycle backfires, like gunshots in our driveway.

"Jim told me about Fox News," I say. "Is this what all this is about? The makeover? The . . . blondeness? All the women are blonde there, right? That's, like, their thing? I've read articles about it."

She touches her hair, a nanosecond of self-consciousness. "They . . . have their eye on me. That's true."

"They have their eye on you for what?"

"For starters . . . subject matter expert. Panelist. Recurring guest. Maybe more."

I don't want to grimace, honestly, but I'm pretty sure that's exactly what I'm doing right now, because her lips tighten. "I know how you feel about what I do, Andy. But I am very good at it. I inspire people . . . I motivate them. I believe this country is in great decline. Moral decline. Financial decline. You name it. It *has* been for a long time, and people need to hear what I have to say."

"Radio voice," I say, petulant and childish.

She stands up. "I'm not going to tell you I'm sorry for caring about something. And I'm not going to apologize for being excited about an incredible opportunity. And I'm not going to let you or your fath—" She stops. There's another backfire outside, which is pretty miraculous timing.

"What?" I say. "Dad's not down with this?"

"He doesn't like change," she says. "You know that. He's an accountant." Her heels make little dents in the carpet as she walks away. She steps over an errant picture of Karen and me dancing our first dance. "All I Want Is You," by U2. More pop music irony at its most jagged.

"Go see your father," she says. "And hey, while you're at it . . . maybe put on some pants. You know . . . shoot for the stars."

I put on one of my old flannel shirts, and, of course, it's way too big, which I blame mostly on Eddie Vedder.

Downstairs, I grab a cold Diet Coke and walk outside through the garage. The deflated sex doll from the other night peeks out at me from a garbage can, and I give it a quick jab to the face.

My dad is straddling the red motorcycle in the driveway. He kicks the starter, and the engine erupts in a cloud of smelly gray smoke. He cuts the engine when he sees me. "Nice shorts," he says.

I look down at my boxers. I've opted to forgo pants as a form of protest against Nancy. Unfortunately, though, her car is just now pulling out of the driveway, so I've missed my window. Therefore, I'm just a guy wearing his underwear in a suburban driveway, underwear that I've just now realized has Santa Clauses on it. "I'm making a statement," I say.

"Profound," he says.

"She said you needed my help with . . . something?"

The engine makes a ticking sound, like a bomb. There are two squirrels in the yard watching us. One is the red one from the other day, I think. The other is baby blue.

"Not really," he says. "I just didn't think you should still be in bed."

"Pretty cool bike," I say.

He sets the kickstand and steps off. "Your mom's convinced I'm gonna kill myself on it."

"Seems like a pretty safe bet," I say.

A neighbor lady walks by pushing a stroller and does a double take when she sees me. "Morning," I say, tipping my Diet Coke. My dad shakes his head.

"So, you know how to ride this thing?" I ask.

"Of course I do. For your information, I used to have one. Before you and Jim came along. Seventy-three Honda CB350. Just like this. Same color and everything."

I try to imagine retro versions of my parents. Nancy, pregnant, with flared jeans and feathered hair, telling him it's time for the motorcycle to go. She pats her swollen stomach for emphasis.

"I thought it would take at least a year to track one down. It was going to be my first postretirement project."

"How long did it take?"

"Five minutes," he says. "I Googled it, and there it was, forty miles away. Guy practically gave it to me." He sounds like he'd rather still be looking, and I can see why. I don't know anything about '73 Honda C-whatever-whatevers, but this one looks pretty rough.

"Are you OK, Dad?" I ask.

"What?"

"*You*. You seem . . . I don't know, down."

"You're asking about *my* well-being?" he says. "Andy, it's almost lunchtime on a Thursday. You smell like alcohol, and you're standing in my driveway wearing Christmas boxers."

"So, you're saying you think I should put on pants, then?"

Perhaps he's about to laugh. We'll never know, though, because Don Johnson, Prairie West Vice, skids to a stop in the middle of the driveway and takes off his sunglasses. My dad stands up straight and puffs out his chest, and for a few seconds, the three of us all stare at each other. The squirrels stare, too. A third has joined them—a yellow one.

"I didn't hear that thing running just now, did I?" asks Don Johnson.

"What thing?" my dad says.

"*That* thing." He points at the motorcycle.

My dad and I look at each other, and then Don Johnson looks at me. "I didn't hear anything," I say.

"You and Nancy signed the covenant, Brad," he says. "No one held a gun to your heads. You know the bylaws. No running motorcycles in the neighborhood proper. You got a problem with it, talk to the board . . . *again.*"

My dad laughs at him—humorless and bitter-sounding—and Don Johnson doesn't like it. He starts walking toward us like he's going to throw a punch or tase one of us. He touches the motorcycle.

"Get your hands off that," my dad says.

"It's warm," says Don Johnson.

"Congratulations, Kojak."

"You think that's funny, huh? Me doing my job? Well, bike's warm, means it was running. I've warned you enough. I'm writing you up."

"Jesus Christ."

"Swearing's not gonna help your cause, Brad." He's furiously scribbling in a little pad. "I hear—or hear *about*—that motorcycle running again in the neighborhood, I'm putting a boot on it. End of story. Done." He tears off a ticket and hands it to my dad.

"Is that even real?" I say.

Now it's my turn to get glared at. "In this neighborhood, son, that's as real as any ticket there is. And you know what? We got a rule about pants, too, now that I think about it."

"Really?" I say. "That seems pretty specific."

"Well, they thought of everything. Rule says you wear pants and shirts in front yards, in driveways, and on sidewalks. So I'm writing you up, too."

And for a moment, I, a grown man, basically, watch a pretend cop write me a pretend ticket for not wearing pants in a driveway that I will likely someday inherit 50 percent of.

"Unbelievable," my dad says.

"This isn't Greenwich Village," says Don Johnson. "We wear pants here."

As he hands me my ticket, I'm genuinely curious about what he thinks goes on in the Village.

When Don Johnson is gone, my dad is squeezing the handlebars of the bike so hard that the blood has drained out of his knuckles, turning them skeletal.

"You know, Dad," I say. "I don't believe I care for that gentleman."

His eyes are actually closed. That's how I gauge his anger. He almost never yelled at us when we were kids. Instead he'd do this—close his eyes and breathe deeply. As a nine-year-old, it was actually kind of terrifying. "I don't care for him either," he says.

"Bylaws?" I say. "A covenant? Did you retire to Soviet Russia? Is the Führer gonna show up, run us all out of the house, load us onto trains?"

He sighs. "You're mixing dictators, Andy."

Across the yard, yet another squirrel has joined the group. It's a whole pack of them now, a tribe, a gang, all beady-eyed, staring. And then they all scatter in different directions. I'm pretty sure they're planning something.

15

The next few days go by very slowly and are very much the same. I wake up late every morning and head to New Beginnings and hang out with my grandpa. I was lucky that first day when we were able to "talk." It hasn't really been like that since. A few times, he's looked at me and somehow acknowledged that I'm there. Today he was able to write "Hi." But mostly he just sleeps, waking occasionally to look at me oddly, like maybe he knows me, maybe he doesn't.

My nights have been even less productive. I've watched the *Worst Best Man . . . Ever!!!!* video a few dozen times. I've poked incessantly around the closet in the Bizarro Room. I called Karen last night. I dialed our old number. No one answered, which is probably good, because I have no idea what I would have said. I got to enjoy the new voice mail message though—*This is Karen and Tyler. Just leave a message at the beep, and we'll get back to you.*

Tonight's different, though.

I'm downtown at a music shop with Daisy, watching her flip through records. And I mean records—like vinyl—the stuff they used to put music on before computers and CDs and tapes and whatever came before tapes.

She texted me two hours ago.

```
What are you doing right this second?
```

No hello, just a question. Given the circumstances, lying seemed appropriate. But for some reason, I opted for the truth.

```
Watching Judge Judy and playing Tetris
on my old Game Boy.
```

She texted back thirty seconds later.

```
Pathetic. Meet me at Drastic Plastic.
Immediately . . . if not sooner.
```

And so here I am, completely baffled that this place still exists. I used to come here in high school to buy music and bootleg concert recordings. The Internet should have killed it years ago, but somehow it's held on, still cluttered and dusty and smelling vaguely of pot. Daisy bobs her head to Death Cab for Cutie as she studies the back of *Lionel Richie's Greatest Hits*.

"So, is this one of your jobs, too?" I say. "When you're not teaching Vagina Fiction? You lurk around indie bookstores and music shops?"

"One of the many benefits of bachelorettehood," she says. "The way I look at it, someday I'll have some dickhead husband and, like, three kids, and I'll long for this kind of freedom. I'm soaking it in."

Samuel L. Jackson and John Travolta are aiming guns off the frame of a *Pulp Fiction* poster. There are hundreds of other posters, too, along with box sets, pirated concert CDs, imported music with Japanese writing on the covers, a life-size Bruce Springsteen cardboard cutout. We're the only people here.

She looks up from her sifting. She's in jeans again and a T-shirt, flip-flops, and maroon lipstick. "So, let's talk," she says.

"Is that not what we're doing right now?"

"No, I mean, talk-talk. *She* . . . the *big* she . . . she who shall remain nameless. She wasn't your first heartbreak, was she?"

"What makes you say that?" I say.

"I have a sense about you. I know your type. You're one of the nice ones. You were even nicer when you were younger, I bet. Less jaded. We must have chewed you up when we were kids."

"We?"

"Girls," she says. "I'm speaking for my people. We're terrible before we learn that we shouldn't be terrible. You're the kind of guy who catches the brunt of that. So, on behalf of bitches and hos everywhere, my sincere apologies."

I pick up a Prince bobblehead doll. It's wearing a little purple suit. On a random shelf of used CDs, I notice a case with a motorcycle on it. It's called *Rolling Thunder*. The caption says, *Classic Engine Sounds of the Twentieth Century*. On the back, instead of songs, there are motorcycle names: Harley-Davidson, Indian, Kawasaki. I think of my dad. "Well, this is pretty sweet," I say.

"What?"

"I think this is a CD of motorcycle engines. How . . . how completely random is that?"

"Yeah, pretty thrilling," she says. "So, your first heartbreak. Number one. What was her name? I know you remember."

She's right of course, I do.

"Why would I want to talk about that?"

"Oh, it's fun, come on . . . War stories. Let's hear it."

"Lindsay Hanna," I say.

"Lindsay," she says, sneering. "Typical. Details, go."

"It was fifth grade."

"Early damage. That's the worst."

"She broke up with me at Skate Land. She gave me a bag of Skittles and told me my face was kind of stupid, but we should still be friends. She was couple-skating with Jason Titus an hour later."

"That *little* whore."

"In her defense, she was the first girl in our school to get boobs. So it was really just a matter of time."

"Next."

"Next?"

"Who was next? I want the whole list—*Misery's Greatest Hits*."

"Freshman year. High school. Andrea Young."

"I've never met an Andrea I liked. Where?"

"School parking lot."

"These bitches and their public places. Who did she dump you for?"

"Scott Grecko, captain of the soccer team. She went to third base with him three weeks later after prom, in the science lab . . . or so I'm told."

"Of course she did. Next?"

I smile. Daisy was right; somehow, this is fun. "Michelle Dundas," I say. "Sophomore year of college. She dumped me over the phone. I was playing *The Legend of Zelda* in my dorm room. Didn't see it coming."

"Bitch," says Daisy.

"She dyed her hair tangerine a month later, started dating the drummer for this horseshit ska band called The Fruit Department."

"OK, that's enough. You're depressing me. I get it."

"I could go on," I say.

"You thought all that was over, didn't you?" she says. "That's what made this one—the big one—so bad. You put a ring on it. You thought all that shit was behind you because you were married, right?"

I nod. Something like 50 percent of marriages end in divorce, everyone knows that, but I never even considered it was something that would happen to me. To us.

We round a long shelf, and we're at the end of Alt Rock. We've been wandering in alphabetical order this whole time. I watch her as she pulls out an LP version of the album *Yankee Hotel Foxtrot* by Wilco. "Probably my favorite album ever," she says.

"You like Wilco?" I ask.

"Of course I do. I'm not deaf, right?" She fiddles with a wrinkled corner. "Their label rejected this. Did you know that? Spectacularly so, actually. They straight up dropped them. Told them to get lost. Wilco produces this incredible, wholly unique, perfect thing, and some fucking suits are like, 'Eh.' Are you kidding me?"

I've heard this story—it's an indie rock legend. The band actually made a documentary about it called *I'm Trying to Break Your Heart*. Her face is reddening, like she's reliving the injustice of it all over again.

"So, what does Wilco do?" she says. "They say *fuck you* and they go and find a new label, and now it's one of the greatest albums ever. The lesson here . . . Sometimes people throw things away. That doesn't mean those things aren't really, really good. Most of the time, it just means that person didn't know what they had."

I'm nodding. I might even be smiling.

"You see what I did there?" she says.

"I think so," I say.

"Maybe you're *Yankee Hotel Foxtrot*. And maybe she's the asshole record label—"

"Yeah, I get it."

And then her face lights up. "Oh my God! Look at this shirt!" She hustles over to a rack of wrinkly T-shirts beneath a sign that says "Clothes, Etc." She holds one up to herself. "Nebraska: Fuck Yeah!" it reads across the chest.

"You can wear it to church," I say.

She finds another one, yellow, and hands it to me. There's a smiling cartoon cowboy riding a corncob like a mechanical bull. "If you don't buy this shirt right now and wear it out of the store tonight, you're making the biggest mistake of your life."

"You think?"

"Go try it on. That's a small."

"Small?"

"You wear mediums, right? You shouldn't. You're a small. Own that shit. It's 2015, small is good. Oh, and you need to shave more often."

I touch my face.

"You need a shaving system. Random isn't a system. Every fourth day. Now seriously, go try this shirt on before I lose my patience."

The dressing room is about the size of an airplane bathroom, with a red velvet curtain and a dusty full-length mirror. I take my shirt off and look at myself for a while, comparing things to the composite I've re-created in my head of a shirtless Tyler. Daisy is on the other side of the curtain going on about shaving.

"The rotation," she says. "Simple. For a whole day, you're clean cut. Clean cut is good, like a restart. The next day is all-day five o'clock shadow, which is nice. Girls love that. They don't know it—at least consciously—but it reminds them of masculinity and their daddies hugging them after work. Et cetera. The day after that, day three, you're officially scruffy. *All* girls like scruffy—it's wired into our DNA. Cavewoman stuff. Then, you start the rotation again the next morning. A slightly different you every day. How long has it been now, like five, six days?"

She's right, again, which is amazing. How does she know all this shit?

"Yeah, well, it's not working for you. You look like you should be selling dope behind a dumpster at 7-Eleven. It's time to shave, Cheech."

"I'm comfortable with who I am," I say, which is a funny thing to say while shaming my own body in a full-length mirror.

"Shut up. No, you're not. No one is. The trick is finding ways to seem like you are. We're all lying. We accentuate what's good, hide what's bad. Like me. My boobs? Average at best. And the left one is smaller than the right one. That's why I draw attention to my ass."

I hear the sound of palm on denim, and I'm pretty sure Daisy just slapped her own ass.

"Jesus," I say. "You should mentor preteen girls about body image."

She snorts. "They should be so lucky."

"I was actually kidding."

"I know you were, but speaking of teenage girls . . . I'm gonna lay it all out for you, OK? Remember that string of movies when we were younger, like mid '90s? The ones where the nerdy girl finally puts on makeup and a Wonderbra and everyone realizes how totally boneable she is?"

"Yeah."

"Well, that's you," she says. "We're in one of those movies. You're my hopeless teenage girl, all stuck in your shell, and I'm here to give you a fresh coat of makeup and a slutty dress. Push those boobies up, Andy Carter, it's go time."

"Do you ever stop talking?" I say. "Seriously, it's like you have a superarticulate form of Tourette syndrome."

"I've decided to take that as a compliment," she says.

I put the yellow T-shirt on. It's too tight, of course, because it's a fucking small, and I'm not a toddler. As I'm taking it off, Daisy tosses the curtain aside and barges right in. "What the hell's taking so long— it's a T-shirt, not a corset."

"Hey!" I cross my arms over my nipples, which is probably not going to help counter the argument that I am an awkward teenage girl.

"Come on, I wanna see it," she says. "Put it on."

"It looks like it's from babyGap. I'm not wearing it."

"Put it on," she says.

We're just a few inches apart, like we might slow dance. She smells like lip gloss, like chemical fruit. I put the stupid thing back on, doing my best not to elbow her in the face. Daisy bites her pinkie fingernail, assessing me. "It's settled, you're buying it. You're officially a size small in novelty Nebraska T-shirts."

"I don't think it's my style," I say.

"And what style is *your* style, exactly, Andy? Sad guy at a bus stop? Divorcee in his parents' basement?"

"Too mean," I say. "And I'm staying in the guest room, actually."

"I stand corrected. However, I think the dynamic we should go with here is where I tell you to do things and then you do them without all the back-sass. It'll save us both time."

"Seems reasonable," I say.

"Your eye is healing nicely, by the way," she says.

I look at myself. It's a little puffy, but everything is basically the color that it's supposed to be. She touches my cheekbone, tilts my head a little, assessing some more.

"You know, if you can manage to stay out of the way of bikes, and if you get this shaving situation under control, I think you'll find that you actually have a relatively nice face, as far as faces go."

I tell her that I'll do my best.

"Now," she says. "We need to talk about your motivation again."

"We do?"

"I don't trust you to do it yourself, so I've come up with one for you. Wanna hear it?"

"Is my motivation to buy more tiny T-shirts? I think I saw an AC/DC onesie out there. I could probably try to jam into it if you want."

"You're going to get over her," she says. "And you're going to meet someone else. And you're going to be happy again."

She's said these three things very slowly, listing them with great emphasis like she's giving a PowerPoint presentation. We're quiet—just two people in a dressing room.

"You'll meet some pretty girl with a Tory Burch handbag and unreasonably big boobs for her size. Nancy will go apeshit for her because she's just perfect and nice and not a man-eating superslut, and you'll be happy."

I allow myself to imagine this. It's nice to think about, but ridiculous, too, like picturing myself atop Everest. And then, with absolutely no warning, Daisy takes her shirt off and the course of our conversation changes dramatically. I try to look up, to look away, to aim my eyeballs in a different direction, but it's impossible in a space this small.

"Relax," she says. "We're old friends, remember?"

"Do you want me to . . . like . . . turn around?"

"Stop being so Catholic. Just go ahead and look. Get it out of your system."

I don't, at least not directly. But it doesn't matter, because the male eyeball sharpens when a girl's shirt comes off. Science, I guess. She's wearing a simple gray bra. There are no tattoos on her stomach or torso. Her skin looks pale and smooth, and there's a tiny scar on her belly button, like it used to be pierced.

"See, nothing you haven't seen before, right? Girl parts."

"I guess," I say.

"I'm kind of worried about these, though," she says. She runs a hand over the skin between her collarbones. There's a triangle-shaped region there of sporadic brown freckles and faint moles. "If I did mentor teenage girls, that'd be lesson number one," she says. "Wear sunscreen, you dumb little bitches."

She puts the "Fuck Yeah!" T-shirt on, and it fits like it was made for her exact shape. She spins a one-eighty and looks at herself in the mirror, striking a pose with her back to me. "What do you think?"

"Not bad," I say.

She rolls it up, tying it in a little ball beneath her breasts, and looks at herself some more. "Is this too slutty?" she says. "You can't really show stomach anymore without looking like a prostitute. It's a shame."

"Beautiful Little Fool" is tattooed in a thin, wispy script across her lower back. Our eyes meet in the mirror. She sees that I've seen it, which is embarrassing, for some reason, even though Daisy seems to care very little about what I am and am not looking at.

"You like it?" she says. "Tattoo number four. It's the best thing a girl can be in this world. A beautiful little fool."

This sounds shockingly poetic, like something out of a movie, but then I remember that I've heard it before. "Wait," I say. "Is that from . . . ?"

"Come on, you know this one," she says. "You can do it."

"*Gatsby*?" I say.

"Ding ding. *The Great Gatsby*, indeed. Well done, sir."

"The girl in the book," I say. "Her name is Daisy, too, right?"

She tilts her head. "Your grasp of basic high school–level English continues to impress, Andy Carter. My parents are teachers. The nurses plopped me on my mom's chest, and my cheeseball dad got all weepy and said I looked like a beautiful little fool. So, Daisy it was, straight to the birth certificate."

"That's . . . that's actually really sweet," I say.

She turns quiet again, and so do I. "You know what," she says. "It's gonna be fun watching you come back to life. I can't wait."

I don't know what to say, because I don't know this girl, and, frankly, I'm a little afraid of her. Generally speaking, it's difficult not to be at least mildly terrified of a girl who might, at any moment, take her shirt off. But I have to admit, it's nice to be out of the house. And I like the fact that five full minutes have passed and I haven't thought of Karen once.

Well, until now.

I bought *Rolling Thunder* for my dad. And Daisy talked me into three more T-shirts and the Prince bobblehead. Then she told me that she had to go to work. When I—quite reasonably, I think—asked her why she had to go to work at almost ten o'clock at night, she told me that it was none of my fucking business, so now I'm walking through downtown Omaha by myself, back toward the Caddie.

"Call me," she said before she left. And then she said, "Or, I don't know, I'll call you. Whatever. Don't forget to shave."

I'm getting a phone call. I can feel it vibrating in my jeans.

It's my dad. "Andy, where are you?" he says.

"I'm at . . ." I try to think of a quick, plausible lie, like I'm sixteen and huffing paint thinner in a cornfield, but then I remember that I'm in my thirties and that I'm allowed to go wherever I want. "Out," I say. "The Old Market."

"Really?" he says. "Well . . . you need to get over to the hospital, OK? Grandpa isn't doing great."

"Oh," I say. "Shit."

"This could be it," he says. "They're not sure yet. Mom and Jim are on their way."

"Are . . . are you gonna be there, too?" I say.

"No. There'll be plenty of time for me later. Go be with them. We'll talk soon."

As I put my phone back in my pocket, I see the Caddie and I remember the last full sentence I said to my grandpa. It was yesterday. He woke up briefly and looked at me. If my grandpa dies tonight, the last words I will have said to him will be: "Why do people like ginger ale so much, anyway? It sort of makes me wanna gag."

16

"Andy! Andy!"

I'm jogging across the New Beginnings parking lot, and Mrs. DiGiacomo is shouting my name. She's standing out in the green space, glowing like a poltergeist in her robe under the moonlight.

"Can't talk now," I say, but it comes out all gaspy because I haven't run in a long time, and there's a fifty-fifty chance I'm not going to make it into the building without collapsing.

"Is everything OK?"

"I'll find you later," I tell her.

She picks up the hem of her robe and starts trudging through the grass after me. I don't have time to wait, though. At least I don't think I do. My dad was vague but serious. Dads have this tone when something is happening; you learn it when you're a toddler and it sticks.

I hit the lobby—all one thousand degrees of it—and I find Nurse Sandy. "Hello again, Andy," she says.

When we make it to Suite #5, she touches my shoulder. It feels nurturing, and I prepare myself with a deep breath. This is a part of life. Death is a part of life. That's what people say. But when she opens the door, everything looks fine. No one's crying, no one's yelling "Clear!"

or performing CPR. Instead my mom and Jim are talking to an Indian man in a doctor's coat who looks like he's about nineteen. All three of them look up at me, and then back down at the chart. My grandpa is in his bed—still small, still gray, but breathing.

"He's stabilized," Nancy tells me.

"Stabilized?" I say.

Jim shrugs at me. He's drinking a Red Bull.

"Your grandfather is a man of will," says the doctor. He doesn't have an Indian accent, which is, for some reason, disappointing. "Hello. Andy, right? I'm Dr. Desai. It's nice to meet you."

Nancy touches the lump of sheets where my grandpa's knees are. "But it could still be . . . any time, though?" she says. She looks tired, a little raw.

Dr. Desai checks one of the tubes. "*Imminent* is a word we use in this business, Mrs. Carter. It's a fancy way of saying *soon*, but we don't really know. He's very weak. There's a chance he won't wake up again. You should know that. And if he does . . . well, his brain is very much affected. For now, though, this is where he wants to be. Here with you and your sons."

Jim and I look at each other. I lean against the wall. There was this one Christmas morning when my grandpa picked up a raw turkey and made it dance. I wonder if Jim is thinking about something like that, too.

Dr. Desai leaves us, and we stand in our little huddle, listening to the respirator or whatever the hell that accordion-looking thing is.

"Dude, where'd you get that shirt?" Jim says.

At first I have no idea what he's talking about. But then I look down at the little corncob cowboy. "I was shopping."

There's a Cubs game on WGN. They're out in San Diego, and they're winning. For the first time in a long, long time, the Cubs aren't terrible, and my grandpa isn't going to get to see how it all plays out.

Nancy touches my arm. "There are a few things of his at the house that I think you might like. Down in the basement."

"What do you mean?" I say.

"Some of his baseball stuff, your grandpa's. Baseball cards, some programs. You should take a look. I think he'd like you to have it."

He used to take Jim and me to Wrigley once a year, a special Chicago weekend. Jim always acted bored because Jim was the kind of kid who was always bored. I liked these trips, though, and I knew enough about the game to talk baseball with my grandpa.

"OK," I say.

"Oh, there's a computer down there, too," says Jim. "Gina and I got it for him when he moved here. We've got, like, five of them at home, so, all yours if you want it."

This feels shitty and morbid. Can he hear us? What would it be like to be lying there listening to your family parceling out a bunch of things you cared enough about to keep for your whole life?

There's a knock at the door—barely a knock, really, more like a tap—and then Mrs. DiGiacomo pokes her head into the room. "Is everything . . ." She stops when she sees him. Her eyes go wide.

"Hey, Marie," my mom says.

Nurse Sandy is here now, too, appearing from the hallway. "Come on now, Mrs. D. You know you're not supposed to be over on this side."

"Is it his time?" she says. "Is he—"

The door closes, so we don't hear the rest of her question. Across the room, on the shelf, more flowers have arrived, more artwork from Bryce and Emma, too, and a smattering of greeting cards. No sunflowers, though. Those are gone.

My phone beeps in my pocket. It's from Daisy.

```
Is he OK? Mrs. D called me.
```

Seven words. Twenty-seven characters. Barely tweetworthy. But I can tell that whoever this weird chick is, she cares very much about my grandpa.

And then my brother flops down on the lime-green loveseat in the corner of the room and puts his legs over the armrest. "Dibs on the couch, sucker," he says. And then, just because, I guess, he says, "Boom."

17

I should really probably be getting back," I say.

I've said this a few times now, but, so far, it's had zero effect. Mrs. DiGiacomo is making me a breakfast Hot Pocket in her microwave. Hers is cooling on the countertop—smoldering really—like something that's bubbled up from the center of the Earth.

"Egg and cheese is the best one for breakfast," she says. "Sausage and cheese sometimes, too. But the sausage doesn't always agree with me on account of my reflux."

"My mom is probably getting worried," I say, trying a slightly different tack.

There are fifty-five seconds left on the microwave, and I take a sip of some gritty iced tea out of a floral old-lady glass. *The Young and the Restless* is on, and I feel like I've failed my father. A man named Victor Newman is talking seductively to a beautiful blonde woman who, according to Mrs. DiGiacomo, is a "class-A tramp."

"Ten seconds," she says. I can hear the thing hissing through the microwave door.

I woke up this morning on the floor of my grandpa's suite. I had an itchy hospital-issued blanket and two folded-up pillows to sleep on. Jim and my mom were gone. My grandpa was asleep, mechanically breathing. I wandered out into the hallway to try to find coffee, and there was Mrs. D., hyperalert, putting together a horse puzzle. "You look hungry," she said. "Do you like Hot Pockets?"

Sometimes in life, it doesn't matter that you've just woken up on a floor. Or that you haven't brushed your teeth. Or that your hair is a mess and you're wearing the clothes you slept in. Sometimes you just have to be polite. "Like them?" I said. "More like *love* them."

She hands me my breakfast on a floral plate. We're on the other side of the building in the nonhospice wing. "Your grandpa used to be right next door," she says. "This was our wall. We shared it."

"Yeah?" I touch my Hot Pocket. It should be cool enough by sometime next week to not completely fuck my mouth up.

"He taught me about baseball," she says. "I kept asking him questions about it, since he was always watching it on the TV in the common room. Those stupid Cubs. One time, I asked him how many points a homerun was worth."

"Runs," I say, a reflex wired into my DNA.

She grins. "I know that. My generation was taught to act dumb to get a man's attention. Not popular by today's thinking, mind you, but it worked. He said, 'Marie, sit your ass down. You're gonna watch this whole game with me and I'm gonna tell you what's what, and you're not gonna ask me any more stupid questions.'"

There are pictures hanging over the television—a man holding a squirming terrier and two senior class photos of a boy and a girl. The photos are all at least thirty years old. The girl has feathered hair and the guy has a heartbreaking little early '80s mustache.

"Genevieve lives in St. Louis," she says. "And that's Anthony Jr. He's in Milwaukee. A lawyer now. Tax lawyer . . . not like lawyers on TV." She takes a bite of her Hot Pocket, and we watch a commercial for term life insurance. I notice the sunflowers on the windowsill, catching some light. "Hey, are those my grandpa's flowers?"

Guilt flashes briefly across her face. "Your mom threw them away. Perfectly lovely and she tossed them. I figured no one would mind."

"Oh," I say. "No, yeah . . . Of course."

I imagine my mother grabbing Daisy's flowers out of all the others and marching them to the garbage.

"So she's on the outs with your sister, then?"

"It's complicated," I say, which isn't a lie, exactly. When the commercials are over, the show comes back. Everyone is beautiful and handsome and spectacularly unhappy.

"Is Henry in pain?" she says after a while. "It looked like it."

"They're giving him medicine. But yeah, I think so."

Her expression is grim as she holds her Hot Pocket over her plate. "Do you think that's going to happen to me?"

I have no idea what to say, so I say, "I hope not," and I realize how utterly amazing it is that we're all able as humans to go about our daily lives without constantly obsessing over the fact that each of us will almost certainly be in a sterile bed someday, medicated and slowly dying. This officially marks the most depressing thing that has ever crossed my mind.

"A lot of people here don't talk to me because they think I'm crazy," Mrs. DiGiacomo says. "Henry always talked to me. I like that about him. Your sister talks to me, too. She's nice. I like her spirit."

I look at the faded pictures in their drugstore frames, and I look at this little room of hers, and I think about the look on her face last night when she saw my grandpa. She's alone here. She's like me really, by herself in a tiny spot that will never quite feel like hers, and she doesn't even have a jerk of a cat to keep her company.

"You know," she says, "I can actually kind of see it now."

"What's that?"

"You and Daisy. You don't *look* alike. Not at all, actually. But you look the *same*. Does that make sense?" I'm not sure, but I tell her that it does because I'm Midwestern and agreeable. She takes the last bite of her Hot Pocket. "Basically," she says, "you both look sad."

When I finally make it back to Suite #5, I open the door quietly. I expect to find things the way I left them—my grandpa sleeping alone, the room empty—but instead, I find Fox News. My mother is standing in front of the TV with a notebook watching Sean Hannity's show. He's talking to Ann Coulter. She's at the desk next to him.

"I don't think people realize," Hannity says on the television, "the amount of drugs that are being smuggled into this country. The amount of criminal activity. And the cost to our criminal justice system, health-care system, and educational system. Is that your point?"

Ann Coulter takes a breath, and I consider backing out of the room, finding Mrs. DiGiacomo, and watching *The Price Is Right*. But then my mom hits "Pause" and starts talking. "Sean, my point is . . . some cultures are more successful than others. It's as simple as that. Obviously, our culture is massively successful. Hugely, thanks in no small part to our freedom."

I'm holding my breath.

"No one can debate our prosperity, and our sheer will to succeed. But what we can't do as a society is continue to flood ourselves with less productive cultures—more primitive cultures, poor cultures, uneducated cultures—and expect them to simply assimilate into our society and become successful overnight. Frankly, it's naïve. And the result of that naïveté, as we've seen, is social unrest and crime. And that's just the beginning. On a larger scale, we're talking about gradually stripping away our culture—the American way of life. Where will we be in twenty years? Fifty years? Will we be the America you and I know and love?"

She hits "Rewind." Hannity is talking in reverse. "Not bad," Nancy whispers. "Slow down a little. It's not a race. Take a breath. Enunciate."

I've just walked in on my mother pretending to be interviewed on Fox News.

"I don't think people realize," Hannity says all over again, and now I am backing away, quickly.

"Andy?" She hits "Pause."

Shit.

"Sorry," I say. "Sorry, Mom. I should have knocked or someth . . ." I trail off and she straightens her blouse. "But what . . . what were you doing?"

"Practicing," she says. "The back and forth. It's the most difficult part. I'm used to being the only one talking. It's more of a challenge when you're dialoguing."

"Dialoguing?"

"Talking."

Hannity is frozen on the TV—eyes midblink, mouth open, crooked. "I made the panelist list," she says. "I found out yesterday, before Jim and I came here. They want to build my brand."

I look over at my grandpa. His chest rises and falls. "What does that mean?"

"They have guests on the talk shows . . . to talk about things, all the issues. I'll start out in spots like that. Talking to the host, establishing my expertise."

"On *Hannity*?"

"Well, I *hope*, of course. Or *O'Reilly*. Those are the big ones. I'll get there. But there are other shows and segments, and everyone needs content. They call . . . day of, usually. It's very topical. The more current topics I can talk about, the better chance I'll get airtime. I'm working on immigration now." She nods to Hannity, who's still frozen, waiting to say things.

"Well, con . . . gratulations?" I say. And then I say it again, all as one word, "Congratulations," no question mark this time.

She's dressed for work, polished, thin, and blonde, and I realize how much I miss the old her. It's probably not fair to feel like this—to insist that our moms and dads somehow exist in suspended animation. But that's how I feel. She was rounder and darker before, softer and brunette, strands of gray here and there, like highlights. Now she's all angles and edges and heels.

"Question," she says. "From your perspective, is *primitive cultures* too much—too, you know, demeaning? I want to strike the right balance."

I stop a few ill-conceived things from tumbling out of my mouth. It's her face that does it—the openness. She's asking for my help, and I'm determined not to fight with her here in this pretend-cozy room, next to my grandpa. "Maybe," I say. "Perhaps it'll come off as hurtful."

She jots something down in her notebook. "I know. Ann Coulter can get away with being mean. It's part of her brand. It's what people want her to be. I don't think I can pull that off yet."

I'm fairly certain she's saying this to herself—either that or to no one in particular—certainly not to me. "You sounded good, though," I say.

This surprises my mother as much as it does me. She scans my face for sincerity.

"I mean it. You're good at this."

Maybe she believes me, maybe not. Either way, she's on to the next topic now. "Did you get a suit yet?" she says.

"What?"

"Jim wanted me to ask you." She looks at my grandpa for emphasis. The machines remind me that they're there with their beeps and hums and compressions. "You need to get on that, Andy. Probably soon."

"I'll do it today," I say.

"Good."

And then she unpauses the TV and starts the whole thing over again.

18

A few hours later, I'm back in the Caddie, parked in front of a pizza place called Lazzari's. The roof of my wrecked mouth is peeling off in gross, rubbery flakes thanks to Mrs. DiGiacomo's Hot Pockets. I watch the YouTube video again on my phone: *Worst Best Man . . . Ever!!!!* I stop it just before the vomiting. There's a big red Ford F-150 pickup truck next to me. The left fender is dented to shit, rusting a little.

> *"We're dealing with an entire generation of people who are absolutely committed to taking zero responsibility for their lives. Everything is somebody else's fault. Classic victim mentality. Don't worry, we'll clean up the mess for you. We'll pick up the check. We'll tip the waiter. You hear it day in and day out from the—"*

I turn the radio off and enjoy a moment of Nancy-less silence. A neon Corona sign hangs at the Lazzari's entrance, and I'm trying to remember if I've ever seen it before. I've probably been here five hundred times. But I've been avoiding it since getting back to Omaha.

The reason? Well, it's complicated. But here's the quick version. The co-owner of Lazzari's is a guy named Neal. Neal is my former best friend—major emphasis on the word *former*. He also happens to be my ex-wife's twin brother. And the last time I saw him, I totally ruined his wedding reception, and I crashed his truck. Oh, and I also punched his dad.

Inside, the place is exactly the same.

Every inch of available wall is covered in Nebraska Cornhusker memorabilia and beer signs. A *Terminator 2: Judgment Day* pinball machine flashes from the corner. The high score still reads "ACC"— Andrew Charles Carter. That's me. Neal's initials are numbers two through ten, and as I stand here taking in the smell of smoldering pizza dough, I'm thinking that this may very well represent my greatest achievement as a man.

There's no one at the register, which is actually a relief. I imagined walking in the door and having Neal standing at the counter and the two of us having a stare-off.

And then I hear his voice. "Just a second," he shouts from some-where. I consider just walking back out to the parking lot and driving away. But instead, I sit down at one of the stools at the tiny bar and pour myself a beer straight from the tap. Speaking from professional experience, this is probably the most annoying thing a person can do.

Neal appears lugging two cases of Amstel Light. There's a pause midstep, but that's all I get. He sets the beer down with a clank by the cooler and points at my beer. "That'll be four bucks," he says.

"It's flat," I say.

He shrugs. If Karen was balding, two shades paler, and a dude, this is exactly what she'd look like, and it's infuriating.

"Come with me if you want to live," says Arnold Schwarzenegger from the pinball machine.

"Still haven't knocked me off on *T2* yet, huh?" I say.

"I stopped trying," he says, which I know is a huge lie.

"Big Red looks a little rough. You should take better care of that thing."

Neal looks out through the window into the parking lot at his damaged truck. "You still owe me eight hundred and forty dollars," he says. "I need to replace the whole front end, thank you very much."

"Go ahead and put it on my tab," I say.

"How's your grandpa?" he asks, and, just like that, our little back and forth is ruined. This is what I hate most about Neal: he's too goddamn nice to properly hold up his end of a feud. I make a face and he seems to get that it means *not good*. He pours himself a fountain Diet Coke and leans against the counter. "So what are you doing here, Andy?"

"How's business?" I say, acknowledging the tumbleweeds blowing across the dining area.

"It's between rushes, you dick," he says. "In fact, I'm actually getting ready for dinner, so maybe you just go ahead and tell me why you're here." His face is slowly darkening. It starts at his neck and works up, the curse of countless generations of Irish Catholicism.

The leftover slices from lunch are bubbling under the heat lamp, which is gross. Neal is looking at me, waiting for an answer. But then Owen, Neal's co-owner, comes schlepping out from the stock room. He's eating breadsticks and wearing a Lazzari's T-shirt that's so dirty it looks like he pulled it from the wreckage of a train derailment. Owen stops when he sees me, his mouth full. "What's up, Andy?" he says.

"Hey, Owen," I say.

Owen, as usual, looks stoned. He lived down the hall from us in college our sophomore year when Neal and I were randomly paired together in the dorms. He's probably the biggest idiot I know, but he makes the best pizza I've ever tasted.

"This is weird," he says. "I was just thinking about you the other day. I was totally watching your YouTube video. I saved it in my favorites. Shit still cracks me up. Like, who knew a human being could puke that much?"

"I'm glad you liked it," I say.

He laughs. "Yeah."

"Oh, and I've been meaning to thank you for posting it on YouTube," I say. "I really appreciate that."

He's still smiling. "BuzzFeed had it as the sixth-biggest wedding fail of all time a few months ago. Like, of all time. That's pretty epic. BuzzFeed, man. That's legit."

"You mean there were five worse?" says Neal. He's cleaning the tops of the Parmesan shakers now, jamming a fork into gunked-up holes. This is also gross.

"You'd be surprised," says Owen. "Number one was this guy in Florida who set himself on fire during the ceremony with some candle by accident. He just burst into flames. It was awesome."

Neal and Owen talk business for a minute, both agreeing to make chicken with goat cheese the special tonight, and then Neal tries to run me out. "So, if there's nothing else, Andy?" he says.

"Hold your horses," I say.

"My horses?"

"Yeah. It's an expression. Just give me a second here."

"I'm busy. This is my job, believe it or not. I take this seriously."

"Do you have a 401(k)?"

"What?"

"Nothing. I have a question about your dad."

"My dad?"

"Yeah. Is he still working over at the Gentleman's Closet?"

Neal rolls his eyes. "No, Andy. After twenty-five years, he sold the place and retired. Now he makes meth out of a Winnebago. Yes, he still works there. Why are you asking me this?"

"On a scale of one to ten, how mad do you think he still is at me?"

"For punching him in the face in front of all his family and friends?"

"Like, what, six? Seven maybe?"

"I seriously don't have—"

"Owen," I say. "You think you can handle dinner prep today?"

Owen is dipping a breadstick deep into a jug of ranch dressing. "I can probably manage," he says.

"Good," I say. "Neal, what do you say you and me go for a ride?"

"Yeah, right," he says.

"Come on, it'll be fun. Owen's gonna whip up the chicken and goat cheese. He's got it covered. We'll be back in like an hour."

"Why in the hell would I go for a ride with you? What do you want?"

"I need you to be a buffer."

"A buffer? What am I buffering?"

"I need you to be a buffer between me and your dad. You know, in case he's still mad at me."

"You're . . . you're fucking kidding me, right?"

Owen joins in before I can answer. "Wait," he says. "What's the expiration date on this ranch?"

"Owen, don't do that, it's really disgusting," says Neal.

"We should probably take my grandpa's Caddie," I say. "No offense, but Big Red has a big fucking dent in it."

19

Their wedding really was lovely.

A textbook union in a nice church with singing and sunshine, an adorable flower girl, tuxedos, a smiling bride. They even had birds, for Christ's sake. Neal's mom, Gloria, released two stunned-looking doves into the sky when it was over. They landed on a nearby power line where they shat furiously and glared at us while we blew bubbles in the church parking lot.

And I was standing next to Neal the whole time.

Karen was there in the front row during the ceremony, next to her parents. She looked so beautiful that it physically hurt to look at her. I did OK, though. I held the rings. I signed the paperwork. I posed for a preposterous number of photos, one of which required me, as the shortest groomsman, to be the top of a pyramid. I even tipped the altar boys. Twenty bucks each seemed a little steep for an hour of standing there with dumb looks on their faces, but I did it anyway. I was friendly and dressed appropriately, and no one could tell that I was, apparently, a time bomb.

We all rode in a limo together to the reception after the ceremony, the whole wedding party, all ten of us. I sat next to Neal, and we were all passing around plastic flutes full of horrible Costco champagne, and everyone was laughing. Kristen's sister made a playlist for the trip, and all the bridesmaids were singing "I'm a Bitch" at the tops of their lungs—some inside joke, I guess.

"How you holding up, man?" Neal asked me.

I downed a gulp of champagne. "All good," I said, even though I'm generally not someone who says that.

"Maybe you wanna go a little easy. Maybe downshift a little."

It was a funny thing to say in a giant car full of drunk people.

"I'm a goddess on my knees!" the girls shrieked.

"We're Catholics, Neal," I said. "This is what we do at weddings. We get drunk and girls sing about blow jobs."

It had been six weeks since Applebee's—six weeks since I moved out of the house—and everyone was treating me like this, all tentative and concerned. "How's the job hunt going?" he asked. "You sending any resumes out?"

"I'm on sabbatical," I say.

At the cocktail hour, I mostly watched everyone and avoided Karen, who, I quickly realized, was avoiding me, too. There were lots of girls there, of course, all dressed up in their wedding best. Some were pretty. A few were beautiful. There were smart-looking girls and party girls, businessy-looking girls, and a few grade school teachers. Every few minutes, I chose one at random and imagined being with her. We'd start dating. We'd have sex for the first time, and it would be OK—a little awkward, but not so bad. I'd meet her parents, and we'd compromise on a breed of dog to buy. We'd argue over the remote and about what color to paint the entryway. Every time I did this, it felt wrong. None of them were Karen. None of them had her silly, wobbly high-heel walk. None of them had her laugh or her weird quirk of holding a wine glass with two hands, like a chalice. None of them had her breasts or her nose or her lips. We made eye contact from maybe fifty feet away. She was talking to a gaggle of interchangeable aunts. She gave me a cautious look. *Hold it together, just for a while longer,* her expression said.

Someone clinked a water glass and Neal and Kristen kissed.

A heart-shaped card sent me to Table #1, which was empty when I got there. It felt good to sit by myself and sip tepid water. I closed my eyes and recited the first line of my toast in my head.

"Wake up, mister." Neal and Karen's cousin Helen slid into the seat next to me. "Party of one here," she said. "Another one of these signature Jack and gingers and I'll be frenching that cheesedick DJ before the father-daughter dance. Mark my words." Helen is tall, perennially single, and prone to odd experiments in eye makeup. She's also the kind of girl who says things like *cheesedick.* She looked coltish and uncomfortable in her lavender bridesmaid dress. I can say with absolute certainty that everything that happened next was entirely her fault.

People started gathering at their tables. Neal and Kristen joined us, and sweat started to pool at odd spots beneath my tux as I thought more and more about the toast I'd soon be delivering.

"I was sorry to hear about you and Karen," Helen said. Someone clinked a glass again, and Neal and Kristen stood and kissed. What an unbelievably stupid tradition.

"Me, too," I said.

"She's making a big mistake with him, you know."

It's funny how you can hear something—every syllable, perfectly clear—but somehow *not* hear it. I was saying my first line over and over again. I'd read somewhere that trying to be funny right off the bat in a best man toast is a mistake. It's best to go with something sincere.

"God, everyone knows it," she went on. "The quarter-life crisis. That's actually a thing now. Talk about white people problems, right? Like we're making up shit to worry about."

I'm sure there were other sounds in that big, drafty room. People talking, silverware tapping on plates, bored waiters and waitresses spilling things. But I didn't hear any of it. It was like the scene in every war movie ever where something explodes and the soldiers stagger around all deaf and confused. "What did you say?"

Her expression turned to quiet panic. "Oh, shit."

"What did—" I said. And then I said, "A mistake?"

She looked around for someone to save her.

Neal gave her a *What the fuck did you just do?* look. "Andy," he said. "Calm down, OK?"

The DJ was blathering, and some asshole was clinking his glass again, but Neal and Kristen didn't kiss this time; they just watched me.

"Helen, what did you say?"

"Helen," said Kristen. "This seriously isn't the—"

"Shut the fuck up, Kristen," I said. Her head snapped back like I'd slapped her. I looked at Helen, waiting. I stared at her. And then my own name was blaring. ". . . Andy Carter!"

Everyone was looking at me, but I was frozen, mounted to my folding chair like a piece of abstract art. The wedding coordinator waved frantically at me, her bangs swooshing across her forehead. The DJ didn't know what to do, so he just repeated his line. "And now let's give it up for the best man . . . Andy Carter!"

When I stood up, my chair made a hideous noise as it scraped along the floor. I took the mic and my stomach churned and flipped. I should have eaten something between all of those drinks. I should have given the microphone back to the DJ. I should have stepped down as the best man. I should have leapt from the limo two hours earlier onto the asphalt and done everyone a huge favor.

People were clapping. Somebody whistled. And then they were all just staring at me. I looked at my speech notes, but they'd turned blurry and foreign. And then my eyes found Karen. My eyes always found her in crowds. Boring work parties, social obligations, all that shit. I'd be alone and shy, and I'd look up and always find her there, chatting with someone, her glass in both hands, and she'd smile, and I would know I was OK. She wasn't smiling now, though. She looked nervous. There was someone next to her. I didn't know who he was at first. He was a guy in a suit—the room was full of them.

"All right, Andy!" someone shouted. It was Owen. He was filming me with his iPhone.

I looked at the guy next to Karen again—like actually *looked* at him. He was our neighbor, the guy across the street and two doors down. The guy who parked an ambulance in his driveway sometimes. What the hell was he doing at Neal's wedding?

It all came together at once. Karen's mistake. The guy next to her. His name was Tyler.

And then I threw up.

A lot.

As much as one could, I think.

Neal and Karen's dad, Jerry—this big Nebraskan of a man—grabbed me, and he took me by the shoulders and hustled me off the stage. I'd puked directly into the microphone. The sound blasted off the walls until the amp shorted into earsplitting feedback. We made it through the lobby, and then he shoved me through some double doors out into the humid parking lot. I actually tried to get back in, but Jerry body-blocked me, and so I hit him.

It was my first punch ever, and it caught him square in the jaw, snapping his head back. No one was more surprised than me.

Neal came running out. "Fucking A, man!" he said. Some others had followed him to gawk. I was convinced that they all knew, like Neal and Kristen had sent out an e-mail blast to get all the guests up to speed on my situation.

I started running.

"Where are you going?" Neal shouted.

I had no idea. How far could I make it like this, sprinting in barf-covered tuxedo shoes?

There was Big Red. It was the first familiar thing I saw. I knew that Neal—dumb, trusting Neal—kept an extra key in a magnet box above the back wheel. It was in my hands in a matter of seconds. Neal's dad was yelling, "Don't even think about it!" But that was as much as anyone did to try to stop me. The truck rumbled to a big, loud start, like it always did. Somebody had written *Just Married* in white block letters, and there were streamers tied to the antenna and bumpers. The tires squealed when I hit the gas.

I made it a few hundred feet—about half the parking lot.

It was the rearview mirror that got me. As I drove away, I looked up and Neal and Kristen were standing there, man and wife. And next to them stood Karen. She was the girl I loved. She was the girl who was going to have my children. She was the girl who loved me even though I'm short and kind of goofy-looking and not particularly good at anything. Tyler put his arm around her. I watched him pull her close to him.

I hopped a curb, pulverized a "No Parking" sign, and smashed into a tree.

20

The little bell above the door at the Gentleman's Closet is shockingly loud.

My former father-in-law is standing by himself in the empty store, running a lint brush over a black suit. He sighs, like he's somehow been expecting me.

"Gerald," I say.

Neal slinks in behind me. Jerry looks at him and then at me.

"Hi, Dad," Neal says. "I'm a buffer."

"Hello, Andrew." Jerry's voice is low and unsmiling. He used this voice on me when Karen and I first started dating. He'd known me for years as Neal's friend, but the moment the concept of me sleeping with his daughter entered the picture, the timbre changed to gravel and threats and storm clouds.

"So we're using formal names, then?" says Neal.

As much as the Gentleman's Closet sounds like it should be a strip club, it's actually Omaha's finest men's formalwear shop. It's been in Neal and Karen's family since the pioneers wore burlap sacks and routinely froze to death in sod huts.

"So, you got any good suits here or what?" I say. It was supposed to be an icebreaker, but no one is laughing. "Maybe something European?"

"Do you even know what a European suit is?" says Neal.

I point to a picture on the wall of a guy with a wedge haircut and a tight blue suit. He looks like a backup singer in a British boy band. "That?" I say.

Both men turn and look.

"Oh, yeah, because that's totally you," says Neal. I'm beginning to rethink bringing him here.

"Andy," says Jerry. He slides his lint brush into his pocket. "Neal is right. That's a very specific look."

"See, this is why I need you, Jerry," I say.

"Not interested," he says.

"I've got money."

"This . . . this isn't about money."

"Done and done," says Neal. "Take me back to Lazzari's. The thought of Owen by himself is actually kind of freaking me out."

"Wait," I say. "Jerry, come on, I'm desperate here."

He folds his arms, clears his throat. "I'm not interested in doing business with you."

"Why?"

"Because you're an idiot. You've always been an idiot. We tolerated you, more or less, because we had to. But we don't have to anymore. And after your little performance at Neal's wedding, I don—"

"Wedding *reception*," I say. "The wedding was lovely."

"Jesus," says Neal.

This would be a much better story if ol' Jerry and Gloria had loved me, if I'd been like their second son. But truth be told, my in-laws were never huge Andy Carter fans. It's not their fault, really. Generally speaking, I tend to underwhelm girls' parents.

"After your little performance at Neal's wedding *reception* . . ."

"Thank you."

". . . I think it's best if you look for a suit elsewhere."

They're standing side by side, Neal and Jerry. They look like a then-and-now photo. "So, you're still mad at me, then?" I say.

"Men's Wearhouse," he says. "Ask for a man named Dwayne. He won't screw you over too badly."

Neal smiles at me. *See?* He's leaning against a table of fanned-out dress socks. The silver of his wedding ring catches some fluorescent light. It's still clean and shiny—unblemished. By the time I took mine off, it was scratched, tarnished, and wrecked. I threw it into a creek off an I-95 overpass somewhere in Delaware on my way to New York last year. It was totally melodramatic—like when Maverick throws Goose's dog tags off the aircraft carrier in *Top Gun.* But I had to do it.

"So, if you don't mind," says Jerry.

"Yeah, Andy," says Neal. "Seriously, let's go."

I had anticipated this. I've got a plan. "OK," I say. "How about this?"

"Andy, it's time for you to—"

"What if I let you punch me in the face?"

This gets his attention—Neal's, too.

"Oh, come on," says Neal.

"I'm serious," I say.

"You're an idiot," says Neal. "Dad, ignore him. I think he's drunk, actually."

I can tell that Jerry is thinking about it.

"We'll be even," I say. "I hit you. You hit me. I buy a suit—it'll probably be marked up a little if we're being honest, right? You'll come out ahead in this deal, Jer. Just . . . could you aim for *this* side here? I'd appreciate it."

"Andy," says Neal. "You can't just show up and have people punch you and think everything's fine."

"Guess what, Neal," I say. "This actually isn't about you. Not everything is about you and your precious goddamn wedding reception, OK?

Other people have shit going on, too. Like me. I'm here to buy a suit—something nice. Apparently not something European—but something respectable, so I won't look like a degenerate at my grandpa's inevitable funeral. But if Jerry here is too big of a pussy to punch me in the face like a man, then I guess I'll go see Dwayne at Men's fucking Wear—"

I thought I was ready for it, but I wasn't. It feels sudden and violent and completely out of nowhere. I'm yelling at Neal, and then fireworks are going off directly in front of my face. And now I'm falling over a rack of dinner jackets.

Thirty minutes later, I'm standing in my underwear in front of a four-way mirror while Neal's dad measures my inseam.

I've got a pack of organic frozen blueberries from Trader Joe's pressed to my face. Jerry made Neal run across the street to get it, which, petty or not, felt like a win.

He's picked a conservative—but still modern—gray Hugo Boss two-button suit, slim-fitted. "Think of it as half-European," he says. I've got the jacket on over a white dress shirt. Neal is on the other side of the store. He got tired of waiting around, I guess, so he's unpacking a box of men's accessories. He takes a break every thirty seconds to glare at me.

Jerry is workmanlike, crouching on one knee, marking things with a chalk pencil. "You certainly aren't a giant, are you?" he says.

"Carter men are late bloomers," I say, which, of course, isn't true. My brother started shaving when he was eleven.

"We have some nice lifts if you're interested," he says.

"Lifts?"

"They give you a solid inch, inch and a half. Movie stars wear them all the time. Red carpets, premieres, that kind of thing. Trade secret."

His mood has lightened since he punched me. Oddly, mine has, too, which makes me wonder if I have a concussion. "I'm sorry I hit you at the reception," I say. "I meant to, I guess, but I didn't *really* mean to."

"I know," Jerry says, talking around a few pins that he's holding in his mouth. "I'm doing this for your grandpa, though. Not for you. He's a good man. I sold him a suit once. Forty-four regular, if I remember correctly. He told me to make him look like Sinatra."

"In case you're wondering," I say. "You hit the wrong side of my face."

"Well, you turned your head. You want some free advice? Next time you ask someone to punch you in the face, stand still."

"I'll remember that," I say.

He looks up from his work and studies my face. "Does it hurt?" He sounds more curious than sorry.

"Not really," I say.

Jerry nods, and for a moment I feel like the type of man he probably wished I was when I married his daughter. But then, when he hands me the marked-up pair of pants, I nearly tip over putting them on, and I wonder if I have brain damage. I imagine the conversation in the ER.

What happened to your face?
My former father-in-law punched it.
Why did he do that?
I asked him to. It should be noted that he's also my tailor.
Did you get a suit?
Yeah.
What color?
Dark gray. Charcoal, actually.
Good choice. Very versatile.

I zip the fly and button up, and then I tuck in the shirt. Jerry picks out a tie—greenish blue—which takes me three attempts to tie because

I can't even remember the last time I tied a tie. Then, when I'm fully dressed, we look at my reflection. Even Neal is interested, despite the fact that he's pretending not to be. And then I have a thought that surprises me. It just pops in there. *What would Daisy think?*

"So?" says Jerry.

"Not bad," I say.

"You look like a short, slightly gay James Bond," says Jerry.

Which is totally the look I was going for.

"Take it off and leave it on the table. I gotta lift the cuffs and take that jacket in a little. I'll call you when it's ready."

"As long as I'm here, I should probably pick up a few other things," I say.

"OK. Like what?"

I start loosening the tie. "Shoes. Brown, I guess. Black, too. I'm a size nine. A few of these dress shirts, maybe. A belt. A few belts. How many belts is a normal amount of belts to have? I don't know. Some socks. Definitely socks."

"OK," he says.

"Oh, and do you have black sport coats and nice jeans?"

"We do."

"Is that . . . Could I pull off that look, do you think?"

"Eh," he says.

"And you were saying something about lifts?"

"That's . . . that's quite a list, Andy."

It takes me a second, but I see what he's getting at. Money. Maybe he's heard about my 401(k) situation. "Don't worry, Jer," I say. "My brother's paying for it."

"Well . . . then let's get started."

21

This is the biggest goddamn car I've ever seen," says Neal. "You could land a helicopter on that hood."

We're on our way back to Lazzari's.

I'm wearing my new sport coat. I look at myself in the rearview mirror, and, even though I'm wearing it over my old T-shirt and jeans and my face looks like partially defrosted chicken breast, I look pretty decent.

"You should probably watch the road?" says Neal.

I steer us back into our lane. "Oh, now you're talking to me," I say. "It took a bribe."

He's got a big brown Gentleman's Closet shopping bag on his lap. I had Jim buy him some shit, too, because I've always been very generous when it comes to other people's money.

"Your brother's gonna kill you, you know," he says.

He's right, of course, but I've decided to let a future version of myself worry about that. "You're the worst buffer I've ever met, by the way," I say.

"Well, you *literally* invited him to punch you," says Neal.

I open and close my mouth a few times and shake my head, trying to silence the ringing in my head.

We drive in silence for a while. Neal looks out the window at the passing this and that. And then he says, "I tried to get ahold of you, after you left. You know that." He's rolling the end of his shopping bag, wrinkling it like a teenage girl on a date.

"I went off the grid," I say.

"You changed your number, your e-mail. I tried Facebooking you. Who quits Facebook? I didn't even know you *could* quit Facebook."

My mother is on the radio again. I have it on her station. I'm not 100 percent sure why.

> "It's sacred. It's not just a contract. It's not a piece of paper that I can tear up when opinions change—when new things come in and out of style. It's a sacred union. When we disrespect that union—that foundation—we all suffer in the end."

"All my friends were her friends," I say.

"What?"

"Facebook. All my friends were her friends. Every time I turned on my computer, I saw her."

He's quiet, thinking about this.

"Fucking Mark Zuckerberg," I say.

"But . . . ," says Neal. That's all he manages to say, though, before a siren goes off behind us. It's probably the loudest thing I've ever heard, and there are lights, too, red and blue, and it's a miracle that I don't run us into oncoming traffic and kill us both. I look up at the rearview. It's not a cop, it's an ambulance, and the driver is waving at me. He's wearing stupid aviator sunglasses, but I recognize him.

"Motherfucker," I say. All around us, cars are starting to slow down and pull to the side of the road, but I hit the gas.

Neal clutches the armrest. "What the fuck are you doing? It's an ambulance, man. Pull over."

The engine roars behind us, pulling right up on the back bumper. Neal turns around and sees what's happening. "Wait, is that . . . ?"

"It is," I say.

It's fucking Tyler.

"Well, this should be interesting," Neal says.

I finally ease off the gas and start guiding us to the side of the road. I put the car in park and watch Tyler get out—tall and V-shaped. He takes his sunglasses off and pushes his floppy hair back.

"You ever notice that like seventy-five percent of the dudes in America look like the bad guy in *The Karate Kid*?" I say.

"Don't do anything stupid," says Neal.

Tyler is standing at my window now—we've got a perfect view of his crotch. I grip the steering wheel and play a quick montage, just to make myself feel better.

There's me rolling down the window and punching him in the balls. There's me turning the car back on and running over his foot. There's an out-of-control FedEx truck running him down, flinging him through the air like the world's biggest Ken Doll. There's me laughing as he flies in slow motion.

He taps the glass with one knuckle. "Roll it down," he says. His voice is muffled through the window.

I touch my ear. "What? I can't hear you. The window is closed."

"Clever," says Neal.

"Roll the window down, Andy."

I do, keeping my eyes straight ahead as the ambulance blinks and flashes behind us like a giant strobe light.

"Hello, Andy," he says.

Next to me, Neal leans forward. "What's up, Tyler?" he says.

"Hey, Neal," says Tyler.

I look at him—at my former best friend—and I'm mortally wounded. Neal shrugs.

Tyler puts his hand on the door and crouches down. His face is inches from mine. "I think we need to talk."

"What would you like to discuss?" I say, struggling to keep my voice from shaking. "Oh, and hey . . . Don't touch the car, please."

"Well, I'd appreciate it if you didn't call my house and creep around my backyard like a psychopath."

"*Your* backyard?"

Tyler looks off to the horizon. Passing rubberneckers are slowing all around us, gawking as they roll by. "Yeah, Andy. *My* yard. *Our* yard, actually. This isn't some new development, believe it or not."

Neal makes a nervous noise from the passenger seat.

"And I loved that Husker gnome, you know," Tyler says. "I've had it since I was a kid, and you fucking destroyed it. And that shit you threw at the house—whatever it was—it stained the siding. I'm gonna have to rent a power washer now."

"It was a Mr. Misty," I say. "Grape."

"Listen," he says. "I've got cop friends. It's trespassing. And vandalism, if we're being technical. I don't want to call them. I don't want to take this in that direction, but . . ."

"You can fix up the yard all you want," I say.

"What?"

"You can buy cool chairs and fertilizer and fucking lawn gnomes. It's not your home. It's not . . . yours."

"Oh, yeah?" he says.

"Because you're a phase."

"I'm a phase?"

"A mistake. A big, dumb mistake."

Neal makes that same nervous sound again. He's serving no practical value here whatsoever.

"A mistake?"

"She doesn't love you. You're just some guy who lived down the street. You took advantage of a situation—our situation. And when she realizes all that, you'll be gone."

He doesn't look happy. "Take your seat belt off, Andy," he says.

"You're not a cop," I say. "I could just drive away right now. What are you gonna do, zap me with your . . . little shock paddles?"

"They're called defibrillators, you moron."

"Woooooooo," I say.

"Take your goddamn seat belt off."

"Why?"

"Just do it."

I do, which I instantly regret, because immediately after the buckle clicks, Tyler is pulling me out the window by my brand-new lapels. I struggle, but it's useless, and when my feet hit the ground, he's still clutching me. I can feel his breath in my face—infuriatingly minty, the son of a bitch.

"Did you seriously just pull me out of a car? What are you, a fucking caveman?"

"Shut up!"

And then he clips me in the stomach. It's just a jab, but it knocks the wind right out of me, and I crumble to my knees. I try to swear, but it comes out in an airless gasp.

"Shit," he says. "Goddammit. Get up. I'm sor . . . Here." He pulls me up onto my feet. I try very, very hard to look like I'm not in agony. "Just breathe normal. It'll come back. Give it a second. Take a breath. Your lungs just need to refill."

"Fuck you," I manage. *Tyler* is stitched into his blue paramedic shirt. God, I fucking hate that name.

"Listen," he says. "I know why you're here. I know why you're back home. I get it. You've got family sh—" Someone honks, and Tyler waves at them to go around us. "Just stay away from her. I mean it."

"Stay away from her? Are you serious?"

"Do I look like I'm joking?"

"You want me . . . *me* . . . to stay away from your . . . your what, your *girlfriend*? Your fucking girlfriend? I guess that makes sense. Wouldn't want to horn in on another guy's chick, would I? Only a real prick would do that."

"She's more than—" He stops himself and closes his eyes. He wants to hit me again, and I wish he would. "She's more than my girlfriend. I think you know that by now."

"No . . . I don't know that. You're just our neighbor. That's what I know. Our dumbfuck neighbor. You're like a jackal. A . . . sex jackal." I hear that, what I've just said, and it sounds so stupid that I now want the fictional FedEx truck to hit me—to just end this, right here, with all these rubbernecking morons as witnesses.

"A sex jackal?"

"Fuck you."

"She doesn't want to see you," he says. "Don't you get that? She doesn't want to deal with your crazy-ass bullshit. You think she didn't know you were out there the other night, sitting on our lawn chair like a serial killer? If she wanted to talk to you, don't you think she would have? Maybe she would have come outside. *Oh, hi, Andy . . . You're not here to murder me, are you?* Or maybe she would have answered the phone when you called. *Oh, hi, is this Andy? Hey, Andy, I'm sleeping, because it's the middle of the fucking night.*"

I'm angry. But I'm embarrassed, too. It's all welling up. "Bullshit," I say. "*You're* the one who doesn't want her to talk to me. You're just scared."

He smiles—just a quick flash of teeth and cheekbones. He puts his sunglasses back on, and I see dual reflections of myself. I look like a beat-up, red-faced kid who's about to cry. "Yeah, I'm terrified," he says.

"You better be," I say.

As he walks away, he turns back. "Nice jacket, by the way."

I smooth out the lapels. "It *was* a nice jacket. Until you got your . . . fucking *bronzer* all over it."

He rolls his eyes and climbs back into the ambulance. "I see you in *our* backyard again—or if you call *our* house—I'm calling the cops. Period. That's a promise."

A car nearly sideswipes another car and they honk at each other. Two more cars behind them honk, and brakes squeal.

"You're a great civil servant, by the way!" I shout. "Maybe you can use your *defibrillator* on all the bodies after the pileup you're going to cause!"

I guess this technically counts as getting the last word. But that satisfaction is short-lived because I'm hit with a wall of street grit and dust as he pulls away. I'm left coughing and covering my eyes.

Fuck him.

Back in the car, I sit for a long time, breathing. I'll remember this, what just happened, for a very long time. I'll be on my own deathbed someday, replaying this in my head, wishing it had gone differently. We hold on to the shitty things the tightest, for some reason. And this is the shittiest thing ever.

"Are you OK?" Neal says.

I'd nearly forgotten he was there. "Not now," I say.

"Look on the bright side," he says. "At least he didn't hit you in the face."

"Get out," I say.

"What?"

"You heard me. Get out."

"Andy."

"You knew," I say.

"I knew what?"

"You fucking knew about that . . . that . . . asshole . . . and you let me walk around like a fucking idiot, letting me think I still had a chance to get her back."

"I knew for like two days! She's my sister. What, you don't think I have any allegiance to her, too? She told me not to tell you yet. I found out the weekend of my wedding . . . and you were my fucking best man. If I told you, you'd have freaked out. I knew you'd go apeshit and wreck something. And guess what. I was right. I was gonna tell you . . . *after*. What do you think I—"

"Get . . . out!"

"What do you want me to do, Andy? Walk?"

"I don't give a shit. Call a cab. And take your shitty clothes with you. Those khakis you picked out look stupid, by the way. No one wears fucking pleats anymore, dipshit."

"Fine." He opens the door and climbs out. "You're not gonna leave me here, Andy. This is stupid. You and I both know it. This . . . is . . . stupid."

I hit the gas and the great car lurches forward, and I hope that these are the last words I ever hear him say—*this is stupid*. But of course, they're not. I make it about five car lengths before I have to slam on the brakes. Traffic is still jacked up from Tyler's dumbfuckery, and we're all waiting at a red light like idiots.

"Motherfucker," I say.

Neal is there in the rearview mirror, shielding his eyes from the sun, looking at me. His shopping bag is sitting at his feet. "I can see you, Andy!" he shouts. "Really smooth exit! Well played!"

I give him the finger through the sunroof, and then I turn my mom's voice up as loud as it'll go. When the light finally turns green, I drive off.

22

It's not books or music this time. And instead of texting, she called.

"Do you like ice cream?" she said.

"Are there people who don't like ice cream?" I said.

"Are you one of those people who answers questions with questions?"

"I'm actually kind of busy right now," I said, which was a lie, of course. At that exact moment I was organizing my CDs by genre and alphabetizing them. This was after a failed attempt at color-coding by album art.

"Well, whatever you're doing, it's not nearly as important as having ice cream with me at Ted & Wally's. Wear your corncob shirt. It'll be fun."

So that's where we are now, standing at the counter looking up at the absurdly complicated ice cream menu. It's another blast from my past, this place. It's as if Daisy Googled *Oddball spots to go in Omaha, Nebraska*, and then just started checking things off.

"I still think this thing is too small for me," I say, tugging at the tight sleeves of my T-shirt. They barely make it past the halfway point of my biceps.

"Shut up," she says. "Most guys our age are fat. You're still skinny. We're accentuating the positives, remember? By the way, did you get taller? You look taller."

I tell her no, that she's imagining things, and then I score one for my former father-in-law, the moody bastard.

The lady behind the counter is waiting for us to order. Aside from two gothed-out teenagers at a booth, we're the only people here. "Sorry," I say. "Just a cup of . . . vanilla, I guess."

"Nope," Daisy says. "Vanilla? No way. Veto."

"Veto?"

"You can't come to a place like this and order . . . *vanilla*. It's like you're ordering a metaphor of yourself. We'll take two cups of pistachio nutmeg, please."

"That doesn't even sound like a real thing," I say.

"Don't listen to him," she says. "He's currently under construction."

The lady nods and gets our ice cream.

We find a table a safe distance from the teenagers, who are full-on making out in the corner. I take a few bites of my ice cream, and it tastes every bit as unnecessary as it sounds.

"So are you gonna tell me about your face?" she asks.

"I'd rather not."

"Did Nancy hit you? I can see her having an abusive side." When I don't say anything, she licks her spoon. "Well, at least you shaved. Day two . . . five o'clock shadow. I like it. The new Andy Carter is taking shape."

"This is the worst ice cream I've ever tasted," I say.

"Well, you're in a mood, aren't you?"

"Sorry," I say.

"You're eating ice cream. It's a sunny day. As my boyfriend Kurt Vonnegut used to say, 'If this isn't nice, what is?'"

She's right, I suppose—it is sunny, and, technically, stupid flavors aside, I am eating ice cream. But I've been like this since seeing Tyler a few days ago. The fact is, he's a prick and a Neanderthal, and I've fantasized about his death a million times, and I've comforted myself with the idea that he's completely wrong for Karen and totally temporary. But he was right about one thing. If Karen wanted to talk to me, she'd talk to me. That's what this has come to—five years of marriage, and she wants nothing to do with me.

"So, I've been meaning to ask you something," Daisy says. "What's your Feel Sorry Flick?"

She's a study in non sequiturs, this girl, and for a second I just stare back, no idea what she's talking about.

"Chapter one, remember? Feeling Better Is Up To . . . *You.*" She points at me. "We're all playing our little Feel Sorry Flicks on our brain TVs. Blah blah. Yada yada. You were so engrossed in it the other night at the bookstore."

"I thought you said that book was bullshit."

"*Mostly* bullshit. She had a point about the flicks, though. Let's hear it. Be specific. And remember, storytelling is about details."

"I don't really have just one," I say.

"Right. There's probably, like, fifty. I get it. But what's your best one? The 'Hey Jude' of Feel Sorry Flicks . . . The one that just makes you wanna go stick your head in the oven and call it a day."

"You first," I say.

She stops eating, spoon in hand.

"Well?" I say.

"Who says I've got Feel Sorry Flicks?"

I tilt my head. "You seem like kind of an expert when it comes to pain and human suffering."

She accepts this without argument and drops her spoon in her cup. "OK, maybe I'm an injured little baby bird, too. I'll make you a deal. I'll tell you mine if you tell me yours. But . . . you first."

"OK," I say, and she claps, genuinely excited, which is weird.

I take a breath. I've actually never told this story to anyone before, and I'm not sure where to start. You'd think it would be easier to articulate the things we obsess over the most. "We were at Applebee's," I say.

"What?"

"We were at Applebe—"

"Nope. Vetoing that, too."

"You can't just keep vetoing things."

"I can. I'll veto that shit all day. In your whole life, Andy, have you ever heard an interesting story that starts in an Applebee's?"

"OK," I say. "I guess that's fair."

"Yeah. Try again."

So I tell her about the blizzard.

It was two winters ago now, and it was legit. A full-fledged snow emergency. A snowbound city. All-day news coverage. A warning from the mayor. It was just us in our little house—*The Shining* without all the scary, disturbing parts.

The first day, Karen and I got dressed and tried to keep our sidewalk clear like good, responsible citizens. We took showers and trudged our way to the gas station for candy and paper towels. But on day two, a Wednesday, we didn't even bother getting dressed. We wore overpriced sweatpants, and Karen bundled up in one of my old hoodies. We ate leftover Halloween bite-size Snickers and drank whatever alcohol we could find in the house. We were watching *Ace Ventura: Pet Detective* on Comedy Central, because that's the sort of thing you watch when you're restless and housebound.

Karen and I were always good at this part of marriage—the lounging-together-and-watching-basic-cable part. It was effortless, and she was beautiful, and I was lucky. I was somehow married to this girl, and I was happy, and I was certain that I always would be. She hadn't started getting solemn and quiet yet. She hadn't started not wanting to go places. Tyler and his stupid jogging shorts hadn't moved in down the street yet. This was before the end started.

Her legs were in my lap. This was our couch position—we fell into it naturally, without discussion—a simple routine of marriage. I sat on the middle cushion, she sat beside me and draped her legs over me, resting her head on the green throw pillows propped up on the armrest. I ran the tips of my fingers along the arches of her feet, somewhere between tickling and massaging. She loved it when I did this. Karen's middle toes are just slightly longer than her big toes. Her E.T. toes. I squeezed her ankles and moved upward, rubbing her calves and then her knees and then her thighs. It was so familiar, her body, all its angles and nuances. Her breathing began to change, the temperature of her skin beneath my hands ticked upward. She lifted her hoodie up for me, and I touched her stomach and kissed her hipbone and that breathing became a small moan, like the letter *m* on repeat.

"Snow day," she whispered.

It was, officially, the last perfect day of our marriage.

I eventually stop talking, and when I do, Daisy says nothing for once, which is a goddamn miracle.

She looks sad, which is new, and I wonder if I should have just stuck with Applebee's. I could have told her about "Wake Me Up Before You Go-Go" and my Sizzling Chili Lime Chicken. But then she leans across the small table and kisses me. It lasts maybe three seconds, and her lips are cool from her silly ice cream.

"E.T. toes," she says. "Good detail. A-plus-plus."

Outside, when we leave, I'm lightheaded, the effects of my first kiss in more than a year. The goth couple from before is sitting on a bench holding hands.

"Can I walk you to your . . . car?" I say. "Is it nearby?"

It's hard to imagine Daisy driving a car. She looks like one of those girls you see in New York, carless, perpetually clomping toward something.

"That's sweet," she says. "But I'm not the kind of girl you need to walk places."

"Clearly," I say.

"You made progress today, you know."

"I did?"

"You kissed a girl, didn't you? Sounds like progress to me."

She touches my face. "Tomorrow's scruffy day."

When she walks away, I watch her go until she disappears around a corner.

I head back toward the Caddie. It's so freaking enormous that its taillights stick out of its parking spot past every other car on the street, which makes it pretty tough to miss. As I get closer, I see that there are some guys looking at it. They're standing there, arms crossed, peeking in the windows like they're going to try to steal something. When they see me coming, all three straighten to full attention.

Parked next to my grandpa's car is a tiny yellow VW Bug. I'm standing there on the sidewalk holding my grandpa's keys.

"Hello, Andy," one of them says. He's wearing jeans and a really nice lightweight sweater. I recognize him from the other night. I recognize the two other guys, too, standing on either side of him. They're the guys who vandalized my parents' yard.

"Hey, guys," I say.

"Nice car," he says. "Don't make 'em like this anymore, huh?"

"No glitter today?" I say.

They all look at each other and smile. "We come in peace. How about a cup of coffee?"

23

I'm Stephen, by the way," the main guy says.

We're sitting at a little table, Stephen and I, at a place called Koba Café. The other two guys are standing over Stephen's shoulder like Secret Service agents.

"This is Ronnie," says Stephen. "Say hi, Ronnie."

Ronnie, the guy on the left, gives me an upward nod.

"And this is Chili."

"Chili?" I say.

"Well, Charles," says Stephen. "But who wants to be a Charles when you can be a Chili, right?"

Chili gives me the peace sign. "Hey," he says.

Ronnie has a well-trimmed goatee, and Chili is wearing rainbow colors on a chain around his neck. They're all about forty, I'd guess, but they could pass for thirty in that way that handsome gay men can seemingly defy the basic rules of nature.

"What are your thoughts on cappuccino?" says Stephen.

I look at Ronnie and Chili, both of whom are glaring at me. "I don't really have any," I say.

"Understandable," says Stephen. "This place has the best cappuccino in the city. Good lattes, too. Tell you the truth, I can hardly tell the difference between a cappuccino and a latte. Or an espresso, for that matter. Coffee and milk, right? Maybe some foam? Who can keep it all straight?"

I happen to agree with him, but I get the feeling we're adversaries, so I don't say anything. I wonder if this is what Tupac felt like right before the bullets started whizzing.

"Ronnie here's a chai tea latte guy, right, Ronnie?"

Ronnie nods, and, on second thought, this is probably nothing like the Tupac thing.

"Too peppery for me," Stephen says. "But that's just my opinion. So what do you say, Mr. Carter? What'll you have?"

"I'm fine," I say.

"Oh, come on. Don't be like that. You have to have something. It's on us. Free coffee."

"OK," I say. "Regular coffee. Whatever size."

"Hey, boys," says Stephen. "Why don't you go order? I'll take my usual—double cap, half-and-half, a little shot of skim." He makes a squirting sound and pantomimes milking a cow. "Our friend here will take a regular coffee. With . . . sugar, Andy?"

"Uh, Splenda."

Stephen shakes his head. "Oh, really? Andy, the chemicals. But then again, sugar's probably no better, right? Just a different kind of bad. There really are no *good* options in life, sometimes, you know. Chili, double cap for me, coffee with Splenda for Mr. Carter. I believe whatever size will do. Let's go with a large. Why not, right?" He winks at me.

Chili takes this all in and walks away.

"Oh, and maybe some biscotti? If it's fresh. Ask Adam if he put them out today, OK? If he didn't, muffins. Blueberry . . . Good?"

The guy at the counter, Adam, is black with cool dreads, and I make a mental note to tell Byron that I saw a black dude in Omaha.

Stephen doesn't say anything for a bit, and I'm very much aware of the fact that he smells terrific—like vanilla and sandalwood and fresh laundry. I am also very much aware of the fact that this is an observation I should keep to myself. "So, are they, like, your goons?"

"Goons?" Stephen smiles. "Well, that's an ugly word, isn't it? Don't call them that to their faces. It'll hurt their feelings."

"But you're the boss? You seem like you're in charge."

"Do I? That's nice. I try to be. There *is* a hierarchy, just like any organization." He surveys the crowd around us. There are a few mothers with their children, some sleepy-looking college kids hunched over Facebook, and a very old man reading the *Omaha World-Herald* with a poodle on his lap. Stephen leans in. "God . . . poodles are so bitchy. I just hate them."

Up front, Chili and Ronnie look back at us, serious and quiet. They seem like they're mad at me.

"Who was that girl you were with back there?" Stephen says.

I start to say something, but then I realize that there is literally no way to describe who or what Daisy is—especially to this guy.

"Well, whoever she is, yum. All those tattoos. Like she wants to fight or tie you up or something. If I went that way, I feel like that's the type I'd go for, someone with an edge—someone my mom would hate. The women in this city are all either chunky monkeys or look like they have a rod stuck up their ass. Daisy's got . . . I don't know . . . spunk."

"Wait," I say. "How do you know her name?"

He sighs. "Well, shoot, I guess you caught me. I know a lot of things, Andy, as you're about to find out. Think of me as the ghost of . . . wait, which ghost was it that knows everything . . . in *A Christmas Carol?*"

"Past, I think."

"Really?" he says. "I thought it was Future. Well, it doesn't matter. Whichever one—that's me. But let's start from the beginning. I'll assume you know who *we* are at this point, right?"

"Not really," I say. "I know what you *did*—you fucked up my parents' yard."

He winces. "Yeah, that was us. I want to apologize for the sex doll. Chili's idea. It was . . . less than professional, admittedly. That thing must have been an absolute whore to get out of that tree. We got it stuck up there pretty good."

"Yeah."

"Those things are so creepy. It's the eyeballs, right? They're like zombie eyes."

"Where do you get that many Ken Dolls anyway?" I ask.

"We buy them in bulk. You can buy anything on the Internet, if you're properly funded, which we are. Miniature tuxedos, too. There are factories everywhere—China and whathaveyou. We *do* have to glue their cute little hands together, though. That can be a pain in the ass. We take turns. Well, Chili and Ronnie take turns. As you said . . . I'm sort of their boss."

I think about the other night—the over-the-top, sketch-comedy gay voices, the lisps and cheerleader chants. It's not like that now. Stephen, other than being hyperarticulate, sounds pretty much like anyone else. "You guys seem . . . ," I say.

"What?"

"Different," I say. "From before."

"What do you mean?

"The other night you were . . ."

He laughs. "What, gayer?"

I shrug. "A little."

Stephen cocks his head and waves his finger at me on a floppy wrist. "What, three fabulous queers in a cute little VW out causin' a ruckus." He puts on an affected voice, drawing out all the *S*'s. "That's all part of the act. We were working. This is more of a social call."

"An act?"

"It's very intentional. All part of our strategy. You take the prej-udice—you take society's worst, most hackneyed, Fox News–loving, backward stereotype of homosexuality—and then you turn it up to eleven. And then you ram it right back down people's throats. In a man-ner of speaking. If they're uncomfortable, good. Mission accomplished. Fuck 'em."

The old guy and his poodle look up simultaneously.

"Sorry, sweetie," Stephen says, using the voice again.

The guy looks away.

"See," Stephen says.

"Right," I say.

"Think of it like this," he says. "Ever been to a pride march? Well, of course you haven't. But you've probably seen them on TV. You think we're all *that* flaming in real life? We're accountants and math teachers and interior designers and quarterbacks, Andy. We have *real* jobs. We work in offices. All the chaps and the chokers, that's just to get the breeders all riled up. Oh, hey, that's a great T-shirt, by the way. I meant to tell you that earlier, but, you know, we kind of had our game faces on."

I look down at my little rodeo man. "Thanks," I say.

Chili and Ronnie are back now with our drinks and a plate of blue-berry muffins. Ronnie gives Stephen his cappuccino, and Chili slams my coffee down on the table in front of me. He tosses a damp Splenda packet next to it, and then the two of them step back and stand with their arms folded, assuming the position.

Stephen takes a sip of his coffee and rolls his eyes with pleasure. "Exactly," he says. "Love this stuff. You'll have to forgive Chili and Ronnie's rudeness. They're nice guys, I promise. They're just, well, I guess they kind of consider you guilty by association."

"Association to what?"

The three of them exchange a look, like a bad-cop, bad-cop, good-cop look. "Andy, you know what, I'm being overly vague here, and I apologize for that," says Stephen. "You need to have all the information if we're going to have a successful dialogue here. Otherwise, we're just wasting each other's time, right? You see, me, Chili, and Ronnie are . . . Well, let's just say we're not big fans of Nancy."

"No shit," I say.

He smiles. "It's more than that, actually. Plenty of people don't like your mother. You probably know that—I mean, growing up in *that* household, after all. But we're members of an organization, Andy. A small but powerful, deeply devoted organization that stands at odds with your mother and her antiquated way of thinking."

"What kind of organization?"

He leans in again. "Have you ever heard of . . . the Glitter Mafia?"

"Glitter Mafia? No."

"Really? Well, that's disappointing. Granted, we're not a household name . . . yet. But I'm sure you know our work. You see Newt Gingrich get glitter-bombed a few years ago in Minnesota on his horrible book tour?"

"Oh, right," I say. "I remember that."

"That was us. We got some of the others, too. Lots of buzz— trending online and such."

"You three did that?" I say.

They look at each other again. Chili and Ronnie scoff.

"No, not us *specifically*, silly," says Stephen. "The three of us handle Omaha. Kansas City a bit, too. Iowa, sometimes, like during the pri- maries. But we're a *national* organization."

"Global, actually." This is Ronnie, his first actual words.

"Oh. Right, Ronnie. Thank you. We're in London now. Fish 'n' chips and pale skin. Beautiful city, though. And we're about to start up a chapter in Toronto. So, yeah . . . we're international. Global. Pretty big deal."

"OK," I say. "So you guys go around pranking Republicans, then?"

Stephen takes a sip of his coffee and holds the cup under his nose, getting a whiff. "I think you'll see that we do a lot more than that."

He holds up his hand and Ronnie springs to action, handing him a manila envelope. Stephen sets it down in front of me.

"What's that?" I ask.

"Patience. We'll get to that. I'm building to something here, Andy, OK? I practiced and everything. You're aware, are you not, that any week now, the Supreme Court will be making a ruling that could, in effect, legalize same-sex marriage in this country?"

"Yeah," I say. "OK."

"And you are also aware that your mother has devoted her entire life and career, as of late, to lobbying against our interests in the case?"

"Right," I say.

"Well, we would like her to stop doing that. Or, at the very least, turn the fucking volume down. I mean, there are plenty of other wing nut causes she could scream about, right? Guns? Trickle-down economics? All those pesky Mexicans stealing our jobs and all?"

I look at Chili and Ronnie, and then back at Stephen. "Guys," I say. "I'm on your side . . . basically. I don't know what you expect me to do."

Stephen smacks his palm on the table. "See, boys," he says. "I told you."

For maybe a tenth of a second, Chili and Ronnie relax their scowls.

"I figured you were one of us . . . Well, in spirit, anyway. You being Mr. New Yorker and all. That's actually one of the reasons we're talking to you."

"How do you know where I live?" I say.

Stephen tsks me. "It's our job to know things like that," he says. "Andrew Charles Carter. New York City resident. Upper East Side, right? Nice. I recommend the Lost Dog Café. You'll thank me. You're divorced. Sorry about that. Unwitting YouTube celebrity. Graduate of the University of Nebraska at Lincoln and Creighton Prep High School. You were an altar boy in junior high. About five-five . . . give or take.

Although you look a little taller than that, now that I've seen you. I'll have to adjust your bio."

"OK," I say. "Google, right? It's a powerful tool."

They laugh, all three of them. "Oh, Andy," says Stephen. "How I love being underestimated. Along with acquiring said information, it is also our job to leverage that information in specific, very targeted ways."

"What the hell does that mean?"

He looks at the envelope sitting on the table between us next to the muffins.

"What?"

"Go ahead," he says.

"Go ahead and what?"

"Andy, this is the part where you open the envelope. Did you really not get that? Don't you watch spy movies?"

Chili and Ronnie lean in, and Stephen wiggles in his seat. I untwist the little metal clip and tear open the top of the envelope. There's a stack of pictures inside, black and whites. I have to squint at the first one, because it's blurry, but it's my dad. He's standing outside of a restaurant.

"We're not fools, Andy," says Stephen. "This is a conservative place—we're not changing the hearts and minds of this big square state. But your mother is becoming a national voice—somehow. And she's a potential threat to us."

I flip to the next picture. It's my dad in his car. In the next picture, my dad is in a restaurant. It's taken from outside, and there's a blurry figure across from him.

"The people who listen to your mother? Lemmings, mostly. Right now they hear her going on and on about how terrible we are—how we're out to convert their babies to the dark side and tear apart the fabric of society—and it charges them up, makes their antigay rage all bubbly and hot. They start e-mailing their congressmen and their senators. The mood gets turbulent. Support begins to slow. Suddenly the

Supreme Court starts getting nervous. They start saying to each other, *Maybe now's not the time.* Maybe they're not ready yet."

"You think Nancy is going to influence the Supreme Court?"

"Maybe, maybe not," says Stephen. "But we're not taking any chances. That's why we want her to put a sock in it. You know as well as I do that marriage equality is inevitable. We just want it to be inevitable . . . now."

I keep flipping through the pictures. And then I see my dad with a woman—a brunette. He's leaning close, talking to her. She's in a dress, and her hair is back in a clip.

"Oh, who's that?" says Stephen. "She's pretty, huh?"

My chest tightens when I see the next picture. They're holding hands, my dad and this woman. She *is* pretty, late forties maybe, she's looking off in the distance. My dad is smiling.

"I'm not a private investigator or anything," says Stephen. "But I don't believe that's Dr. Nancy Knows, huh?"

I put the stack of photos down. They're walking into a hotel. My father is looking back over his shoulder. "Where did you get these?" I say.

He runs his fingers along the rim of his cup and puts a dollop of foam in his mouth. "Not Google."

There are more pictures in the stack, maybe a dozen, and I don't want to see them.

"The husband of Nancy Carter—*the* Nancy Carter—defender of the sanctity of old-fashioned America, embroiled in a seedy affair? That'd be a big story right there, Andy? People would wanna read about that. Oh, and that last one right there . . . outside the hotel. You guys were all at the hospital with poor sick Grandpa Henry. That is *not* a media-friendly detail."

"So, you guys . . . You're threatening my family?"

"Oh, don't be so dramatic." Stephen holds his empty cup in the air and Chili takes it. "Listen, we're not monsters. We have little interest in ruining your family. Your mother, well, no offense, she's awful. I wouldn't mind seeing her go down in flames. Your dad, though, he doesn't seem so bad. Kinda sweet. Your brother, Jim, too. I mean, I doubt we'd be buddy-buddy, but he seems fine. Adorable kids, too. The little girl one is a doll. And you . . . Well, I like your style, Andy. You have good taste in T-shirts, and I suspect deep down you're as horrified by your mom's rhetoric as the boys and me are. But this is bigger than just us. And it's bigger than the Carters. So if Nancy continues her campaign to persecute us . . . these pictures will make their way to the *Omaha World-Herald*, I promise you. And not just there. *Drudge Report. Huffington Post. Gawker. Daily Beast.* The list goes on and on. She's not some local kook droning on about the evils of the Kardashians, Andy. This is the big time. And I think we both know that she doesn't want this stuff out there."

This, of course, is true, and we all know it. Nancy would be devastated—and, worse, she'd become a joke. "So what am I supposed to do? I'm just . . . visiting."

"You'll figure something out," he says.

He gets up and drops a few dollars on the table. Chili and Ronnie leave first. They open the door and step out into the parking lot, putting on their sunglasses. Stephen lags behind. "It was nice to meet you, Andy," he says. "Sorry about your grandpa. He seems sweet, too."

I'm looking at a new picture now. They're coming out of the hotel. The woman is walking a few paces behind my dad. They don't know they're being photographed.

"He looks happy in that one," says Stephen. He straightens his sweater and smoothes out the front of his jeans. "The heart wants what the heart wants," he says. "Feel free to take a muffin."

And then all three of them are gone.

24

Nancy stabs a green bean, looks at it, and then puts it in her mouth. She chews and chews, like she's pretending there's more there than there is. There's a skinny piece of grilled chicken on her plate and a limp stack of soggy vegetables. This is how she eats now.

My dad and I are splitting lasagna—a premade thing from the grocery store. He's reading an article about birds, and she's reading an issue of *National Review*, and I'm pretty much just sitting here. The grandfather clock is ticking in the entryway. I clear my throat, but neither of them looks up.

This is the third of these meals the three of us have endured together since I got back to Omaha. I imagine going up to their bedroom and having it be '60s sitcom style, with two twin beds and long, elaborate dressing gowns.

I look at my dad and think of the man in the pictures. The whole stack is in my room, the manila envelope jammed into my old desk drawer. I looked at them last night as I was lying in bed and tried to imagine my dad having sex with whoever that lady is. And then I tried to imagine Nancy having sex. I didn't have the advantage of a photograph, though, so my brain chose Sean Hannity from Fox News as her partner. So now that's there in my brain, probably forever, the image of Sean Hannity having sex with my mother.

"So," I say. "Dad, you said you're serving on . . . a board?"

He looks up and nudges his reading glasses to the bottom of his nose. There's a little hair of cheese hanging from his lip.

"What . . . kind of company is it?" I ask.

He looks at Nancy and takes a bite of lasagna. All of my talking has messed up the creepy silence. "An accounting advisory board," he says.

As far as conversations go, that's not much of a jumping-off point. I liked yesterday better, and all the days before that. Back then, I didn't think about the complexities of my parents' lives because I was busy obsessing over mine.

"Is that where you were today?" I say.

He swallows, and, unless I'm imagining things, it looks like a difficult swallow, a gulp. I watched him leave earlier this afternoon. I was watching *Judge Judy*, and he hopped on the motorcycle and wobbled out of the driveway. If he hadn't been wearing a tucked-in yellow polo and khakis with pleats, and if he hadn't nearly sent himself crashing into the shrubbery, he would have actually looked like a badass.

Nancy sets her magazine down.

"Yeah," he says. "We had a meeting today. There are some conferences coming up."

"Oh," I say. "Well, next time, let me know. Maybe I'll go with you."

He looks surprised. That's actually an understatement. He looks stunned. "Really?"

I put some lasagna in my mouth. I'm like a poker player, bluffing with whatever cards equal a really shitty hand. I should mention that I have no fucking idea how to play poker.

"You want to come with me to a meeting about helping organizations integrate modern accounting best practices into their quarterly business plans?"

I'm not entirely sure any of that was English. "Yeah," I say. "I do. Why not?"

We continue eating, and I wish Jim was here. When we were kids, there were no magazines at the table, no TV or radios, either. Nancy forbade all that. The four of us sat together and talked about our days, like a Norman Rockwell painting. Sometimes Grandpa Henry and Grandma Dot would visit. They were only a few miles away, and they'd pop over in the Caddie, and Grandma Dot would bring one of her horrible Jell-O molds with mango or ominous blueberries floating inside.

"Well, I have some news, Andy," says Nancy. Her microdinner is all gone, her little plate empty. "Remember the list I told you about?"

I look at my dad. He's watching us. He clearly knows about this already.

"Yeah," I say.

"I got the call."

"You . . . The call? Really?"

She's biting back a smile. She's a bad poker player, too. She's clearly delighted.

"On Fffff . . ." The word, *Fox*, catches in my mouth, a sudden speech impediment.

After dinner, I shock everyone by volunteering to clean up. When I'm done clearing and then piling the dishes into the dishwasher, I call Jim, who answers on the first ring. "This is Jim Carter."

"This is Andy Carter," I say, trying to sound as obnoxious as he does.

"Jesus," he says. "Andy."

"Well, hello to you, too."

"I'm about to get on a conference call. I thought you were Asia."

"The whole country?" I say.

"It's a continent, genius."

"I know. Are you at work? Do you have a life? Are you a sophisticated robot sent from the future to have conference calls?"

"I'm in my office at the house," he says. "I just gave the kids a bath . . . Now, back to work."

"What time is it in Asia, anyway?" I say.

Jim is quiet, thinking. "Hell, I don't even know. I accept the Outlook invite, I get on the phone, I kick ass. That's the job. Karate lessons and Range Rovers don't pay for themselves. Anyway, they're supposed to call . . . um . . . thirty seconds ago. Did you get a suit yet?"

"Yeah," I say. "It should be ready in a day or so."

"How was it seeing Mr. G. again?" he says.

"Rough at first, but then he punched me in the face, so we're cool now."

"Good for him," says Jim. "So, seriously, what's going on?"

"You sound weird," I say. "Are you wearing one of those awful headsets?"

"I always wear headsets on work calls. I can pace around the room and yell at people more effectively."

"Can you yell, 'I love black people,' and 'Show me the money'?"

"What?"

"It's from *Jerry Maguire*. You know . . . 'You had me at hello.'"

"Andy, I don't have time for this."

"I think there's something up with Mom and Dad," I say.

"What do you mean *up*?"

"Do they seem . . . *weird* to you?"

"No. I don't know. Why? You're the one who's living there. You tell me."

"Something . . . happened yesterday," I say. "We need to talk, OK? I need to talk to you about something."

"About what? Are you menstruating? Did you get your period?"

"Stop being a dick. I don't want to talk about it over the phone."

"Is the phone bugged?"

"No. They're . . . here, you asshole. I don't want to talk about them while they're here. Jesus. Mom's doing push-ups in the other room. Our mother is doing push-ups, Jim, to a workout DVD. That, in and of itself, is weird. They hardly talk to each other. Dad is shooting at animals in the yard. Mom ate, like, three little grilled pieces of vegetable and a cracker for dinner. And . . . have you seen the extra bedrooms?"

"Are you in trouble or something?"

"Trouble? That's what you got out of all the things I just said? Why would you think I'm in trouble?"

Jim laughs. "I've been your brother for a while now. I've learned to expect certain things from you."

"Can we meet tomorrow? Like lunch or whatever?"

He blows some air into the phone, and I can hear him shuffling with something, flipping some pages. "Lunch . . . no. Not tomorrow. Early dinner? It's my evening to deal with the kids. Like . . . six? Take it or leave it."

I tell him OK.

"But here's the deal," he says. "I get to pick the place."

"OK, fine. Where do you—"

"And I don't know about you, but I'm in the mood for some pizza. Lazzari's sound good?"

"No, Jim. That's not a good idea. There was . . . There was an incident the other day."

"Ooo . . . Sounds interesting."

"Come on, I don't—"

But then there's a click on the line, a quick drop in and out. "That's them," he says. "They're beeping in. I gotta go yell at like five Korean guys right now. Shit's a mess over there. Six o'clock at Lazzari's. See you there, punk."

And then he's gone.

He's such a dickhead.

25

The next day, after spending some time with my grandpa in the morning, I very briefly considered digging my old running shoes out of the closet and going for a jog in the neighborhood. I had it all planned out. I'd find one of my running tapes and the Walkman that I used in high school. I'd wear shorts, and I'd sweat, and I'd feel good about myself . . . just like the old days. Maybe I'd get lucky and see Don Johnson and give him the finger.

But instead, I'm sitting in the gazebo in my parents' yard destroying a box of Teddy Grahams and watching the battle between the squirrels and the birds. Generally speaking, the birds are much angrier than the squirrels, and they're blessed with the ability to attack from the sky. But the squirrels, decked out in rebel war paint, look like miniature Mel Gibsons from *Braveheart*, so it's difficult not to pull for them.

I throw them a few Teddy Grahams, which they accept begrudgingly. When my phone rings, I see that it's Daisy. "Hello," I say.

"Quivering flower," she says.

"Excuse me."

"Quivering flower."

"Should I say *excuse me* again?" I say.

"You strike me as a guy who knows a thing or two about vaginas," she says.

"I'm basically an expert."

"Have you ever once thought of a vagina as a quivering flower?"

"No," I say. "Actually, the first time I saw one in real life, I thought of the Great Pit of Carkoon in *Return of the Jedi*."

"OK, well, I officially take back my previous comment about you knowing a thing or two about vaginas."

"Understandable."

"What are you doing right now?" she says.

"Volunteering at a soup kitchen," I say. "Then it's off to hot yoga." I watch one squirrel pounce on the bird feeder and scatter seeds onto the ground for his friends.

"I'm at the mall. What size pants do you wear, by the way?"

"Thirty-two, thirty," I say.

"OK . . . Thirty, thirty it is," she says. "We're streamlining you, remember. I've decided you're gonna start weaving chinos into your rotation. Not like the horrible things you probably wore when you had a real job. Casual, wrinkled, but not too wrinkled. Think of them as the pants you see on guys who look like they don't care but secretly care very much."

"I hate those guys," I say.

I hear mall sounds behind her, chimes and people milling about. And then she says, "I actually feel kind of bad."

"About what?"

"Normally I don't feel bad about things. It's this talent I have, like I'm a dead-inside robot when I want to be. But the other day, I duped you into telling me about your worst Feel Sorry Flick, then I took off."

"Yeah, that was pretty shitty," I say. I lean back against one of the gazebo pillars and think about what she looks like now, talking on her phone in some store. She doesn't come into focus, though. It's just frayed jeans and a blurry face. She's like a password that I haven't totally memorized yet.

"He tried to teach me to play the guitar this one time," she says.

"Who?" I say.

"Who do you think," she says. "Him—and he, too, shall remain nameless."

There are more mall sounds. "So you're like me, after all, then?"

"A shell of a girl," she says. "Cast aside."

"So, a guitar player," I say. "Why doesn't that surprise me?"

"He's really good. Was. Is. I don't know. I prefer to use the past tense sometimes, like he's dead."

"He probably listens to vinyl, doesn't he? And he's totally self-righteous about it."

"*Exclusively*," she says. "Total record snob. But shut up, OK, because this is my story."

I agree to shut up, and she tells me about how he was trying to teach her how to hold her fingers—where to put them on the strings—but she just couldn't get it. "I kept staring at his fingers, but it was reversed, like when you look in a mirror. So he told me to turn around, and he sat behind me and held my hands and put my fingers where they were supposed to go. He smelled like cigarettes and this leather polish he used to use on his boots. Smell can be used as a weapon sometimes. Guys don't seem to get that."

"So, that's it?"

"On repeat. Over and over and over. I close my eyes, and I can feel his breath on the back of my neck. It's pathetic."

"I don't mean to marginalize this, Daisy, I promise. But you do realize that your Feel Sorry Flick is just a hipster version of the pottery-making scene in *Ghost*, right?"

There's quiet, and then, "Shit. I never thought of that."

"Don't beat yourself up. Nothing's new anymore. We've already experienced everything there is to experience by watching movies. We're basically all just going through the motions."

"Kenny's here, by the way," she says.

"Your stalker?"

"Yeah. Malls are prime spots for creepers. Lots of shit to lurk behind and mirrors to peek around. How far is a hundred yards, anyway?"

I tell her that it's the length of a football field, and then she asks me if I've seen Henry today.

"This morning," I say. "I read him some *Clear and Present Danger*. He never woke up, though. He hasn't for a while."

"I saw him last night," she says.

"Really? When?"

"Late. Mrs. DiGiacomo sneaks me in sometimes. Nancy banned me. She put me on some kind of blacklist. So I have to do what I have to do."

"Daisy," I say. "Why would my mom ban you from seeing my grandpa?"

She ignores this, just skips right over it. "He thought I was your grandma," she says. "He was awake for a little while, kind of. I got his pad for him, and he . . . he called me Dot."

"Jim said that he gets confused sometimes."

"Yeah."

"Did he say anything?"

I listen to her breath.

"He asked me when we can go home."

26

When I get to Lazzari's, the table is destroyed.

Partially eaten triangles of pizza are scattered everywhere, like they've been launched out of a T-shirt cannon. A sippy cup of milk lies on its side, dripping. The top of a cheese shaker has been pried off, and Parmesan dust is scattered like snowflakes.

Jim squeezes his forehead. "You're late."

"By seven minutes. Not sure that even counts." I assess the table. "This is some pretty impressive destruction."

"I fed the kids first. As you can see, that went well. Eating with children at a restaurant is like eating with a live grenade. It's going to explode every time. You just don't know when."

Emma is at the table, jamming a peach-colored crayon into her nose. Her T-shirt is covered in tomato sauce like movie blood. She smiles brightly when she notices me. "Annnndaaaaaa!"

I sit down next to her. "What up, girlfriend? You got a little something on your shirt."

She looks down at herself and then pokes her own bloated toddler belly.

On the other side of the restaurant, Bryce is in full karate gear again, hammering away on the *Terminator 2: Judgment Day* pinball machine. Arnold Schwarzenegger's head lights up, his one red eye blinking.

"Does he ever take that robe off?" I say.

"Nope," says Jim. "He went to church in it last weekend. That was great. He tried to karate kick the statue of the Virgin Mary."

"Well, in his defense, ninja assassins have to be ready for all kinds of shit."

"It!" says Emma.

"Oh, crap . . . Sorry."

Jim looks too beaten down to care about minor swear words. "Hey, Neal!" he says. "His majesty has arrived." He turns back to me. "I took the liberty of ordering for you, by the way."

Neal is behind the counter. Not surprisingly, he doesn't look thrilled to see me. "Your pizza's coming right up, Jim," he says.

"Burying the hatchet, I see," says Jim.

"Like I said, there was an incident the other day."

"No kidding. You dumped him at the side of the road? On Dodge Street? Seems a little extreme, doesn't it? Poor guy had to walk, like, two miles."

"My heart weeps for him," I say.

Jim shakes his head. "Hey, Em," he says. "Sweetie-pie?"

Emma has removed the crayon from her nostril and is now furiously scribbling with it on her paper kiddie menu.

"How about you go watch your brother play?"

"Plah?" she asks.

"Yeah, over there, babes." He points to Bryce. "Daddy's gonna have a little chat with your idiot uncle."

"Anndaa?"

"Yep, that's the idiot I'm referring to. Go ahead, hon. Watch Brycie play his big-boy game, OK?"

Jim and I watch as Emma toddles off. She's wearing tiny pink Under Armour sneakers and jeans with elastic on them. And unless I'm mistaken, she has quite a load in her pants.

By the look on Jim's face I can see he's disappointed in me, but also kind of amused, too. He's looked at me like this a lot over the years. "I didn't know people could get pulled over by ambulances," he says. "You might be the first. Congratulations."

There's a beer in front of him, just sitting there, mostly full. I look back at Neal, but he pretends to ignore me as he rings up some woman. "Jabberjaw over there has been telling stories, I see."

"Yeah. And I'm glad he did. As your brother, it's important for me to know exactly how fucked up you are. The guy—the other guy? What's his name again?"

"Tyler," I say.

"Yeah, Tyler. He accused you of . . . sneaking around his yard in the middle of the night, calling the house? Something about a lawn gnome? Is that true? Don't tell me it's true."

"It used to be *my* yard," I say.

"Well, it's not anymore. And she's not your wife, either."

"Thanks," I say.

"It's called tough love. Oh, and trespassing is illegal, by the way. It's creepy as hell, too. You weren't wearing a mask made of human skin, were you?"

I grab Jim's beer and take a long sip. "By all means," he says. "Help yourself." He shouts across the restaurant again. "And another beer, too, Neal."

The beer is flat, but it's reasonably cold and exactly what I need right now. I take a moment to feel it dull my senses as it works its way outward from my stomach. Over at *T2* pinball, Emma pinches Bryce's arm, and he slaps her hand away. Emma looks briefly devastated but then launches into a flurry of angry nonsense. The volume of her voice is set to Rape Whistle.

"Bryce!" says Jim. "Don't hit your sister."

"But she pinched me!"

"I don't care."

This goes on for some time. People at other tables pretend not to watch my brother and his children yell at each other, and for a moment, I imagine that Bryce and Emma are mine. Jim is no longer sitting across from me. Instead it's Karen, and we're laughing at the mess and the tomato fingerprints and all the scattered cheese. We're laughing at how tired we are, because being tired is part of it. It's probably unhealthy to miss a life that never actually existed—to miss an imaginary family that you've just cobbled together on the fly from mismatched parts.

Jim picks up a discarded pizza crust and takes a bite. "Sometimes, it feels like I went to the zoo and they gave me two chimpanzees, and now I have to take them places and buy them food and raise them like they're my own."

As if to somehow prove this, Emma starts tugging at the lump in her pants.

"Oh God. Gross. No, honey, don't touch that. We'll change your diaper, OK? Just give Daddy a minute."

She scowls and then slaps her brother again for no good reason. Bryce shouts, and Jim threatens to take away their "special treats." It works, because they both go silent and rigid.

"What're special treats?"

"Oreos," he says. "They get one every night if they're good. You can get kids to do basically anything for an Oreo. Parenting is mostly bribery . . . and yelling. I yell more than I imagined I would. Dad never yelled. I wonder if he wanted to."

"Probably," I say. "You were kind of a dick when you were a kid."

"I'm being punished for it," he says. "Anyway, what did you want to talk about? I need to make this fast. Emma's got bath time, then story time, then cuddle time, then bed. It's a process. We're about thirty minutes from a nuclear meltdown here."

I assess the state of the table again, the state of my brother, and the state of his two monkey children. "Should we do this . . . later?" I say.

"Later?" He laughs. "There is no *later*. This is my life. You dodged a bullet, if you ask me. You've managed to skate through life this long without kids. Congrats." But then he looks at Emma and Bryce and scolds himself. "I don't really mean that. I love them. I kind of hate them, too. It's complicated. Hey, did you check out that computer yet?"

"What computer?"

"Are you drunk all the time? Grandpa's computer. I told you about it. It's in Mom and Dad's basement with Grandpa's stuff. Yours if you want it. It's a pretty nice one."

"OK, yeah, I will," I say. And then I pull out the manila envelope and set it between us.

Jim's eyes narrow. "What's that?"

"We have a problem."

He tosses the pizza crust onto the table. "Shit," he says.

"What?" I say. "I haven't even told you the problem yet."

"What's in there?"

"Pictures."

"God . . . *dammit*," he says.

"Why are you preemptively pissed?"

"Because I know what's in the envelope, you dipshit. They got to you, didn't they?"

"Got to me? Who? Wait? You know about . . . *them*?"

"Yes, I know about *them*."

I have to recalibrate. I didn't imagine the conversation going like this. I finish the rest of the beer I just stole from Jim. "Are we talking about the same guys?" I say.

"Yeah. They've been harassing our family for months. You've been in New York doing God knows what. We've been *here*, dealing with the gay *Sopranos*. They showed up at my office a while back. My fucking office. Showed me . . . those. I assume they're pictures of Dad with . . ."

"So you've seen them?"

He nods.

"What'd you do?"

"What do you mean, *What'd I do?* Nothing, that's what I did. What, did they tell you they're going to the media? Jesus. Woodward and Bernstein–style? I told them to fuck off . . . and then you know what happened next?"

"What?"

"Nothing. They didn't do shit."

"They seemed serious," I say.

"They *seemed* like amateurs. And that's exactly what they are. Trust me. Nancy's famous. Infamous a little, I guess. But people know who she is. You've gotta accept that. And it's only gonna get worse. You heard she got the call-up, right? Officially. Fox . . . like the Yankees of twenty-four-hour news. Tomorrow night, I think. Shit's about to blow up."

Jim is one of those guys who speak with absolute authority, no matter what he's saying. I usually admire this about him, but right now it's making me nervous. "I don't know," I say.

"People come out of the woodwork when you're famous. Extortion, that's what it's called. Throw those pictures away. All of them. And forget about them. Now. Today."

Owen appears at our table. He's got two beers and a large pepperoni pizza. He sets everything down, which must be like a high-wire act considering he's obviously stoned again. "You're lucky, Andy," he says. "I made Neal promise not to do anything gross to your half of the pizza."

"I appreciate that, Owen," I say.

"And this beer's on me, man," he says. "You crossed a million views on YouTube. Congrats. That's . . . like . . . a milestone. Like, cat-video territory, man."

"Couldn't be prouder," I say.

Jim and I grab slices. The pizza is so good that it's like a piece of nostalgia, like a goddamn Bryan Adams song, and I think of all the hours the younger version of me spent here, eating and drinking and laughing and manhandling *Terminator 2: Judgment Day* pinball. Neal and I met freshman year at the University of Nebraska. We became friends the way guys do when they're eighteen—quickly and totally. When I found out he had a twin sister named Karen who went out of state to college in California, I told him that she'd someday be mine. I was kidding of course. But when I finally met her a few years later at a party, she smiled at me and held out her hand and said it was nice to finally meet me, and I didn't breathe for twenty seconds.

"So," I say. "You really don't think we should say *anything*? Like, not even as a precaution?"

"To who?" Jim says.

"I don't know. Them. Our parents. Jim, Dad is . . . Dad is having an affair, right? That's what these pictures are. We can't just . . . let it happen. Mom should know. Shouldn't she?"

"Or maybe she shouldn't."

"What?"

"Think about it. Karen was having an affair on you, right, with that douchebag Travis or Trevor?"

"Tyler."

"Whatever. You found out, and look at you. You're a fucking mess. No offense. Why put her through that? Maybe it'll just . . . work itself out."

"That's stupid," I say. But maybe it isn't. Maybe, in fact, it's brilliant. My parents are Catholic. Technically Jim and I are Catholic, too. Maybe this is how Catholics do it. We accept a certain level of unhappiness— like we have an unhappiness equilibrium built into our brains—and then, one day, we drop dead.

I'd like to keep thinking about this. I'd like to spend hours turning it over in my head and justifying why keeping Nancy in the dark is the way to go. But I can't right now, because I've just noticed that my niece is dangling from the neon Corona sign at the front window. No one else sees it yet. Not Neal—certainly not stoned-to-bejesus Owen. Not the other customers or her father. Not even Bryce. Just me.

"Uh-oh," I say.

27

The next night, when my dad walks into my room, I'm on the floor rebuilding the Lego Ewok Village and listening to my old-school stereo on full volume.

> *This motherfucka's got a score to settle.*
> *And guess what . . . This motherfucka be packin metal.*
> *This motherfucka's got—*

I hit "Pause," and I'm embarrassed. Admittedly, though, if your dad is going to walk into your room without knocking, there are worse things he can find you doing than building Legos and listening to violent rap music.

"What are you doing, Andy?" he says.

I look down at a dozen or so Lego Ewoks. I've lined them shoulder to shoulder next to the instruction booklet. "Believe it or not," I say, "this is a collector's item."

"It's almost time," he says.

I look at my watch . . . but I'm not wearing a watch. "Do we know when she's going to be on . . . *exactly?*"

"Probably the second segment, but they could shuffle. We should watch from the beginning."

"Do you know what she's talking about?"

He shakes his head. I haven't said anything to him about the pictures. This wasn't so much a decision as it was an indecision. I almost did, today, but then I didn't. It's the sort of thing you can't unsay.

"If you're hungry, I heated up some chili," he says.

And then, as if he's just noticing where he is, he looks around the room. He assesses the N.W.A. poster, my wedding photos piled in the middle of the room, my random new clothes on the windowsill. "I like what you've done with the place," he says.

"This room is three times bigger than my whole apartment," I say. "I don't know what to do with all the space."

His knees crack as he crouches down to inspect my Ewok Village. I've spent most of the evening trying to figure out how to put it back together. He pokes one of the ledges and C-3PO falls to the carpet. "I remember when we got you this for Christmas," he says.

"It was a pretty sweet gift."

"Yes, it was," he says. "You were eleven."

I suppose I deserve that.

Mitch Cameron is talking about immigration.

The TV is loud and colorful with all its graphics and talking. There are two guests on split screen, one in Arizona, one in Boston. Cameron and the woman from Arizona agree with each other. The guy from Boston looks like he's not quite sure how he ended up here, like he lost some confusing bet.

The host, Mitch Cameron, is pretty high up, apparently. I just Googled him on my phone. He's not O'Reilly or Hannity, but he's got the fifth-highest-rated show. He's a divisive member of the Fox family, according to Wikipedia, because he tends to be more of a moderate—perhaps even a left-leaning moderate. He's a good-looking guy, with graying hair and blue eyes.

"I understand that argument, sir," he says. "I honestly do, and, frankly, I sympathize." He's got a slight Southern accent. "We're a country of immigrants. But countries change—and so do the times. We're a two-hundred-and-fifty-year-old, well-established superpower, and there are people out there in every corner of the world who want to hurt us. At some point, the floodgates simply have to close."

My dad was gone most of the day. Another *meeting*. To his credit, he *did* ask me if I wanted to go. "I'm sure it's not something you'd want to do," he said, hedging. "But you're welcome to come along." I'm sure he was going to see her, the woman. Nobody looks that excited to go to a meeting about accounting.

I take a bite of chili. We're sitting in dual recliners, eating off TV stands, and I have a brief vision of our future as father and son if my parents get divorced. Christmas Eve. Recliners and Hungry Man turkey dinners.

"Are you . . . nervous?" I say.

He looks at me like I'm weird, but I don't really have a baseline for this—for seeing one's mother on Fox News. I'm nervous that she'll do badly, that something will go horrifically wrong and she'll look like a fool. But I'm also nervous that she'll do well—really well—and she'll look like someone who belongs on Fox News. I have no idea what I'm rooting for.

When a block of commercials ends, the show comes back, and some chili shifts precariously in my stomach.

"And welcome back to *Cameron PM*," the host says, staring right at us. "Will it be activist judges . . . or will it be a victory for states' rights? Will it be a group of unelected judges upending one of mankind's oldest institutions, or will it be a nod to the sanctity of marriage? With the Supreme Court set to hear arguments on the legalization of gay marriage, we'll all know soon enough. But what does it all mean? And more importantly . . . what's at stake for you and me?"

And there she is, my mother, smiling on television.

"Joining me now from Omaha tonight—and making her Fox News debut, I might add—is Dr. Nancy Carter of the popular *Nancy Knows Radio Show*."

She looks nice. Pretty. My dad is watching with his mouth open.

"Welcome to Fox, Nancy. We're excited to have you. How are things out there in flyover country?"

She laughs. "Hi, Mitch. Thanks so much. And yeah . . . I'll take flyover country any day of the week, thank you very much."

"Well said. Sometimes I wish I could join you. So let's get into it here. You know what's going on. You've been an outspoken voice for the defense of marriage for a lon—"

"And I have the scars to prove it."

Cameron seems thrown, but he recovers fast. "I'm sure you do. Welcome to my life. Anyway . . . the ruling will come whether we're ready or not, and a lot of experts are predicting a win for progressives on this one. What say you?"

Nancy clears her throat. "Well, with all due respect to the *experts*, I'm convinced the sane, nonactivist wing of the court will take a stand for America and stick with the true—proven—definition of marriage. And that's a union between one man and one woman."

"Well, I admire your optimism," says Cameron.

I hate this. I hate seeing her like this. I hate that it's documented on television and that it will exist always.

"I'm keeping the faith, Mitch," she says.

"Be that as it may . . . let's take a step away from the talking points, here, if you don't mind. Let's just have a chat."

Nancy's brow tightens. "OK," she says.

"Ruling or no ruling, the numbers do seem to be shifting, and shifting fast. Most polls are showing at least half the country supporting gay marriage. And an overwhelming number of young people say they support it—even those who identify as conservative. And let's face it, they'll be running the place when you and me are gone, right? What do you and your listeners know that they don't? Make the case for me here, Nancy. I'm all ears."

"Well, Mitch," she says. Her eyes fall. She's looking at her notes, I can tell. She clears her throat nervously. "If we based all public policy on what young people think, we'd be in big trouble. It's like I used to tell my boys when they were kids . . ."

"Oh Jesus," I say.

"Just because the cool kids are doing it, that doesn't make it right . . . Right?"

"She never said that," I say.

"Andy, quiet."

"I think there's a lot of what I call me-tooism when it comes to this issue. The *cool kids* have it in their heads that all love is good love. And let's be frank, all *lust* is good lust, too. If it feels good, do it. You and I know that's foolish and shortsighted. But young people think that way because it's easy to think that way when you have no perspective."

"It's about youth, then."

"Partially—and our culture, our gay-friendly media. We can't ignore that. Gay is cool if all you do is watch popular TV."

"So, if it's just youthful indiscretion—or a lack of perspective, as you say—are you suggesting younger Americans who support gay marriage *now* will become *less* in favor of it as they get older? They'll do a reverse-evolve, so to speak?"

"I'm *sure* they will," she says. "Not all of them, of course. But many. And don't forget, there's precedent here. The '60s, remember them?"

"Barely." Cameron laughs. "I was a kid. You can't blame me for that one."

"Well, I'm a little older than you. The free-love hippies, the age of hedonism? You know what most of them did? They put out their joints, got jobs, and had kids. They became adults. The same thing will happen here. When they start having kids, start trying to raise good, upstanding members of society, let's see how they feel about having to explain why every TV show coming out of Hollywood is full of homoeroticism. Let's see how they like their kids' third-grade teacher marching in a pride parade. Let's see how they react when little Timmy or Johnny wants to wear a dress or play with dolls. *Cool* or not, they won't like it. They'll want their kids to be normal."

"Normal?" says Cameron. "Interesting choice of words. So I assume you're debunking the idea of the new norm—"

"They can try to redefine the word *marriage* all they want, Mitch. But they can't redefine the word *normal.* Everyone knows the gay community is more promiscuous than the straight community. That's documented. That's just fact."

I look at my dad. His eyes have gone wide.

"Oh, shit," I say.

"Well, you're casting a wide net here, Nancy. We weren't talking about promiscuity, we were talking about what you define as normal. But I think we can all agree, this is more than just an issue of two people living in a house and calling themselves married. It's changing the fundamentals of society."

"Absolutely, it is," says Nancy. "And not for the better. As conservatives, what we need to do, collectively, is refuse to let it happen. Stop looking the other way. We need to make noise. You're Catholic, Mitch, right? So am I. I'm a proud Catholic, and I believe in God, and I believe that marriage is sacred—a bond. But quoting Bible verses and putting an 'It's Adam and Eve not Adam and Steve' bumper sticker on your truck isn't going to work. The word of God won't sway people who don't believe in God in the first place. Secular progressives have no God."

That hitch is gone. She's vibrant, her voice forceful and steady.

"So, let's put religion aside and focus on biology, on thousands of years of civilized society, on thousands of years of hardwiring. A male and a female are biologically engineered to come together and propagate the species. It's that way with humans—and it's that way with animals, too. Even insects. So, what, we're supposed to flip all that because of a genetic mistake?"

"A mistake?" he says. "That's a controversial—"

"Fine," she says. "We're on semantics again, Mitch. Call it an anomaly if you want. Abnormality. You can call it lots of things. It doesn't matter—it's all the same. Some things are just wrong. Some things are just mistakes of nature. That's my point. Ninety percent of the country shouldn't have to alter their lives because ten percent are damaged."

Silence on television is different from silence in real life, which is why it seems like minutes before anyone talks. They're on a split screen, Cameron and my mom, and they both look shocked at what she's just said.

"Well," says Cameron. The split screen changes to a single shot of him. "Some powerful words indeed—and food for thought from our newest colleague. Time will tell if her theory is correct. But quite frankly, I have my doubts. And if I was a betting man, my guess is the Supreme Court will, too."

28

I find him a half hour later, standing in the middle of the living room, looking out onto the dark front yard.

When *Cameron PM* went to commercial and Nancy's segment was over, he set his tray aside and quietly got up and left the room. I sat staring at the television, my chili cooling into a lump. I had this idea that if I didn't acknowledge what we'd just watched, maybe it will not have actually happened.

"Dad," I say.

He doesn't turn around. A car drives by, briefly lighting up the room, and he cranes his head to look.

"You want a beer?" I say.

He holds out his hand by way of an answer, so I give him one of the two I brought with me.

"They're gonna be coming soon," he says.

I wonder if the Glitter Mafia has someone assigned to Fox News twenty-four hours a day, some poor intern maybe, a kid tallying offensive statements in an Excel doc. I hope Jim is right. I hope they're all talk, Stephen and his crew.

"He cornered her," he says. "She was flustered. That's what they do, they poke and prod until you say something you regret."

"Do you agree with her, Dad?"

I've never asked him this question, and I instantly regret it. I've never wanted to know. And now I've gone and ruined it.

"Marriage isn't easy, Andy," he says. "You love someone in a specific time and place. But you have no idea what they'll become. People change. Sometimes, they change so much you hardly even recognize them anymore."

For the millionth time, I think of Karen in her pajama pants and hoodie, lazing on the couch, giggling at Jim Carrey talking out of his butt. Everything would be so much better if she'd just stayed like that.

"Is there something you want to tell me, Dad?" I say. He's still watching the window. "You can, you know. Remember when I was in high school, and you said if I was ever drunk at a party or whatever, I should call you instead of drive? You'd come get me, no questions asked. Think of it like that."

He sits down in a reading chair and rubs his eyes.

"I know about the . . . the girl . . . the woma—"

"That's part of the deal, though," he says.

"What?"

"That's what you sign up for when you're married. It's a gamble, like anything else."

"Did you hear what I just—"

"No matter how much they change, they're still yours. Do I agree with her? That's what you asked, right?"

"Yeah."

"It doesn't matter. Marriage isn't about agreeing. It's about staying. That's what I'm doing."

And then he goes outside to stand guard on the front porch.

29

The basement in our old house scared the shit out of me when I was a kid.

It was a dark, musty dungeon of a place, and every once in a while we'd find a spider the size of a tennis ball. Jim liked to push me down there sometimes and hold the door closed. I'd scream and cry and be scarred irreparably. He thought it was hilarious.

The new basement isn't scary at all. There's a flatscreen on the wall, nice carpeting, an expensive treadmill, and a pool table. The whole place smells like lemons.

My grandpa's things are stacked neatly in the corner, each box marked with my mother's handwriting in Magic Marker. Baseball Things. Tax Returns. Social Security Info. House Info.

Nancy was right about the Cubs stuff. There's a ton of it. I flip through programs and scorecards. There are commemorative plastic soda cups, yellowed by time, and a mini ice cream helmet. There's a signed picture of Harry Caray that Jim and I got for Grandpa when we were kids. I pick up a tattered stuffed bear cub that smells like mildew, and one ancient, broken-in glove. It's sad to see it all, a lifetime fan's lifetime of stuff jammed into some boxes.

I find the computer that Jim told me about. It's an Apple laptop. I pick it up and it's light and sleek and beautiful. He's just giving it to me, apparently, and I briefly feel bad for charging an extra five hundred dollars at the Gentleman's Closet. I hit the power button, but the battery's dead.

And then I find a box that stops me.

It's a lighter, more faded cardboard than the other boxes, and "Dot" is written across the top in my grandpa's handwriting. I don't even have to open it to know what's in there, and I think of the box currently upstairs in my Bizarro Room, the one filled with hundreds of pictures of me and Karen. Maybe this is how all marriages end up—the good ones and the bad ones alike—in a box in a basement.

"Andy."

Nancy is standing at the bottom of the stairs. "What are you doing down here?" she says.

I nod at all the boxes, and she tells me to take whatever I want.

"Dad still on the porch?"

She sighs. "I sent him to bed. He was drinking." She looks at my beer, which I've set on the floor. "I see you are, too. You're having quite an influence on your father."

"We had a beer, Mom," I say. "Having a beer isn't *drinking*. Besides, we needed it."

She crosses her arms, defiant. "You watched, then, I gather, with your father?"

My answer is all nonwords and body language.

"Well, what'd you think?"

"You were . . ."

She cocks her head, eyes raised, ready to defend herself from whatever it is she assumes I'm going to say.

"Mean," I say.

Her jaw flexes. She's still wearing her TV makeup. It's strange, like her features have been shifted and blurred. "I wasn't mean. I was unapologetic. I was compelling."

"Compelling?"

"I was articulate," she says. "I was forceful . . . but forceful without being too threatening. Not an easy line to walk. The marketability is in the balance."

"What are you talking about?"

"The network called after the show. My contact at Fox. He said they were very pleased. He said I was the kind of woman they could see themselves getting into business with."

30

I'm standing outside the Gentleman's Closet.

I received a very businesslike voice mail this morning from Jerry telling me that my suit is ready.

Through the window, I see him standing behind the desk, looking all official. The place is totally empty. My back pocket vibrates.

```
Are you happy yet?
```

It's Daisy. It sounds more like an accusation than a question, like something you say to someone immediately after they do something spectacularly stupid. I scroll through some emoticons until I find something stupid and cheery. It's a small cartoon dog wagging its tail—the emoticon version of "Wake Me Up Before You Go-Go."

She texts back instantly.

```
I'm bored. I'm prepared to allow you to
hang out with me today.
```

I text her back and tell her that I'm running errands.

What kind of errands?

More thumb typing. I tell her that I'm picking up my suit at the Gentleman's Closet. And I include an emoticon of a man dancing in a suit. And then I tell her that I'm going to do everything in my power not to get punched again. Three seconds later, she tells me to wait for her. I don't know what that means exactly.

I look through the window again. Jerry has a pencil behind his ear. I've always been a little afraid of him. He's a big man, and he rarely smiles and, of course, he doesn't like me. I remind myself that I used to help pick out birthday and Father's Day presents for him. I remind myself that I went golfing with him once even though I hate golf. On the eleventh hole while we ate cheese crackers I told him that I loved his daughter more than anything else in the world and that I wanted to marry her.

I shove the door open and step inside. "In the Air Tonight" by Phil Collins is playing, which couldn't have worked out better if I'd planned it, even if it is only the Muzak version. I put up my fists, boxer-style. "Wanna make it two out of three, old man?"

For several minutes I stand looking at the photos of handsome men on the walls while he rummages around in the back. At one point, I hear him mutter, "Oh, for Christ's sake." Eventually he comes out with my suit.

"Should I . . . try it on?"

"I wouldn't bother. I know what I'm doing."

"OK, well, thanks for the help. I'll give you a shout if I ever need anyone to punch me again."

"Wait," he says. He goes behind the counter and rummages around in a drawer. And then he pulls out two tumblers and some murky brown liquid. "How about it? Time for a quick one?"

I look around. We're the only two here. "You . . . drink at work?"

"Routinely," he says. "Weekday afternoons it's just me. I could hire a golden retriever to man the register. It wouldn't matter."

It's scotch of some sort, I think, something that's way more man than I am. "Good stuff," I say through the burn.

"I was thinking about your grandpa this morning," he says. "The suit I sold him . . . two-button, navy blue. Solid. Ended up being more Steve McQueen than Sinatra, but he was happy."

He takes a drink, closing his eyes as he swallows, savoring it. I do the same, and it burns a little less this time. I suspect scotch is something you have to convince yourself to enjoy, like sushi or the last few Radiohead albums, but I can't deny the result is nice.

"You know, I really am sorry I hit you at the reception," I tell him again.

If I was in charge of all things, this is where he'd apologize for punching me in the face the other day, but instead he says something even more surprising. "You know, I never disliked you as much as you think I did."

"Really?"

"Karen could have done worse. You meant well, basically. Her mom and I always knew that."

Maybe the alcohol has gone straight to my head—all I've eaten today is a bowl of my mother's horrible cardboard diet cereal—but I'm going to go ahead and take that as a compliment, because, to date, it's the nicest thing he's ever said to me.

"Daughters," he says. "You raise them and watch them grow up, and you love them so much it makes you crazy. Then one day some guy shows up. Maybe he's nice. Maybe he's got a good job. Maybe he's got his shirt tucked in and he calls you *sir*. But he's never quite what you're hoping for. If you have one someday—a daughter, I mean—you'll know what I'm talking about."

We're quiet for a few sips, two guys drinking in an empty men's clothing store listening to soft rock, and I wonder what Jerry thinks of Tyler. I imagine the two of them together on a deck drinking whatever the hell this is. What is it about me that makes me hope that he likes me more?

"Well, if it's any consolation, Jerry," I say, "I guess I wasn't quite what she was hoping for, either."

He gives my tumbler a look, but I've still got some work to do. "Son, you're not the first. She hurt you. Badly . . . obviously. I mean, look at you."

He's being rhetorical, I'm sure, but there are, like, twenty mirrors in this place, so I actually do look at myself. Do I really look as bad as everyone seems to be saying I do?

"Kindergarten," he says. "First . . . second grade. Early on. These stupid boys were enamored with her. Once when she was a little-*little* girl, I was at one of those horrible school pageants. Wintertime. Cold as hell. After the show, all the parents were trying to get their kids in coats and gloves. This one little boy—he was dressed like a camel or a wise man, something stupid. He comes running across the gym with his arms out, pure love on his dumb little face. He tried to give Karen a hug. Just a hug. Perfectly innocent. Kid stuff. And you know what? She just shrugged him off. Couldn't have cared less. Little boy burst into tears, of course. 'Mommy, mommy, why won't Karen hug me?'"

"I know the feeling," I say.

He smiles, and I can tell that he's proud of all this, his daughter's wake of male wreckage. "Junior high and high school were worse," he says. "There was this poor exchange student when she was a freshman. French kid, I think. It got ugly. I had to talk him down off the roof of our garage. Even the guys she *liked* . . . She got tired of them. Every time. Don't know if that makes you feel any better. Maybe it makes you feel worse. Who knows? But it's something to think about. Sometimes the cards are just stacked against you. Nothing you can do about it."

Outside, an old guy peeks in over the "Open" sign. He seems to briefly consider shopping for men's formalwear, but then he wanders away, and Jerry looks relieved.

"All that stuff I just told you," he says. "That's about Karen. Between you and her. None of it is Neal's fault."

"Who said it was?"

"*You*, apparently. Karen hurt you, you're depressed. But why does that mean you get to hurt my son? Who wins there?"

I take a drink. "It's more complicated than that."

He rejects this, waving it away. "You were the only real friend he had—a lot better than that stoner moron Owen. That's why we tolerated you. Neal finally had a buddy."

Collegiate montage. Neal, tall and ridiculously pale. Me, short and skinny. The two of us standing in corners at parties, avoiding talking to girls, arguing about who was the best James Bond.

Goddammit, Neal.

When the door at the front entrance opens behind me, I hear the little bell ring, and I watch Jerry's face. His expression is professional—the go-to look he's been using for years, courteous, knowledgeable, authoritative. But then it turns to surprise. "Hello there," he says. "Can I help you, miss?"

"There you are, Andy."

It's Daisy. She's smiling, her lips shiny. She's startling, like a bank robber in a sundress. Jerry is looking at me, his face all questions.

"Sorry I'm late." She's walking toward me now. Her body is doing that insane, side-to-side thing that female bodies do when they're wearing heels. "Hi there," she says. And then she kisses me on the lips.

"Um," I say. It's different from the one the other day—it lingers, and the tip of her tongue finds space between my lips.

"Did you cut yourself shaving again?" She touches my face and looks at Jerry. "He can't be trusted," she says, like this is a thing I do. I cut my face. "Hi. I'm Daisy."

Jerry looks at me again and takes her hand.

"Did you try it on yet, babe?" she asks me. Babe?

"What?" I say.

"Your suit, silly. Did you try it on?"

"I'm sure it's fine."

"Well, get in there." She points to the sign that says "Dressing Room." "Chop-chop." She doesn't sound like herself at all. She's cheery and bright eyed, and it's a little scary, like maybe she's lost her mind. Maybe that's her secret. Maybe that's the question I've never asked. Maybe Daisy's just plain crazy.

"No . . . seriously, it's fine," I say.

"I'm sure it is. But I didn't drive all the way over here to *not* see you wearing it." She turns to Jerry. "No offense. I'm sure you did a great job. But I've got veto power over these kinds of things. You understand."

"I certainly do," he says. "You heard the woman, Andy. Get in there."

And so I head to the dressing room.

When you're used to wearing jeans and T-shirts, a suit feels like something you might tear right through like the Incredible Hulk, so I dress slowly and then squint at myself in the mirror. I can hear them out there talking. I can't make out the words, but Daisy sounds charming, and my lips taste like her lip gloss.

I button the top button of the jacket and look at myself. Jerry's little chalk lines are gone—the extra fabric hanging at the sleeves has been trimmed away. It fits perfectly. I put on a tie, and I get it right on the first try.

Daisy is giggling. She touches Jerry's arm, smiling. "No, no," she says. "Not me. I'm actually from . . ." But she stops when she sees me.

She puts her hand between her breasts, holding her breath. "Well now," she says. "Hello, handsome."

Blood rushes to my face. I feel silly. Teenage girl. Nineties movie. Slutty dress. I'm being unveiled.

"I believe my work here is done," says Jerry.

"That was . . . interesting," I say.

We're in the parking lot walking to the Caddie. She's holding my hand. She grabbed it on our way out, and she hasn't let go. "That? *That* was exhilarating," she says. "You should have seen the look on his face."

"Who were you in there?"

"I'm good, right? I could have been an actress. I should have been."

"But why were you acting?"

She lets go of my hand. "Because she deserves to feel like shit, that's why."

"Who?"

"Andy, I apologize in advance for using her name. I know I said I wouldn't do that, but it's necessary for emphasis. How many times in the last year have you imagined Karen having sex with the ambulance driver. Like what, conservatively . . . A hundred thousand? And it sucks, doesn't it? Every . . . fucking . . . time. Right?"

I'm thinking about it now, actually, and it does suck.

"Tonight, when the suit man gets home, the first words out of his mouth when he sees his wife are going to be 'Guess what happened at work today, honey.' And he's gonna tell . . . Wait, what's your mother-in-law's name?"

"*Ex*-mother-in-law," I say. "And it's Bonnie."

"Bonnie? Jesus, really? That's perfect. Like she was born to be someone's mother-in-law. Anyway, he's going to tell *Bonnie* all about me and how I kissed you right there in his store, right in front of him, and how

I maybe even used a little tongue. And then, you know who Bonnie's gonna call?"

She touches my chest again—the same spot she touched at the Bookworm, but this time it's her fist, kneading into me. "She's going to call Karen. And that feeling you feel all the time, the one right here? That's what she's gonna feel. And it's gonna hurt like a bitch."

"Oh," I say.

"She deserves it. Because she had *Yankee Hotel Foxtrot*. She had something unique—something indie and great. She had this special thing that wasn't like everyone else. And she gave it away. Now she gets to suffer a little, too. You're welcome."

31

And here's what I'm not going to do.

I'm not going to look at Facebook. I'm not going to look at Facebook.

I'm in the Bizarro Room, telling myself this, over and over, like a mantra. My new free laptop is open on my chest, and I'm lying on the bed, and I'm not going to fucking look at Facebook.

I've given it some thought, and, seriously, there's just no way Facebook can be good for you. I'm sure there have been studies, so this probably isn't some brilliant revelation, but I'll say it anyway. On the surface, it's harmless enough, I guess. How bad can it really be with its endless baby posts, food pictures, and beachy foot selfies? But it's not that simple. Mixed in with all of its silly bullshit, Facebook is the literal manifestation of all our regrets, looping and looping, for free, on our computers and phones. People who should be gone and safely out of our lives forever are there again, one cryptic little glimpse at a time, reminding us of all the things we should or shouldn't have done.

Then again, maybe I could just look for ten seconds.

Technically, I deactivated my Facebook account two weeks after I moved to New York. I saw a picture of a bouquet of flowers on Karen's wall. It had been liked forty-seven times; there were six comments. I immediately Googled *How do you deactivate fucking Facebook?* Not surprisingly, I wasn't the first to search this, f-word and all. I followed the instructions meticulously. I clicked "Yes I'm sure" a dozen or so times. But we all know that my page is still there, buried somewhere in all the digital 1s and 0s, waiting to spring up like a movie villain you thought was dead but was totally just pretending.

"Goddammit," I say.

My left index finger strikes *f*. I'll go to Karen's page, and I'll look at her pictures. Not all of them, just a few—however many you can look at in ten seconds. But before my other finger hits *a*, a URL appears automatically in the browser window, and it stops me: "freegirlcamslive.com."

I hit "Enter." I don't even mean to really; I just do, and the page loads, and two seconds later, dozens of images of girls appear, each in an individual box, lined up in a grid across the screen. Some of the girls are smiling. Some are nearly naked. A few actually are naked. "Whoa," I say.

I'm a male in the twenty-first century. I've seen girls on a computer screen before. But I don't know what this is. After a moment of scanning, I do know what it is. It's a cam girl site. Each girl has a name—obviously fake. Miss Cox. LadyNeon. JessyAdorbz. And then I see her. My eyes somehow go right to where she is, drawn there, a brunette somewhere in the middle of the grid. She's not smiling in her picture, but she's not frowning either, exactly. I've seen this expression—a kind of joyless intelligence. Her eyes are big and brown and familiar. I squint and pull the monitor to my face. Under her picture, it reads "LovelyDaisy."

The screen changes when I click her name. Her image blurs and expands, and then she's there, on the screen, on video. It's Daisy. She's barefoot, sitting Indian-style on a bed in short shorts and a T-shirt. "Nebraska, Fuck Yeah!" it says across her breasts, just in case I needed proof that it's actually her. At the corner of her screen, it reads "LovelyDaisy Is Live."

"Daisy," I say, aloud.

Below her, messages appear and scroll upward and off the screen.

MR.O-FACE: *OMFG, Daisy . . . you are an angel sent from heaven.*

Guest12388: *Beautiful beautiful girl.*

KnightLife: *Look at those eyes.*

MattyICE: *How many tats?*

MR.O-FACE: *AN ANGEL! Swear . . . to . . . GOD!*

Daisy smiles. "Fifteen tats, Matty," she says. She holds up her wrist and shows her "Read." tattoo. "But this one is my favorite."

These messages are constant, relentlessly scrolling up and up. People are talking to her, and she's talking back.

There's a little chime, like something from *Super Mario Bros.*

MR.O-FACE has tipped 85 tokens.

Daisy blows a kiss. "Thanks, Mr. O.," she says.

They're paying her. Forty tokens. One token. Thirty-seven tokens. Sometimes she thanks them, sometimes she doesn't. Men with random, ridiculous names call her beautiful. They tell her how gorgeous she is, and all the while, she just sits. Occasionally she tilts her head or bites her lip, and whenever she does this, more chimes ring. More tokens. I watch as she slowly applies lip gloss, and there's another flurry of chimes.

RavenNATION: *Can I please see your tongue, D?*

MattyICE: *Marry me?*

RavenNATION: *Pleeeeeeease.*

"No, Raven," she says. "And you know the rules. No requests. And no begging. Act like a grownup or you're getting banned."

RavenNATION: *But... But... But...*

Guest(M)Can'tSLEEP: *Fav place to be kissed?*

Questions like this flow and flow. Guys asking to see things—odd, superspecific things, like her feet and hip bones, her belly button, and her lower back. Guys asking her about sexual things. There's a number at the top right of the screen—the number of viewers. Roughly seven hundred and fifty people are watching her. I am one of them.

I find my phone on the floor and scroll through my text messages until I find one from her. I text her one word.

Hey.

I watch. Seconds pass, maybe five. She looks down and then picks up her phone. I see her smile and start typing.

RavenNATION: *Who are you talking to??????*

Johnson&Johnson: *Can I text you, too? 100 tokens for your number!!!!*

RavenNATION: *It's just a tongue. No big whoop, right?*

Guest31222: *Can I make you cum? PLEEEEEZE GOD! Fav way to cum?*

Guest44923 *Have you ever kissed a girl?*

```
Hi there. What's up?
```

I watch her wait for me to text her back. A strand of hair falls across her forehead. She's watching her phone, waiting for me to talk to her. I can't take my eyes off of her. She's beautiful. I text her again.

```
I can see you.
```

"What?"

```
Daisy . . . I can see you. On the computer.
```

She looks directly at the camera, like she's making eye contact, like she's looking right at me. Her smile is gone. "Andy?" she says.

Johnson&Johnson: *Who's Andy?*

RavenNATION: *Suck it, Andy! She's mine!*

I actually start talking, out loud, like she can hear me. But then I text back a question mark. What in the fuck is going on?

She unfolds her legs and rises up to her knees. She tugs at the bottom of her shirt, flashing a glimpse of her skin. She types on her phone.

`Are you looking at me right now?`

She runs her hands through her hair and lets it fall across her shoulders.

The sound is out of control. Chime after chime—tip after tip. RavenNATION thanks me, whoever the hell I am. Daisy starts typing again, her thumbs working, and then she tosses the phone down on her bed and looks back into the camera.

"Is there gas in Henry's Caddie?" she says.

As a bunch of questions flood the page about who the hell Henry is, I blank, stupidly. My grandpa. He has a name, and it's Henry, and his enormous Cadillac is currently parked outside in the driveway, waiting to be driven. Just as I put all these things together, I receive another text from Daisy. It's an address.

32

It's just after ten p.m., and Siri tells me to turn left.

I'm all the way downtown now. In Omaha terms, I'm a million miles from my parents' place, and I feel a little sick to my stomach with nerves.

What exactly is it that you plan to do, Andy?
I don't have a plan, Siri. I don't want to think. That's the point of this. I'm tired of thinking. I just want something good to happen for once.
You don't know this girl, Andy.
Quiet, Siri.
Why was she on your grandpa's computer, Andy? Why haven't you asked yourself that question yet?

I do my best to block all this out, which isn't difficult, since Siri isn't actually talking.

"You have reached your final destination," she says.

I'm stopped in front of a long row of warehouses that have been converted into apartments. At the front entrance, I find "12" on a crowded board and push the button. There's a loud buzz, and a big lock clicks. I walk through a cool, silent vestibule and down a hallway of apartment doors until I find hers. The door is ajar. Wilco is playing— *Yankee Hotel Foxtrot.* I push the door gently, and it opens. She's standing in a little kitchenette, sipping a glass of wine. She's not in short shorts anymore or her Nebraska T-shirt. Instead she's in a baggy pair of sweats and a hoodie. Her hair is up on top of her head in a haphazard bun. She looks like she just woke up.

"It's your album," she says, and she sways a little to the music. She asks me if I want a drink.

"Why were you on my grandpa's computer?" I say.

"You should have a drink," she says. She pours me a glass of wine.

"Daisy," I say.

She hands me a glass of red wine. "Relax," she says. "I'll tell you, OK? In a bit. Let's just relax for a minute."

She leads me to the big, overstuffed sofa. I sit and sink into warmth and comfort. I look around the place. The walls are bare. The furniture is stark and white. "Is this where you live?"

"It's where I'm *living*," she says, which is an odd thing to say. She putters around the room for a moment, humming along with Wilco. She stops at a turntable. She touches the needle but leaves it. "You know, I've been thinking," she says. "What if we're not supposed to turn off our Feel Sorry Flicks? Have you ever thought about that?"

"That's pretty unhealthy," I say, "according to the bullshit book of mine."

She rolls her eyes. "Andy, look at us. I think the healthy ship sailed a long, long time ago."

I sip my wine, making a conscious effort not to guzzle it. Perhaps she has a point.

"What if instead of trying *not* to think about . . . *them* . . . What if we're actually supposed to accept that we're always going to think about them? What if that pain is never going to go away, no matter how hard we try? And what if we don't actually want it to go away?"

She sits down beside me on the couch. She settles herself and stretches her legs across my lap. Her feet are thin and pale, her toenails bright pink. She looks at them and smiles. "You should touch them," she says.

"Your feet?"

"The arches." She bites her lip. "With the tips of your fingers. Gently."

"What's going on, Daisy?"

She shushes me. "Come on," she says. "It'll be fun. We can talk later."

I touch the arch of her foot and her legs go stiff. "Be careful," she whispers. "I'm very ticklish. I'm gonna do my best not to kick you in the face, but I can't make any promises."

I lighten my touch as best I can. She takes a breath, holds it, and then lets it out. "That actually feels good," she says. "Wow. OK. I get this. I like it." And then she clears her throat. "All right. I'm going back into character now. But keep doing that."

"Character?"

She settles her head on the armrest and closes her eyes. Somehow, I understand what this is. The hoodie. The sweatpants. Her legs across my lap. I think of Karen and our blizzard, but I push it out of my head even though I'm pretty sure it's exactly what Daisy wants me to be thinking about. She wants me to think about Karen, no matter how much it hurts. That's her point. I run my fingers along the ball of her right foot, the spot that Karen loved so much. And then I move up her legs to her soft, smooth calf.

Daisy reaches for her laptop on the coffee table in front of us. She taps some buttons, and a video starts playing. It takes me a moment to realize that it's *Ace Ventura: Pet Detective*. "Netflix has it," she whispers. "Lucky break, huh?"

"Daisy, this is—"

She shakes her head, and an inch of stomach appears as she tugs her hoodie up. She started the movie randomly in the middle. It's the part where Jim Carrey is making dolphin sounds in an empty swimming pool. She tugs farther and farther, and then she pulls her sweatshirt off and over her head. "It's OK," she says. She takes my hand and rests it on her breast. "We're pretending."

I say her name again, and again she shushes me. She takes my other hand and hooks my fingers on the waistband of her sweats. I pull them down slowly, following along, playing my part in this. She kisses her finger and then touches my lips, and I can practically smell what our old house smelled like, like this weird potpourri that Karen bought at the drugstore. This feels so strange, what I'm doing. But it feels better than missing her, which is nice.

"Snow day," Daisy says, and then she pulls me on top of her.

My eyes open, and suddenly I'm awake.

Most mornings since I moved to New York, it takes me at least five seconds to remember where I am when I first wake up. This same phenomenon has occurred each morning in the Bizarro Room, too. *Where in the hell am I?* I've wondered. Sometimes I look for Karen beside me—still, after all this time. But not now.

I'm in Daisy's bedroom, lying in her soft bed, divorced and in my underwear. I've just had sex for the first time in more than a year, and the effect is dizziness and a vague sense of shame. That second one I blame mostly on Catholicism. Words come into focus; they're written on cards and stuck to a board above my head.

The delicate place.
This pretty pink flower.
The center of me.

Secret spot.
My thornless rose.
The forbidden canal.

There must be fifty others. It's Daisy's wall of awful vagina euphemisms.

My forbidden garden.
Her velvet slipper.

Yeesh.

My wonder spot.
My special wetness.

Daisy is lying beside me, propped up on a pillow in her Nebraska T-shirt again, reading *The Son of Hollywood* by Curtis Violet. "You mutter in your sleep," she says. "It's sort of creepy."

"Sorry," I say. "How's your book?"

"Sad," she says. "Well, actually, it's kind of happy. It's a sweet book, really. But it's sad that he's dead. He was my favorite writer."

"Yeah," I say.

"He hit on me once."

"Who?"

She flips the book over and touches the author's small black-and-white photo. "I drove like five hours all by myself to see him read at the University of Iowa when I was, like, nineteen. When he signed my book, he told me I was the prettiest thing he'd seen in Iowa City since John Irving. He invited me to the bar at his hotel for a drink."

She doesn't say anything else for a while, leaving me hanging.

"Well," I say. "Did you go?"

She tells me that it's none of my fucking business.

Directly across from the bed sits a desktop computer. Atop that is an elaborate web camera mounted to the monitor. I have a lot of questions.

"So that's your job, then?" I ask, nodding to all the equipment.

"One of them," she says. "Cam girl. That's what it's called. I say 'model' on my W-2s, like how strippers call themselves dancers. But that's the proper name for it. Cam girl. I get to telecommute. And I can write off my wireless bill. Strippers can't do that."

"But why do you—"

"I'm not gonna justify myself, Andy," she says. "I am an adult. I'm thirty years old. I go on my camera at night and men look at me and talk to me and ask me questions. It's as simple as that. Other girls do things and show things. I don't. Not because I would be ashamed to or afraid to. I just choose not to. And I don't have daddy issues, either. My dad isn't really an English teacher. I made that up. But he's a very sweet man. He and my mom live in Minneapolis."

I wonder how many times she's delivered versions of this speech. In my insurance days, on the rare occasion when someone asked me why I did what I did, I'd just shrug and say something about limitless office supplies and paid vacations. "How did you . . . get into it?"

She takes a patient breath and sets the book down open on her lap. "You ever been to O'Hare in Chicago?"

"The airport? Tons of times. I was just there, actually. Layover."

"You know how it's a total clusterfuck, right? Well, I had a delay, and I was stuck there for, like, seven hours one day. I was sitting by myself, waiting for my stupid plane. At some point I dozed off. When I woke up, I stood up and stretched, to get the blood going. No big deal. But then I realized that all these guys were looking at me. I couldn't believe it. All of them. And these weren't dirtbags, like, leering at me and drooling. They were just normal, perfectly harmless guys, sitting with their wives and reading magazines. A few of them were just kids, like twelve-year-olds. They all stopped what they were doing and stared at my body, and all I did was stand up and lift my arms over my head. I was wearing jeans and a T-shirt, flip-flops. I couldn't have been trying less."

I briefly try to calculate the number of times I've looked at a girl like this, and I feel bad.

"At first I was annoyed, you know? I mean, fuck them. What gives them the right to stare at me? But then I started thinking about it. Is it their fault? Every centimeter of the female body has been sexualized. I could bitch about it. I could write a diatribe and send it to the *Huffington Post*. I could claim all men are creeps and wear a snowsuit every day and cut all my hair off. Or . . . I could look at it as an opportunity."

"So they pay you?"

She shrugs.

"Do you like it?" I ask. I realize that this sounds like an accusation.

"If I do, is that bad?" she says. "Let's reverse things for a sec. If you were in an airport or a restaurant or wherever . . . and you realized that every female within, say, a hundred feet was sexually attracted to you, would you like that? If all you had to do was sit quietly on your bed and chat and smile, and women would send you money, would you like that?"

I don't say anything. Instead I think of my grandpa, an old man in a lonely little room, watching a girl. This girl.

"Some of the men are assholes," she says. "I block them, and then they can't see me anymore. I'm in charge. Queen of my virtual kingdom. And to be honest, most of the guys are actually very sweet."

"My grandpa?" I say.

She smiles. "The sweetest of them all."

"How did he find you?"

She rolls onto her side to face me. "How many of these questions do you have?"

"I don't know," I say, honestly.

"OK," she says. "I asked him that once, how he found me."

"And?"

"He didn't want to tell me at first. I think he was embarrassed. He told me he Googled *How to find a girlfriend when you're alone.*"

The sadness is sudden, and it arrives with significant weight into my sternum, knocking the breath out of me.

"The site popped up, and he found me. He said he watched me for a while—a couple of weeks. One night he sent me a private request."

"Private request?"

"When I'm in public chat, anyone can see me. That's how you found me earlier, you dirty boy. People can send me private requests, though, and if I accept, it's just the two of us, cam to cam."

"You could see him?"

She nods. "That part shocked him, actually. He didn't know he had a camera on his computer."

"You talked?" I say.

"We did. A lot. We became friends. He was very sweet to me. The first time we talked, he told me I looked cold, and that I should put something on. You don't hear that a lot in this job."

"But," I say.

"What?"

"I don't mean to sound like a dick. You're . . . Well, from what I saw, you're very good at what you do. But . . ."

"Why did he like me?"

I nod, and she touches my arm.

"I'm going to show you something, OK? And it might seem weird at first. But . . . it'll explain a lot, I think."

She picks up her Curtis Violet book off the bed and pulls a photograph from the pages, her bookmark. When she hands it to me, I see a girl in one of those 1950s-style swimsuits—frills and buttons. She's smiling at the camera, shy, with her feet in the water.

"Kinda looks like me, huh?" she says.

"Yeah," I say. "It does. Is it, like, your grandma or something?"

"No," she says. "It's yours."

"It's my what?"

She lets me work this through on my own, and I do my best.

"*Your* grandma. He thought I looked like her. Dot. That's why he started watching me. He found me among all those scantily clad girls because he thought I looked like your grandma when she was young."

"Jesus," I say. She gives me another second as this information settles. "Is that why he keeps asking for her?"

"I don't know," she says. "But I'm glad this happened because I'm gonna see him later, tonight. I'm gonna say good-bye to him. Mrs. DiGiacomo said she'd let me in. I think you should come with me."

"Me? Why?"

"It's different at night," she says. "It's quieter, and you can actually almost talk to him."

"It's late," I say.

"What, you have plans?" she says.

I don't, of course. I don't have anything, actually. I can't remember the last time I had to be anywhere.

She lays down and rolls on her side toward me so we're eye-to-eye, her breath smells sweet, like wine, and she puts her hand on my arm and lets it rest there. It's embarrassing when she asks me if I was thinking about Karen before.

"A little," I say. "At first."

"Felt nice, didn't it, to just give up for a few minutes and stop fighting it?"

I admit that it did.

"Lie on top of me, OK?" she says. She pushes her pillow to the floor and rolls onto her back. She kicks the covers to the end of the bed, and then she's laid out there in her underwear and a T-shirt, pale and skinny and beautiful and sad.

I touch her leg. I run my hand down the elaborate tattoo there on her thigh. I don't even know what it is, just colors and swirls, and she makes a sound. When I'm on top of her, she closes her eyes and tells me to kiss her, and so I do. And then she tells me to suck gently on the tip of her tongue, and I do my best, and it feels soft and alive in my mouth. She tugs her tongue out from between my lips. Her eyes are still closed, like she's asleep and dreaming. "Tell me I'm your sweet girl," she whispers.

"Daisy," I say.

"Just say it, OK?"

I kiss her collarbone. "You're my sweet girl." I whisper it into her neck.

She sighs. It's the same sound I made earlier on the couch. It's the sound of letting yourself feel good again, if only for a few minutes.

"Is that what he used to call—"

"Shhh," she says. "Shut up."

I kiss the tip of her nose. I kiss her forehead and bite her earlobe. I'm playing my part—pretending to be someone who loves her. She wraps her legs around me and I kiss her lips. I close my eyes now, too. I close my eyes and think of Karen while Daisy thinks of him—whoever he is—the guy who cast her aside. "Tell me how much you've missed me," she says.

"My God. I've missed you so much."

33

Mrs. DiGiacomo is waiting for us when we get to New Beginnings. We find her at an entrance around the side of the building, wide awake in her robe. She and Daisy hug, and I get the sense that this happens a lot. This is how Daisy visits him, at night, in secret.

"Hi, Andy," she says.

"Hey, Mrs. D.," I say.

"Your mother was here earlier," she tells Daisy. "She'll be back first thing, so maybe you want to hurry?"

She says this to both of us, but then I remember the variables here. Daisy and I are brother and sister. Nancy is our mother. I barely know Mrs. DiGiacomo, but I feel bad lying to her like this. I make a mental note to watch *The Young and the Restless* with her the next time I'm here.

I follow them both through a door and up some stairs, and then I recognize my grandpa's floor. A nurse is working at the front desk, a lady I've never seen before.

"Hi, Nadine," says Daisy.

Nadine looks up and offers a brief, efficient smile. I've seen bouncers give girls this look before, girls who probably aren't twenty-one.

"Nadine understands our situation," Mrs. DiGiacomo whispers to me. I have no idea what that situation is, exactly—what elaborate story Daisy and Mrs. DiGiacomo have told her—but, apparently, it worked, because we've breezed right in like hospice center VIPs.

Mrs. DiGiacomo has set up a little spot in the hallway outside my grandpa's suite. She has a blanket and two chairs and one of her floral glasses of tea sitting on some magazines. Daisy slides her shoes off and sits in a chair beside her. "You should go in first," she tells me.

"I thought you wanted to—"

"I'll go after. I want to be alone with him. Go talk to him."

He's asleep when I go in, of course. The machines are making their noises, doing their thing. I sit on the uncomfortable chair at the side of his bed and watch him sleep for a while. The "I ♥ NY" mug is by the window next to all the flowers and cards, and I think of him telling Google that he's alone, and I feel terrible again. "I'm sorry, Grandpa," I say.

I watch to see if his face changes, but it doesn't.

"I'm sorry I left. And I'm sorry I didn't call you more. And I should have gotten you more than a coffee mug. And I hope now that the goddamn Cubs don't suck so horribly and they actually win something someday. You've been a really great grandpa, and you deserve better than this."

I reach for his hand and hold it awhile. I wish he'd wake up again—if just for a few seconds so he'd know that I'm here. He doesn't, though. But I'm not ready to leave yet, so I pick up *Clear and Present Danger* and start reading from where Nancy left off. A few pages in, I fall into the story. It's fun to read about Jack Ryan. He's cool and smart, and I imagine him as Harrison Ford, like in the movie. And the best part is, no matter how much danger he's in . . . he'll never die.

Back in the hallway, Daisy stands up when she sees me. "All done?" she asks.

"Yeah," I say.

She's wearing a clingy black sweater and jeans. She's pulled her hair back, too. Her tattoos are hidden. I notice she took her nose ring out. She doesn't really look like herself.

"Why tonight?" I ask.

"You guys are probably gonna start spending the night here—you and your family. Nancy. There's something I want to do for him, and I want to make sure I can."

"What are you going to do?" I say.

"He thinks I'm your grandma," she says. "I'm gonna let him keep thinking that."

"OK, yeah. But what does that mean now? What are you going to—"

She kisses me on the cheek. It's not a kiss a sister gives her brother, but Mrs. DiGiacomo seems oblivious as she leafs through an old magazine. "I'm gonna be who he wants me to be," she says.

And then she walks into my grandpa's suite and closes the door behind her.

When I sit down next to Mrs. DiGiacomo, she holds out a paper plate. There are two shriveled little Hot Pockets there.

"They're cold," she says. "I hope you don't mind."

I take one, and somehow, despite everything I know to be true in the world, it tastes really good.

34

I turn the headlights off as I pull into the driveway.

I close the car door as quietly as I can. It's after three a.m., and I don't want to wake my parents. I sneak up the porch stairs like I'm about to rob the place. And then I see a body sprawled out on the front porch and nearly pass out.

It's my dad. And unless I'm mistaken, he's not dead. He's at his post, sitting in a deck chair, protecting the house from the Glitter Mafia. And he's fast asleep.

"Dad." I give him a shake. "Dad."

It's pointless, really. My dad is impossible to wake. He always has been. I look out at the neighborhood. I watch the trees and the lawn. I'm not even a little bit tired, and the idea of sitting up in the Bizarro Room until the sun rises seems daunting. So I go inside quietly to grab some supplies: two blankets, a pillow, my new computer, some Teddy Grahams.

When I return, my dad murmurs something as I angle the pillow under his head. I settle into the deck chair beside him. My new, gently used computer starts right up with a satisfying little ping.

Daisy and I parted ways at her apartment about half an hour ago. She was practically asleep on her feet. I asked her how it went with my grandpa. She was in there with him for more than an hour. I asked her if he was awake. I asked her what she said to him. But she didn't answer.

I guess I'll never know.

When I moved to New York last year, I really did go off the grid—my former grid, at least. I killed off all my social media accounts in one drunken evening with my window open and the sounds of the city honking and blasting outside. It was the most liberating thing I'd ever done. I never officially deleted my old e-mail account, though. I tried, but I couldn't figure it out, so I started a new account and gave the address to my parents, Jim, and my grandpa. Somehow, I managed to never go back to the old one again.

Until now.

I type *gmail.com* and enter my old password, which happens to be Karen's birthday. When my inbox appears, I scroll and scroll, deleting things as I go—spam and e-mails about erections. Eventually I make it to the days around Neal's wedding—my last days in Omaha.

There are some e-mails from one of the other groomsmen, a guy named Dave. Apparently the tux deposits went on his credit card and I owe him seven hundred dollars. My sister-in-law sent me a message, and so did the Gap, Banana Republic, and the University of Nebraska. I delete these, and when the next page appears, I see Neal's name over and over again. I count from the bottom up. He sent me twelve e-mails.

The first few are very long with very little punctuation—ranting mostly. But as I work my way through, his anger starts to fizzle. You can tell by the subject lines.

WTF?!!!!!!!

SERIOUSLY!

ARE YOU GOING TO ANSWER ME?

You Left???

Are you even getting these???

New York????

Until, finally, the last one says just "Fine."
I scan one of his e-mails toward the end of the list.

> The whole thing is stupid, if you think about
> it. I mean, we were friends before her, right?
> I don't understand why we can't be friends
> after her, too. Maybe we can just skip over
> the entire time period—THE KAREN ERA.
> It can be like Godfather 3 or Jar Jar Binks
> or New Coke. We can just collectively both
> agree that it didn't happen. I can do that.
> Can you do that?

There's more there, but I stop reading. Maybe I'll go back and read
it later—along with all the others—but it's too much right now. I close
my eyes and try to remain pissed at him. I try to tap into the bubbling
cauldron of resentment that's been fueling me all year. It's gone, though,
dried up. He had the audacity to share a womb with Karen, so I threw
up in front of everyone he knows, punched his dad, and wrecked his
car. Maybe we're even.

I open his last e-mail, the one with "Fine." as the subject line.

> I guess you're gone. I'll stop e-mailing you
> then. I don't even know if you're going to
> read this, or if you've read all the other

e-mails I've sent you. But if you are reading it, the thing I'm most pissed about is that I didn't get to hear your speech. I know you worked really hard on it. I bet it would have been good.

Neal.

I close the laptop. I pull my blanket up and think about the logistics of skipping over the Karen Era. Is it even possible? Maybe that's just what moving on is, not *getting* over, but *skipping* over.

And then I notice the Ken Doll.

It's been sitting here this whole time, hiding in plain sight a few feet away from my chair. I set the computer down and untangle myself from the blanket. I look at my dad, but he's still racked out. Stephen must have been here—maybe they all were. But instead of wrecking the place like last time, they just left this.

I pick up the smiling doll. There's a pink index card rolled up and jammed under his little tuxedoed arm. I squint to make out the handwriting.

Andrew:

I wish you had taken us more seriously. Just remember, it didn't have to be like this.

Sincerely,
The Glitter Mafia

35

Daisy and I are in the Caddie, parked outside of Lazzari's, drinking enormous iced coffees from Koba Café.

I've just told her everything. All of it. It just sort of spilled out—this caffeine-infused tsunami of words. I told her about my dad, the Glitter Mafia, the envelope of pictures, my mother's appearance on Fox, even the Ken Dolls.

She doesn't look particularly surprised. All she says is, "You don't normally drink this much coffee, huh?"

"That's it?" I say. "I tell you all that, and that's all I get?"

"Andy," she says. "I'd probably cheat on your mother, too." And then she reaches over and takes the coffee away from me. "You need a little break from this."

We went to Koba Café in the idiotic hope that we might find Stephen or his henchmen there. I thought maybe I could talk him down from whatever it is he's thinking about doing. But he wasn't there, and I have no idea how to find him or how to get in touch. So I'm pretty much screwed.

We sit for a while. I'm drumming my hands on the steering wheel like a coke fiend.

"Man, somebody really messed that window up," she says. She's looking at the spot where the Corona sign used to be. Emma tore it off the wall the other night, which cracked the glass. Neal's put some half-assed duct tape over it, but it looks like someone tried to go through it with a battering ram.

"Probably some drunk asshole," I say.

I pull the wrinkly index card out of my back pocket and look at it for a second, running over my opening line again. It's been a while, but it's still a good line, a year later. I found my speech in the closet in the Bizarro Room, tucked safely into the pocket of a torn, puke-stained tuxedo jacket—the one I never returned.

"What's that?" she says.

"A best man speech," I say.

"For who?"

"None of your fucking business," I say. "Wait here, OK? I have to go do something."

"Hold on," she says.

"What?"

"Kiss me."

"Now? Like, on command?"

"Don't think. All you do is think. Just do it." I'm worried about my breath because of the half bucket of coffee I just shotgunned, but she's drinking coffee, too, so maybe that cancels everything out. The fact that I'm thinking about this perfectly proves the point Daisy just made, because what I should be thinking about is Daisy's mouth and how it feels against mine.

When I pull away, she appears also to be thinking. She looks like a girl in a fancy restaurant who's just sampled something weird.

"OK, go," she says. "I'll wait."

～

Lazzari's is busy. Too busy.

I imagined walking in and finding a midweek ghost town. But it's not midweek. It's Saturday. I've completely lost track of the days of the week.

An adult softball team is eating at a big table, talking loudly. There are kids and families here, people milling around the counter, waiting for their food, shouting orders. Owen and Neal are slinging pizza and filling up beers and doing their best to keep up.

He sees me and does a double take. Jesus, why does he have to look so much like Karen?

"Neal!" I shout.

He sees me and rolls his eyes. "Dude . . . what?"

"I need to talk to you. Just for a minute."

"Are you serious? Now?"

"Hi, Andy," says Owen, waving at me like Forrest Gump. "One point one million views, bro," he says.

"That's great, man," I say. "Seriously, Neal, just give me like five minutes, OK?"

"Andy, go home," he says. "Believe it or not, this is my job. I do this for a living."

The people in line seem to agree. They all look at me, telling me to shut the hell up with their eyeballs. This is going to be harder than I thought.

Owen announces an order into the microphone under the "Pick Up Here" sign at the other end of the long counter. "Eight twenty-two," he says, and a girl grabs her food in a takeaway box and rushes off. I reach into my back pocket and take out the note card. My plan was to give it to him and tell him I'm sorry, but clearly I'm going to need to switch things up. So I step through the line of people. In New York, a move like this would warrant a throat punch, possibly a stabbing, but in Nebraska everyone just glares. "Excuse me," I say. "Sorry. I know. I'm sorry . . . I'm not cutting, I promise. Just give me a second here."

I push through a little half door and step behind the counter. Owen and Neal don't notice, and I think of that Billy Joel song, but instead of a beer, the microphone smells like pizza, which is gross. I look at my notes and take a breath and clear my throat. And then I deliver my first line. "No offense to anyone here, I'm sure you're all great, but Neal is a better person than all of us combined."

If there was a turntable here—some big, dusty monstrosity like Daisy's ex-boyfriend probably listens to—the needle would slide loudly off the record. Everyone in the restaurant has stopped what they're doing, and now they're looking at me. I'm relieved to discover that I have absolutely no urge to vomit. Yet.

"Who's that guy?" someone says.

"He work here?" someone else says.

I start talking again. "He's kinder. He's gentler. He has a bigger heart. He would do anything for any of us, and he wouldn't ask for anything in return. Because that's who he is. And I'm proud to stand here, on one of the most important days of his life, and say that he is my best friend."

Neal is frozen at the register, his hands at his side, a pencil behind his ear. I look away from him, though, and out into the confused crowd of people, pretending, for some reason, that this really is his wedding day. One of the softball players has stopped midbite to stare at me— some cheese hangs from his mouth. Other than a toddler about Emma's age babbling from one of the back booths, it's totally silent. Even Arnold Schwarzenegger is quiet.

"I remember the day I met him, actually. Freshman orientation at Nebraska. It was a hundred degrees out, and we were at this hor- rible freshman mixer. I was wearing a Yoda T-shirt and shorts and these dumb Tevas. I know . . . guys wore Tevas back then. I felt like an idiot, because everyone else had dressed up like it was a yacht party or some- thing. I didn't know anyone and I was completely lost and so . . . so short. Everyone in this state is tall, if you haven't noticed."

I look up. I'm pretty sure people would have laughed at this at the reception—it's a good line. But I'm in a pizza shop, and I think most of these people are trying to figure out whether or not I'm insane, so everyone just keeps staring.

"Anyway," I say. "I was trying to make small talk with this group of guys. They all looked like Abercrombie models, and they were pretty much ignoring me. And then I looked over at this tray of shrimp cocktail in the corner of the room, and there was Neal . . . tall, skinny Neal, shoveling shrimp into his mouth like a trained seal. He was wearing a *Ghostbusters* T-shirt, and he looked every inch as totally out of place as I did. And I said to myself, *I've gotta go talk to that guy right there. Maybe I can make him be my friend.*

"And fifteen years later—or whatever the math is—I'm glad I did. Because I wouldn't have made it through college without him. I probably helped him a little bit, too. But he helped me more. And I hope all of you appreciate how lucky you are to know him. And Kristen—"

"Who's Kristen?" someone says.

Fuck it: I'm sticking to the script.

"Kristen, I hope you realize that you've got a great guy here—one of the good ones. He's going to be a wonderful husband and a wonderful father someday. And to me, he'll always be a great friend. So if you'll raise your glasses . . ."

To my surprise, a few random people actually do—they lift their domestic beer bottles and plastic soda cups. A little kid sitting with her parents lifts a juice box. Neal is rubbing his own eyebrows.

"Cheers . . . to Neal and Kristen."

The mic is mounted to the counter, so I can't hand it to someone or drop it like a rapper, so I just step away. Silence follows, of course, because no one has any idea what to say or do. And then Owen—smiling, stoned-ass Owen—starts clapping. Everyone just watches him, confused, Neal and I included. He does this for a few seconds and then gets annoyed. "Jesus, people!" he says. "Clap. That was beautiful."

Maybe five people clap—or at least kind of clap—and Neal is embarrassed to the point of looking like he might faint. Finally, he waves me back toward the pizza ovens. The regular noise level returns as people realize that our odd little performance is over.

"Nice speech, moron," he says.

"I think I delivered it pretty well."

"I wanted to tell you about him," he says. "I mean, you know that, don't you?"

"Yeah," I say. "You should have, but I get it."

"But here's the thing . . . What she did to you was shitty. She's my sister, though."

"I know."

"And I love her. I always will. That's just the way it's going to be. She and I shared a womb. You and I shared a dorm room."

"That's fair."

"And it was a *Star Trek* T-shirt," he says. "I never had a *Ghostbusters* shirt. *Ghostbusters* shirts are totally cliché."

"But I fucking hate *Star Trek* because it's so stupid. And it was my toast. So deal with it."

Maybe we should hug or high five. Something. It doesn't matter, though, because just like that, we're mostly fine. Not totally fine. That will take a while. I was a dick. He was a dick, too, but probably not as much of a dick as I was. We can figure that all out later. We talk a little more, and I suggest that if he wants to organize some sort of installment plan, maybe I'll eventually pay him back for Big Red, but maybe he should leave it the way it is for a while because there's something pretty badass about a big, dented-up truck. He's not paying attention to me, though. One, because I'm yammering, and two, because a beautiful girl with great big eyes is standing next to *Terminator 2: Judgment Day* pinball. She's smiling in a way that leads me to believe that she's been standing there for a while.

36

I pull the Caddie into a spot at New Beginnings.

I see Nancy's car a few spots over, and I stand there in the parking lot and prepare myself mentally to see her. I scan the lot for my dad's car—Jim's Range Rover, too—but there's no sign of either, and I wonder if other sons do this. Do other sons have to gear up to see their own mother? I've been doing it for years, as if seeing her is the equivalent of lifting the heavy end of a piano.

Daisy and I had pizza and a few beers at Lazzari's after my best man speech earlier today. When the rush slowed, Neal and Owen took turns hanging out at our table. They were both self-conscious and silly around Daisy. They fumbled and flustered and stammered a little, because this is how men like us behave around women. It's how we've always behaved around women.

"So where did you . . . go to high school?" asked Neal.

"Nowhere near here," she said, enjoying the intense power of his awkwardness.

If it's possible, Owen was even worse. "What does this one here mean?" he said, touching the inside of her wrist.

"It means read, Owen," she said.

"Oh, yeah. Right on. I like reading. Do you read any *Star Wars* books?"

And so on.

When I drove her home, as we floated east toward downtown, she reached across the big plush armrest and took my hand. I was startled by it at first, but I played it cool. What did it mean, exactly? How do I feel about it? And more importantly, is it fucked up that she looks like a version of my grandma that I never even saw, or that my grandpa watched her on his computer? These are difficult questions.

I don't go into New Beginnings the secret back way like last night. I enter through the main lobby, taking in the full oppressive weight of the heat there. The usual suspects are watching movies and playing checkers. I spot Mrs. DiGiacomo in her favorite spot by a window looking out onto the bocce ball court.

"Hey there, lady," I say.

She turns and says hello, but she doesn't smile, and her voice is different.

"Everything OK?"

"Sure," she says. "I've never really understood this game."

We look out at the bocce. A man tosses a ball, the other men shake their heads. I have no idea why.

"I think it might even be more ridiculous than baseball," she says. "Men and their balls."

"Thanks for . . . last night," I say. "Daisy really appreciated it. Me, too."

Her eyes go vacant, but only for an instant. "When my Anthony went, that's what we did. Me and the kids . . . We took our turns, went in one at a time. He told me to make sure I keep the grass watered. That's what he told me to do. So I did for as long as I could."

"You maybe wanna watch some *Y and R* a little later?" I say. "I think I'll be here for a while. Might need a break in a few hours. We'll drink some tea. Get a little wild. Maybe cause some trouble."

She looks back at the grass and sighs. "You could have told me she's not your sister, you know."

My stomach goes tight. "What?"

"I know every family has its . . . its unique situations. But it doesn't mean you have to make up stories."

I consider denying it, simply lying to this old woman. But that doesn't make sense. "I actually tried to tell you," I say. "That first day I met you, out in the parking lot."

She frowns, thinking. "Well, I guess you didn't try as hard as you should have."

"Sorry," I say.

"Why did she tell me she was his granddaughter? That's the thing I don't understand."

I remember what Daisy told me that first night at the Bookworm, how she said she just let Mrs. DiGiacomo believe what she wanted to believe. "Did she actually tell you that? Or did you just—"

"That's *exactly* what she told me. I was on my walk, and she came up to me out in the yard—this girl I'd never seen before. She asked me if I knew Henry. I said I did, and she told me he was her grandpa. She said she wanted to see him, but your mom had forbidden it. It wasn't my business. But I didn't think it was right for a girl not to get to see her grandpa when he was sick."

"Are you sure that maybe you didn't . . ."

I think it's the first time I've ever heard her voice like this—clear and certain—and I believe her. Daisy lied to me, and she lied to Mrs. DiGiacomo.

"Henry told me all about you and Jim. Never her, though. I believed her, because why would somebody make up something like that? I guess I shouldn't have."

"Mrs. DiGiacomo," I say. "How did you . . . ?"

"Your mother," she says.

"My mom?"

207

"Nancy told me everything. She's upstairs, by the way. Sounds like she's interested in having a little chat with you."

I don't wait for a nurse. Instead I head down the long hallway myself toward hospice. I tap my grandpa's suite door twice, tentative, and I hear, "Come in." She's in the chair beside him, Tom Clancy in her lap. "Oh, good," she says vividly, but with an edge.

"Hey, Mom."

"I hear you've been a very busy young man," she says. "You must be tired."

"Mom."

She looks at her watch. "I'm glad you made it actually. I was about to call you. I'm planning a little family dinner party this evening. It's a shame we haven't all had a chance to be together."

"You've . . . Mom . . . you've kinda got the crazy eyes going."

She smiles. "Don't be silly, Andy. My eyes are fine. An impromptu thing at the house, that's all. Jim and Gina will be there with the kids. Your father. You should invite . . . your little friend. What's her name again?"

"Mom."

"Dani? Daphne?"

"Daisy."

She snaps her fingers. "Right. I keep forgetting that. What an unusual name. You don't hear it much anymore. Anyway, give her a call. Tell her six thirty. No need to bring anything. Just herself."

"That's in, like, three hours," I say. "A little last-minute, don't you think?"

It's a pathetic attempt to derail this, whatever it is, and we both know it. She tilts her head, her smile laser focused, like a sophisticated weapon. "You know what?" she says. "I wouldn't worry about it. Something tells me her schedule is open."

37

It's later now, dinnertime, and Nancy is wearing a dress.

It's not a power dress. It's not a Fox News dress. It's just a nice yellow-and-light-blue thing that a reasonable woman might wear. For some reason, I find this ominous. She's smiling and being friendly, too, which is equally as frightening. She's chatting with Jim and me while we sip beers in the kitchen.

"Why are you in such a good mood, Mom?" Jim says. I guess he finds this weird, too. "Are you drunk?"

She laughs. "It's just nice to have us all together."

Jim looks at me—*What the fuck?*

I decide to pretend to be as ignorant as he is. I should be able to pull this off convincingly for at least twenty more minutes, I figure. Jim's wife, Gina, is out in the backyard, chasing Emma and Bryce around. My dad is out there, too, seeming to enjoy himself. I should work my way out there. It seems safer. And while I'm there, maybe I'll go ahead and set the house on fire to prevent this dinner from actually occurring.

"So when's your *friend* coming, Andy?" my mom says. "Jim, has Andy told you about his new friend?"

Jim looks vaguely interested. "What? No."

"Well . . . it's a girl."

And now he *is* interested. "No sh—really? Who is it? A girl? Like, a girl-girl?"

I should probably be offended that he finds this news so utterly stunning, but I get it. "No one," I say.

"I hear she's quite pretty, actually," Nancy says.

"Nice, man," says Jim. "No wonder you're all dressed up. Look at you."

I decided to go all in tonight. I'm wearing my new jeans and a new button-up shirt. Jim paid for both of them, along with my new shoes and lifts, but there's no reason to get into that right now.

Two minutes—and about twenty questions from Jim—later, the doorbell rings. I realize all at once how horrible an idea this is. When I called Daisy to invite her to dinner, I figured she'd laugh in my face and tell me hell no. But instead, she agreed instantly. She told me she's tired of hiding from my mother.

"Uh-oh," says Jim, clapping his hands.

"That must be her," says Nancy. "Go let her in. Don't be rude."

When I open the door, she's in a green peasant dress, and she's holding a classy bottle of red wine. Her hair is blow dried and wavy, arranged carefully down either side of her face. I've only seen it either wild or tied up, like an afterthought. She hands me the wine, and I'm not sure what to do with it, exactly. One option is to pry the cork out with my bare hands and start guzzling it.

"You look . . . ," I say.

"Am I stoned, or is there a squirrel in the yard wearing a tiny sweater?" she says.

I look out into the grass. It's standing beneath a tree, watching the house. It looks almost sophisticated, like a young urban professional in a tasteful green jumper. "It's a long story," I say.

"OK, then," she says. "I interrupted you. You were about to tell me how good I look."

"You look," I say, taking it from the top, "really great."

I probably could have done better, but she thanks me anyway. She touches the sleeve of my new shirt, which is tucked in and everything. "Nice," she says.

I could stand like this for a while, the two of us in the doorway, half smiling, and I try to stretch it for as long as I can, but then she says, "Maybe I should come in? I drove all the way out here and all."

Jim's reaction to Daisy is similar to how Neal and Owen reacted—surprise mixed with disbelief mixed with mild confusion. He shakes her hand. "Nice ink," he says.

When my mom appears from the kitchen, she's wearing her same weaponized smile. "And you must be . . ." She lets this hang there for an awkwardly long time. For some reason, my mother has committed to not remembering Daisy's name.

"Daisy," she says.

"Oh, of course. Welcome."

They shake hands while Jim and I watch stupidly. He looks at me—a different kind of *What the fuck?* this time—and, mixed in with all the swirling anxiety and low-level terror, I feel a twinge of pride. This shocking girl is here to see me.

"Thanks for inviting me, Mrs. Carter. You have a beautiful home."

Nancy laughs. "No need for formalities here, Daisy. Please . . . call me Nancy."

I give Daisy a quick tour of the house, because that seems like something people do in situations like these. I show her the TV room and the dining room. We breeze through the laundry room, the basement, and the enormous bathroom on the first floor. She follows along, being appropriately impressed with everything. In the hallway, leading up the stairs, we stop at a particularly somber portrait of Jesus. We've had it for as long as I can remember. It hung in our old house, and now it hangs in this one. He—capital *H*—is perfectly Caucasian with great cheekbones and a beautifully trimmed beard. He's serious, staring off into the middle distance.

"Who's this handsome guy?" says Daisy. "Friend of yours?"

"No, actually," I say. "It's Barry Gibb. My parents are huge Bee Gees fans."

Eventually, we make it to the Bizarro Room.

She spends a few minutes looking through my things, studying the crap from my youth. She slides out of her heels and sits cross-legged on my bed holding a Lego Ewok. She looks at the posters and my small furniture.

"So," she says. "They decorated your room with all your old stuff?"

"OK, good. So it's not just me who thinks that's weird. Jim's room, too."

"It makes sense," she says.

"It does?"

"That's what her kind of politics is all about, right? The past is this sacred, glorified thing? Even though it never really existed in the first place."

I hold up my duct-taped Walkman. "I'm not sure what you mean."

"All the stuff she says on the radio. It's just fear. The world is leaving people like her behind, and it scares the shit out of her."

Over the years, I've been so busy being horrified by the things my mother says that I've never really thought about *why* she says them. Maybe Daisy's right. Either way, it's a funny insight coming from the two of us, a couple of people who know a fair bit about longing for things long gone.

"So how many times, conservatively speaking, do you think you've masturbated on this bed?"

I look at my old twin, small and juvenile, a kid's bed dressed up with big-boy sheets. "What? You mean, like, today? Not that many."

She looks at the pile of photographs and albums. They're hard to miss. I didn't imagine we'd be up here, Daisy and me, so I just left them all piled on the floor. She hops down off my bed and curls up beside them. She starts with our wedding album and flips through the pages quickly. A picture of Karen by herself stops her. It's one of those casual shots that wedding photographers love to get. She's standing at the back of the church waiting for Jerry to come walk her down the aisle. She looks stunning, a little nervous.

"Why didn't you tell me how ugly she is?" says Daisy.

"It seemed in poor taste," I say.

Daisy closes the album and runs her palms over the soft leather cover. "The first time I saw . . . *him*," she says. "The very first time, he looked so gorgeous that I walked up to him and told him that if he didn't kiss me by the end of the night I'd kill him and then slit my own wrists."

"Oh, that old line?" I say.

"You haven't seen her yet, right? Since you've been back?"

"There's a slight chance I saw her silhouette from the yard. But . . . no, not really."

"Well, don't worry, because you will. That's how it works. Right when you find yourself not thinking about her at all, there she'll be, right at the end of the story to fuck with your head one last time."

She holds her hands out to me, so I help her up off the floor. We're face-to-face. We could kiss or slow dance or high-five if we wanted to. I'm about to ask her why she lied to Mrs. DiGiacomo. It's been bothering me all day. But before I can, she says, "What's that?"

It's a picture on my bookshelf—one I forgot I even have. It's Jim and me from a random Halloween when we were kids. I was ten-ish; he was fourteen-ish. We're dressed as Batman and Robin.

"Jim and me," I say.

"Oh, man," she says. "This explains a lot."

"A lot of what?"

She pushes the picture off its little kickstand and lays it down glass-first. "A little boy shouldn't dress up like a sidekick for Halloween."

Another montage—fall, cold, winter coats over costumes. There's Jim dressed as Batman, me as Robin. There's Jim as Superman, me as Jimmy Olsen. There's me tripping over a tree root as I chase after him in someone's yard, Snickers bars flying from my Halloween bag. There's Jim as the Lone Ranger, me as Tonto. Jim as Sherlock Holmes, me as Watson. Jim as Mario, me as Luigi. Jim as a football player, me as a cheerleader. I'm about 95 percent sure that last one didn't actually happen, but still . . .

"I want you to promise me something, OK?" Daisy says. "From here on out, no matter what happens, even if I'm not around to keep drumming it into your head, you're Batman. Always. Never Robin. Never again. Deal?"

I wish I'd met her when I was younger. She could've given me these little speeches and set the course of my life in an entirely different direction.

I tell her, "Deal," and she says, "Good." And then she says, "Now take me downstairs. If my instincts are correct, I think we're gonna want to start drinking sooner rather than later."

This house is huge. We've established that. The rooms, the yard, the driveway, the TVs. The dining room table, though, for some reason, is quite small. At least that's how it feels.

Daisy and I are seated side by side. Directly across from us sit my parents. My brother, Gina, and the kids are at the end. Bryce, still in his karate gear, is complaining loudly that he doesn't like sauce on his spaghetti, and my brother and Gina are rattling off the impressive list of things that'll be taken away from him if he doesn't eat it. Emma is oblivious. She's planted in her booster seat beside Daisy, and most of her spaghetti is on her face or in her lap. At present, she's carefully tracing each tattoo she can reach with her tiny index finger.

"Clooor?" she says.

"You like those?" Daisy asks.

Emma nods with great, wordless certainty.

"Do you give high fives?"

Emma slaps Daisy's palm and laughs. She does it three more times and laughs harder each time.

"She likes you, Daisy," Jim says.

"I guess she's too young to know any better, right?" Daisy replies.

"That's a good point," says Jim. "After all, she does seem to like Andy a lot."

"Anndaaaa!" says Emma. I like this little girl very much, and I make a silent agreement with myself to be the cool uncle who buys her beer in, like, sixteen years.

And then my mother says, "Well, you are quite a novelty, Daisy. I think it's safe to say she hasn't seen quite so many tattoos in her life. We're not really a tattoo crowd."

Daisy holds her smile, refusing to let it fall.

"Emma," says Gina. "Let's leave Miss Daisy alone, OK? She's trying to eat her dinner."

"It's OK," says Daisy. "I don't mind. She can trace all she wants."

"So how did you guys meet, anyway?" asks Jim.

I have no idea how to answer this, so I freeze.

"We were at the Bookworm," Daisy says.

"The bookstore?" Gina says. "That one in Midtown? I love that place." She tears some crust off a piece of Italian bread and gives a white glob to Bryce.

"He asked me about the book I was reading."

"Seriously?" says Jim.

"Yep, he walked up and just started talking to me. He was very intellectual."

"Well, Andrew Carter . . . making moves. I'm impressed."

Despite the fact that this isn't true—not even close, actually—I feel myself swelling with pride. "It looked interesting," I say.

"So are you from Omaha, then?" Gina asks.

"No, actually. I'm . . . not. Nearby, though."

"Kansas City isn't exactly nearby," Nancy says. "Three hours, at least. Depending on traffic."

We all look at my mother—except for my dad, who's studying his pile of spaghetti.

"Kansas City?" Gina says. "That's a fun town."

Daisy is pretending that I'm not looking at her.

"Ityyyyy," Emma says.

"She still can't talk yet," says Bryce.

"She's doing her best, Bryce," says Gina. "So what brought you to Omaha?"

Daisy ignores Gina's question. She leans in eye-to-eye with Emma. "You know, Emma," she says. "I didn't talk until I was four and a half. My parents thought there was something wrong with me. They tested me and everything. Then one day, out of the blue, I just started talking in big full sentences. I wasn't ready . . . until I was ready."

"See, there's hope, Em," says Jim, touching the top of his daughter's head.

Gina starts to ask her question again—what brought Daisy here—but Nancy cuts her off. "What an inspirational story," she says. "I guess I find myself wondering whether or not we're supposed to believe one single, solitary word of it."

"Nancy," my dad says.

She swirls her wine, which is the only movement at the table. The rest of us have gone still, frozen by the tone of my mother's voice, even the kids, and I'm wondering, for the first time in my life, if I actually dislike my mother. It's a startling thing to have cross your mind so suddenly. Can you dislike the woman who gave birth to you—who is your reason for being alive? Maybe I do. Maybe everything has led up to this moment, at this table, eating this spaghetti, and I'm going to officially be someone who doesn't like his mother.

"Nancy," my dad says again, trying. "Not now."

"Nincccyy," says Emma.

"I guess I can't make you believe me," Daisy says. "If you choose not to."

The sounds of knives and forks and chewing follow. The tension in the room feels like something that might burst into flames at any second, like a slow gas leak. And then my sister-in-law, God bless her, clears her throat. She's just trying to be nice. She's just trying to fight through the sudden, inexplicable awkwardness. "So," she says. "What do you do, then, Daisy?"

"OK, that . . . is . . . enough!" says Nancy.

"Mom?" I say.

"Nancy, you invited me here," Daisy says.

"I am not going to sit at my own table and listen to my family continue to refer to you as *Daisy*. It's embarrassing. You're making asses of all of them."

"What?" I say.

"Daaaaaarzzy," says Emma.

"Your name is Stephanie Fitzgerald. You live in Kansas City. You dropped out of college. You're thirty years old, and your sole source of income is preying on vulnerable men from your computer."

"What the hell's going on?" Jim says.

"Mom, Dad said *hell*."

Gina puts her hand over her son's mouth. Daisy and Nancy are staring at each other across the table.

"What, did you think I wasn't going to look into you, *Stephanie*?" she says. "Did you think I was just going to sit and let you bleed my dying father dry?"

"Daisy," I say.

"Stop calling her that, Andy. You sound like a fool. What? Was Andy going to be next? You're nearly done with my father—he'll be dead any day now, right? Better sink your claws into the next one. Well, I hate to spoil this for you, Ms. Fitzgerald, but he doesn't have a dime to his name."

"I think I should go," Daisy says. She puts her napkin down and slides away from the table, but she doesn't get up. She looks at me.

I put my hand on her elbow. "What is—"

"I never liked the name Stephanie," she says. "It's so boring."

"Tell him how much he gave you," my mom says. "How much money has my father . . . *tipped* you?"

"It's not the way she's making it sound," Daisy says. She's just talking to me, no one else.

"One hundred and eighty-five thousand dollars."

For some vague period of time, I don't move, my heart doesn't beat, my blood doesn't flow, and I don't breathe.

"But that wasn't enough, was it? You got yourself into his will, too. Congratulations. You're a *real* professional."

I take my hand away from her.

"I did everything I could not to have to tell you guys," Nancy says to Jim and me. "I didn't want you to know that your grandfather has been watching . . . *this* person on the Internet and giving her his life savings. I didn't want that to be your lasting memory of him. But I guess I don't have a choice, do I?"

"He was lonely," Daisy says. My mother scoffs. "He was alone. By himself. You put him in that home. And where were you, Nancy? Where were you while he was getting sick? Where were you when he was scared? You were too busy dyeing your hair and exercising. Too busy saying horrible things on the radio. Too busy ignoring everyone in your life, apparently." She looks at my dad.

"Daisy," I say. "No."

"Yeah . . . How's your marriage going, Nancy? Sacred? A sacred bond?"

"How dare you talk about—"

"You took Grandpa's money?" Jim says.

"And where were you, Jim? At your office?"

My brother doesn't know what's going on, but he knows when he's getting called out. "Now, hold on a second," he says.

"Daisy," I say. "Is this . . . A hundred and eighty-five thousand?"

"And you," she says. She holds her stare, she doesn't blink. "You ran away. What, you send him a letter—a coffee mug? You think that's enough? All of you. You all left him behind and went on with your lives. Some family. He was alone and lonely and scared . . . and I was his friend."

There are tears in Nancy's eyes, pooling there, glistening under the dining room chandelier, but she's too angry to let them fall. No one says anything; we all just stare at each other, afraid to move. And then there's a chorus of odd, electrical sounds. My pocket goes first. Then there are matching robot beeps from Jim and Gina, like R2-D2. My dad's pocket honks, and from the serving table across the room, there are three distinct chimes. It's our phones, all at once. We've each gotten a text message.

Jim and I fumble for our phones. My dad does, too. My mom gets up and grabs hers. Because, of course, it's my grandpa. It's what we're all thinking. The world has chosen this difficult, confusing moment in Carter Family history to take him, and, for some reason, the hospice center is texting us about it. Which is ridiculous, of course. They would call, right? They wouldn't text us like teenage girls. I look down at my phone. I see a link on my little screen with a message.

Sent with love. Courtesy of the Glitter Mafia.

"What's this?" Jim says. He's looking at his phone, too. I click the link, and my browser tries to open a page. My mother is standing, reading her phone. Her face doesn't change. She sighs and looks at my dad. "Bradley," she says. "You idiot."

He stands and leaves the room, and we all watch him as he goes.

"Where's Grandpa going?" asks Bryce.

Emma waves. "Bah-bah!"

The motorcycle starts in the garage, shaking the entire house. My mother looks at Daisy and tells her to get out of her home. Home, not house.

Daisy looks at me, and in her eyes I can see that she's asking for my help. She's asking for me to believe her. But I look away, and I don't get up. I just sit and watch her leave.

38

The last few days have been strange.

    The link the Glitter Mafia sent to all of us was to some political blog I'd never heard of. It looked low-rent and thrown-together, like one of those sites where people post cat GIFs and vacation pictures. The shots were pasted up there at random, grainy and ominous. The headline read:

Betcha Nancy Didn't Know *This*

I guess that's reasonably clever, a play on *Nancy Knows*.

The production quality of the source didn't really matter, though. That's modern journalism, I guess. Because, from there, it spread. The *Omaha World-Herald* ran with it. The very paper that's been publishing Nancy's op-eds for more than a decade was now running gossip about her, complete with screen-captured images of my father and his "apparent mistress." For a day or so, it seemed like maybe it'd just be a local story, something that would cause some mild embarrassment at the grocery store and blow over. But then *Salon* picked it up, and in a matter of hours, thousands and thousands of people who didn't even know who in the hell Nancy was were reading about the details of her troubled marriage.

It's hard to keep track of the order—like charting which trees burn up first in a forest fire—but it looks like the *Mother Jones* piece came next. It wasn't just about Nancy. Instead it documented a long list of social conservatives around the country who've fallen on their faces at the hand of some scandal—earnest conservative lawmakers soliciting blow jobs in seedy bathrooms, corruption charges, infidelity, that sort of thing. She was on the home page of the *Huffington Post* this morning. *Morning Joe* mentioned the story, too, in passing. They seemed ashamed of themselves for doing it, like they were sullying their airwaves, but they did it nonetheless.

And so on.

I Googled her name today. A few years ago, I promised myself I would never do that again. There's something unhealthy about reading horrible things about your mother or seeing JPEGs of her with penises drawn next to her face. But curiosity got the better of me, and I found link after link to snide liberals making fun of her, essentially rolling around in her unhappiness like puppies in the snow.

And all the while, I haven't spoken to Daisy. Or, well, Stephanie, I guess.

Nancy has known about her for a while, it turns out. About three months ago, Nancy found her name, Stephanie Fitzgerald, in the latest version of my grandpa's will. After several meetings with our family's lawyer, a private investigator got involved. My grandpa's credit card statements were pulled. I'm not exactly sure if that part was legal, but the bills were astronomical. He'd been giving her money every day— thousands of dollars a week. Along with the money he gave her through tips to her page, which Daisy has already paid taxes on, she is currently set to inherit an additional one hundred thousand dollars upon my grandpa's death.

My mother is fighting it all, of course. From what Jim has told me, it could take years to figure out, and, since my grandpa isn't crazy, he's not sure if she has a leg to stand on.

I know how all this sounds. It sounds very bad. My lonely, dying grandpa slowly giving a beautiful, tattooed girl from the Internet pretty much all his money. But here's the thing. I can't stop thinking about her.

39

The door to Koba Café opens, and Stephen walks in.

I can see the VW outside in the parking lot. He asked me to meet him here. I planned to tell him to fuck off. And then I planned to slash his tires. And then I planned to stand him up entirely. But now I'm not doing any of those things. He's looking for me in the crowd of tables and loiterers, so I give him a little wave, which is ridiculous, waving at this guy who rolled a grenade into my family.

I probably should have stood him up, but I have to admit, it's nice to be out of the house. My mom and dad are staying away from home, and when they are there at the same time, they avoid each other, keeping to separate wings, which, now that I think about it, isn't that much of a change actually.

Stephen sits down across from me. He waves to Adam, the barista, and gives him a little wink. "Yep, just a pinch of brown sugar," he says. And then he looks at me. "Hello there, Andy."

"No goons today?" I say.

"Gave the boys the day off. Not thinking I'm gonna need any muscle. Besides, this is more of a personal errand, actually."

"Well, looks like you got the job done," I say. "Nancy is humiliated. You've probably ruined her career. Do you get, like, a bonus or something? Profit sharing?"

He takes this in, smirking. "Your mother will be just fine, Andy. Rich white people have a tendency to land on their feet, historically speaking."

"You could have told me you—"

"What, Andy?"

"You could have told me you were serious."

A full-on smile now. "I told you, we love being underestimated. It's our greatest weapon. But seriously, I'm not kidding, she'll be fine. Republicans rally when shit like this happens. Jesus, Dick Cheney practically blew his best friend's brains out—and they loved him for it. My guess is there's a whole bunch of *Nancy Knows* bumper stickers being printed right this very second. She's their girl. Besides, she'll probably just be the victim in all this. Your dad . . . He's the one we really screwed over."

"Then why'd you bother?" I say.

"That's a fair question. It's like this. When you make a threat, you have to see it through. Rules of war." He leans in and squeezes my forearm. "Listen, you love her. You have to. All that maternal stuff . . . Breast-feeding, I assume. I get it. But try to ignore all that for a second, if you can. You know that we did what needed to be done. You know that old black-and-white footage of protesters during desegregation? All those people in the background mad about black kids going to school? In ten—maybe fifteen—years that's what Nancy's gonna look like. She's gonna look like a bigot in the background of history, booing progress. She's a symbol of everything you and I should be fighting against. And you know it. Even if you did happen to once live inside her."

Adam brings Stephen his drink, and I take a sip of my plain, perfectly boring coffee and watch a Nancy montage in my head.

She's making my lunch when I was a kid, packing it into my G.I. Joe lunch box. She's sitting up with me every night that one summer when a dipshit babysitter let me watch *Poltergeist* and I was convinced that the oak tree in our backyard was going to come through the wall and eat me. She's teaching me to ride a bike because my dad traveled so much for work. She's waving at me from the crowd at my high school graduation.

She's not a symbol. She's just my mom.

"Why did you want to see me, then?" I say. "Why am I here?"

"Oh, I don't know," he says. "I'm a softy, I guess. I just wanted to tell you, no hard feelings."

I take another sip. This was all just a stunt.

"You ever think about just . . . *moving*?" I say. "Just going somewhere else? I mean, I live in Manhattan. I'm like the only straight guy there. Couldn't you just go somewhere and be happy . . . Forget about this place?"

He's warming his palms with his mug, watching me. "Ms. Parks, did you ever think about just getting your tired ass up and going to the back of the bus?"

I sigh. Mostly because he's right, but also because I want to throw my coffee in his face.

"What, too much?" he says. "OK. I'll admit, I thought about it when I was younger. New York, San Fran, Chicago maybe. But it turns out I really like it here. This is my home, Andy. And I have season tickets to the Huskers."

I do my best to keep my face even, not at all shocked.

"Oh, stop it . . . Don't look so stunned. We get to like football, too. You people don't own that." And then he turns in his seat toward the window. "And here's another thing," he says. "Just look at that motherfucking sky."

I haven't looked at it since I've been back. Hell, even when I lived here, I didn't look at it. But I'm seeing it now, remembering again. The sky in Nebraska is bigger than any other sky on earth. It's absolutely enormous.

"Where else am I gonna find a sky like that, Andy Carter?"

I want to throw my coffee in his face slightly less now. He's a good-looking, confident guy, secure in who he is. But at one point in his life, I'll bet, when he was a kid, things were probably pretty tough for him. "You know, for the record," I say. "I don't think you're damaged."

He laughs and puts his hands on the table. A few pieces of glitter cling to his skin, which is perfect. "I appreciate that," he says. "But I absolutely am. After the age of about . . . what, sixteen? We're all damaged. Every single beautiful, stupid, precious one of us. Damaged, damaged, damaged."

When he gets up to leave, I stop him. "Wait," I say.

"Really? That was such a good line to end on. You totally spoiled it."

"Sorry," I say. "The girl. The one I was with last time. You knew who she was, didn't you?"

"The elusive cam girl with the heart of gold?"

"Right. Yeah. Dai . . . Um, Stephanie."

"We looked into her," he says.

"What does that mean?"

"We were gathering intel on Nancy. I love saying that—*intel*—like we're a bunch of little James Bonds. We found out about her. We figured it was her thing, like she must have a long wake of dead sugar daddies behind her. So we did some digging."

"Well?" I say.

He shakes his head. "Nope," he says. "Just a pretty girl from Kansas City trying to make it in this big, bad world. Who'da guessed, huh?"

And then he really does leave.

40

When I dock the Caddie back in my parents' driveway, I see my dad's motorcycle. It's tipped over on its side, just lying there, handlebars askew, and I immediately assume that I've arrived at the inevitable crash site. My dad is probably stumbling around the yard, dazed and bleeding, and I'm going to have to rush him to the emergency room, and my scorned mother is going to say, "I told you so, you idiot."

But no.

The poor old bike hasn't been wrecked—it's been booted. It's this big yellow thing clamped to the front tire, choking it into submission. There's an open toolbox beside it. I find a miniature handsaw, completely destroyed, its little teeth worn to nubs. Two sets of pliers have been ruined, too, one snapped in half and the other bent beyond recognition.

Don Johnson.

That ballsy motherfucker booted my dad's motorcycle.

Inside, the house is empty, but through the kitchen window I see my dad sitting out in the gazebo, drinking a beer. I call for him from the deck, but he doesn't look up. When I sit down next to him, he says, "I've tried everything."

I'm not really sure what he's talking about.

"I think I just have to give up. I concede. I mean, how many times can I shoot them?"

The paintball gun is sitting at his feet, and he's looking out at the bird feeder. The squirrels are working in pairs, stealing and eating. Pretty much every square inch of yard around them is splattered red, like a killing field.

"Get out of here!" I shout.

The squirrels freeze. And then I watch as each of them, simultaneously, gives me the finger.

"You see?" he says.

"How about we take one thing at a time here?" I say. "The motorcycle? What happened?"

He looks defeated. His hands are raw and blistered, the tips of two fingers bleeding. I imagine him sawing at metal like a fool, swearing alone in the driveway. "I found it like that," he says. "I left it out. I can't believe I was so stupid. Why didn't I put it in the garage?"

"You have any more of those beers?" I say.

"No. But you can have the rest of this one."

"That's pretty gross," I say, but I down it anyway in one lukewarm swig. I attempt to throw the empty can at the squirrels, but it turns out empty beer cans don't travel very far when heaved across yards by chronically unathletic men in their early thirties.

"Are you OK, Dad?" I say.

For the first thirty-something years of my life, I never once asked my dad if he was OK . . . and now I've done it twice in one week. I wonder if this is just the way it is. Are all our parents, collectively, fucked up? Have they always been fucked up, and it just takes us until our own adulthood to figure that out?

"I was in love with her," he says. He's looking out at the trees. "It's important to me that you know that . . . that it wasn't just about . . ."

I've never heard my dad say the word *sex* before, and I'm glad he doesn't now.

"And it only happened a few times."

"Dad, I don't need to . . ."

"We have a relationship. Had. We *had* a relationship. We went on . . . dates. Restaurants were good. Lunches, mostly. How bad can lunch be? That's what we told ourselves. No harm in lunch. It was wrong, though. We're both . . ."

"Married?" I say.

He nods.

"And then we had dinner once. We drove fifty miles and we had dinner. And when you drive fifty miles to have dinner, it gets harder to tell yourself that you're not doing something wrong. But it was nice to talk. It's been a while since I've really had someone who wanted to talk to me. It's not a justification, I know, but it's the truth."

I don't know what to say. I wish I had another beer. I should have brought a wheelbarrow full of them.

"So it's over now?" I ask.

"It's for the best," he says.

"Best for who?"

"Everyone."

This is what we've become. My dad is pining for someone he barely had—a brunette lady with a nice smile in photographs. I'm pining for a girl who got bored of me and told me she didn't love me and then fucked the exact physical opposite of me. My grandpa is pining for a woman who is dead. We're three hopelessly sorry people. If we were characters in Vagina Fiction, Daisy would circle us in red and demand that we . . . *do* something, for fuck's sake.

And now, for some reason, I'm thinking of N.W.A.

I think of the poster tacked up crooked, four hardcore motherfuck-ers who just don't give a shit. Would they allow themselves to be this pathetic? No. Would they let themselves be this wounded by a girl? No way. And would they let some punk-ass pretend cop in a golf cart tell them what's what in their own neighborhood? No motherfucking way.

"Andy," my dad says. "Why are you smiling?"

Am I smiling? I am smiling. Why? Because I'm brilliant. I can't do anything about Karen. I tried as hard as I could, and she's gone. Maybe my dad is equally as screwed, and Lord knows my grandpa is, too. But there is something my dad and I can do. And that's get back at Don Motherfucking Johnson.

"Your motorcycle," I say.

"What about it?"

"How heavy is it? Do you think we could lift it?"

"It's not that heavy. Why would we want to lift it?"

"I need you to give me, like, forty-five minutes," I say. "I'll be right back. I have to get some things."

"What? Where are you going?"

"Dad, sit tight. I have an idea. But we're gonna need a truck."

I'm all business when I get to Lazzari's, which makes one of us.

The place is empty again, and it smells like there's been a fire. Neal and Owen are loudly playing what appears to be a high-stakes game of *Terminator 2: Judgment Day* pinball.

"Andy," says Neal over the sound of the robot apocalypse. Owen is manning the controls, and he's got a look of intense determination on his face as he slaps the little silver ball around the battlefield. "I'm coming after your record, Andy C.," he says. "It falls today." He says this last part in a pretty decent Schwarzenegger.

"Good luck, dude," I say. "Hey, Neal, can I talk to you for a second?"

"You seem tense," says Neal. "Do you want breadsticks? I just made some."

"No. Thanks. But listen, we're friends again, right?"

"I feel like talking about how you're friends again kind of ruins it," says Owen.

"He's actually right," says Neal. "We should just let things progress naturally. It's an organic process. I definitely dislike you less, though. That's something. And I don't want to punch you like I usually do."

"Fine," I say. "Fair enough. So I kinda need a favor."

"Well, there's a surprise," he says.

"It's too soon for favors, man," says Owen.

I ignore this and give Neal my grandpa's car keys.

"You're giving me a Cadillac?" he says. "That's your favor? Seems easy. Done."

"Sweet," says Owen.

"I'm not giving it to you . . . I'm trading it. Just for a couple of hours."

"Trading it? For what?"

I pause, mainly to heighten the drama. I'm starting to get excited about my plan. I think parts of it might be illegal, which makes it even better. "Neal" I say. "I'm taking Big Red."

He's supposed to be instantly cool with this and say something like *Fuck yeah, you are.* But instead, he says, "Wait. Why? For what?"

"That's not important."

"I strenuously disagree."

"I need to move something with my dad."

"What are you moving?"

"His motorcycle."

I've gone ahead and made this sound incredibly harmless, and I can see that he's considering it. "Do you promise to be really careful?" he says.

"How come you never let me borrow the truck?" says Owen.

"Well, you've never traded me a Cadillac for it before," says Neal. "And you're also stoned most of the time."

"Reasonable," says Owen. "But last time he drove your truck he was wasted, and he crashed it right in front of you and your entire family. Andy, you used to be in the insurance business, right? Who's a better risk? Me, or you?"

"Owen, concentrate on your game," I say.

"I don't need to concentrate. At this point, it's a matter of destiny."

I take a short break from my plan and watch Owen play. A second ball has entered the scene, zigzagging. Eventually, Neal nods to the door, and we walk outside. Perhaps it's a bad omen that we stop about two feet away from the window that Emma totally wrecked.

"You should get that fixed," I say.

"The Carters are a very destructive family," he says. "Speaking of, how's Nancy?"

"You saw the—"

"What, you don't think I'm up on current events? Is that why you need the truck? Is your dad . . . moving out?"

I almost say yes, just to move things along, but lying to Neal at this point in our renewed friendship is probably a bad idea. "I have no idea," I say. "Not yet, at least. Truth is, I need Big Red because my dad and I are getting even with someone."

"Doesn't sound worrisome at all," he says. "Who?"

"Don Johnson."

Neal frowns. "Wait," he says. "That guy from *Miami Vice*?"

My dad and I are in the driveway now, looking up at Big Red, which looks bigger and redder than ever at the moment. He tugs his beard, thinking. I know this look very well. He's about to say something negative and completely reasonable. "I don't know about this, Andy," he says.

"I've thought it all through, Dad."

"Have you? Because, it seems . . . stupid. Doesn't it?"

"That's the insane beauty of it. It *is* stupid. Profoundly stupid. But so is telling a grown man that he can't ride his motorcycle in his own neighborhood."

"I don't know."

"Come on, Dad. I need this, OK? No. *We* need this." As I listen to what I've just said, I discover that I truly mean it. I care about this.

When I got back from Lazzari's with the truck, I went straight up to the Bizarro Room and started digging through the closet for supplies. I pulled out my old boom box and loaded it up with batteries. I riffled through all my old CDs until I found my copy of *Straight Outta Compton*. I found bungee cords in the garage and used them to secure my boom box to Big Red's roof. I found the *Rolling Thunder* CD I bought at Drastic Plastic but forgot to give my dad. And then, finally, I put the inflatable sex doll in the passenger seat and hung one of its creepy arms out the window. Now all I need is for my dad to have a little faith in me and help me deadlift this goddamn motorcycle into the bed of this giant truck so we can completely redeem ourselves.

"You really want to do this?" he says.

I tell him that I do.

"OK, then," he says. "Why not?"

Getting a forty-year-old motorcycle with a parking boot on its front wheel into the bed of an F-150 pickup is harder than I imagined it'd be. But after a few minutes of struggling and swearing, we figure it out. With all the parts now assembled, my dad hops up into the truck bed and climbs onto his bike. "You're not going to go *too* fast, are you?" he says. "This thing isn't secured at all. It's just dead weight."

"I'll go slow," I say. "Trust me."

"And you don't want me to start it?"

"No. That's a direct violation of the bylaws, remember?"

"OK," he says.

"That's what *this* is for." I show him the *Rolling Thunder* CD, and, finally, he gets it. "One last thing," I say. "I need to take my pants off."

"Why would you do that?"

"You're not the only one who's been wronged here, Dad," I say. "I feel like a neighborhood that has a specific rule about pantslessness needs to reevaluate some things." I shimmy out of my jeans. I'm wearing seasonally appropriate boxers this time, which seems to please my dad, despite himself.

I climb in behind Big Red's wheel and start it up. I hit the gas a few times, just to maximize the noise. "Ready, Dad?" I shout.

"I think so!"

"OK, hit 'Play' on the boom box!"

When he does, a blast of engine sounds ricochets off the house, across the driveway, and out into the lovely, suburban neighborhood. It's perfect. In the truck stereo, I eject Neal's Pearl Jam CD and replace it with N.W.A. I skip to track number two and turn the volume up as high as it goes. It takes a second, and then, as N.W.A.'s "Fuck tha Police" comes on in all its obscene glory, I'm filled with a wave of happiness so powerful that I feel like I might start crying right here next to a life-size sex doll.

"OK!" I say. "Hold on!"

I turn out of the driveway and onto the street, easing up on the gas, and we're off. The engine roars, the engine sounds roar, N.W.A. roars. As we coast along, winding from street to street, avenue to avenue, people stop what they're doing and watch us—a man mowing his lawn, a woman watering flowers, a girl walking a dog, two kids playing basketball in their driveway. The ball bounces between them and rolls into the grass as they watch, befuddled.

The word *fuck* is said over and over. *Nigga*, too. It's ridiculous, the entire thing, and I start laughing. I'm pretty sure my dad didn't know the lyrics to "Fuck tha Police" when we started this mission, but he's hearing them now, and in the rearview mirror, I can see that he's laughing, too. He's gripping the handlebars, pretending to drive, and his hair is blowing in the wind. He's smiling like he smiled in those pictures, like a genuinely happy person. He's not a happy person, and neither am I, but right now we are, and that's all that matters.

We turn around in a cul-de-sac, and people are actually starting to come out of their houses to watch us. People stand side by side with their children and dogs. My dad and I wave, but they just keep staring. They're all thinking the same thing; you can see it on their confused faces. *What . . . in the hell?*

"Fuck tha police," the song tells them, again and again and again.

I look at the sex doll. By chance, its body has contorted so that it's looking at me, and its head is bobbing along with the truck.

My dad shouts, "Uh-oh" from the back. I can hear joy in his voice, like a kid laughing. Behind us, Don Johnson and his Prairie West Security golf cart come tearing out of a driveway, lights flashing, which is exactly what we both hoped would happen. He's screaming at us to pull over, but his words are lost in our tidal wave of idiotic noise. I've forgotten where we are, exactly, but I start to recognize things. After loops and blind turns, we've somehow ended up back near my parents' house.

"He's gaining on us!" my dad yells. "Faster! Go faster!"

It's a relative term, since we're only going about twenty miles per hour, but I tap the gas and we lunge forward. I look at Don Johnson in the side mirror, falling back. He's furious, and it's wonderful.

For a year, I've been so sad, so trapped in this murky, sludgy cesspool of misery, that I've barely been breathing. But I'm alive now. And it feels fucking good. Everything is going to be OK. I'm going to get better. I'm going to be happy again.

Then I hear my dad yell. His voice is different this time. He's not laughing.

I look again at the road in front of us, and there's something there, scattered across the pavement. Reflexes take over. I grab the wheel and hit the brakes at the same time. Big Red's front tire hits the curb, and I feel the truck's weight shift. A mailbox explodes into a million shards of wood and brick and plastic.

N.W.A. raps about putting a clip in a gun. And then they say "Boom, boom."

As we start to flip over, I think of my dad behind me. And in the slow motion tumbling that follows, I see him airborne out of the corner of my eye. I see the sex doll ejected from the side window. There's a flash of white pain, like a lightning strike, and my wrist snaps against the steering wheel, flopping at a hideous angle, like it's no longer attached. The second before the windshield shatters, I can see clearly out onto the street. Arranged there in V-formation, together, tiny and determined, red and yellow and blue and silver and gold, united against us, stand five squirrels.

41

I had hernia surgery in high school.

It wasn't from lifting something heavy—not that kind of hernia. It was just something I was born with, this painful little flaw that needed to be fixed. It wasn't a particularly dangerous or frightening surgery, but I was nervous anyway. The anesthesiologist wore a Nebraska Cornhuskers doctor mask. He put an IV in my arm and told me to count backwards from one hundred. I made it to ninety-eight, and then, seconds later, it seemed, a nurse was shaking me awake. It was like I had traveled through time.

This doesn't feel like that.

As I'm waking up, I'm aware that time has passed. Maybe this is what a coma feels like. Maybe I'll wake up and Daisy will be there, but she'll be middle-aged—her tattoos sunken and faded on her flesh—and there will be flying cars and robot butlers.

I remember flashes of things. Don Johnson shouting at us. Don Johnson shouting at my dad. *Brad! Bradley! Can you hear me? Andy! Son! Andy!* And then there was the word *ambulance*. And then there was an actual ambulance—the sirens and all that bullshit—and then I was being lifted and told not to move.

I open my eyes and there's a ceiling. And on that ceiling is a water stain that looks very much like the state of Texas. So I'm pretty sure it's not the future, because in the future we probably won't have water stains on ceilings. We will have figured that out by then with some sort of all-new ceiling technology.

I turn my head. I must be hallucinating or dreaming or having a nightmare, because Tyler is sitting in a chair beside my bed. He's wearing his paramedic uniform.

Fucking Tyler.

"You awake?" he says, even though there's no way he can really be here.

"No," I say.

He sighs. "You're awake."

The fog clears pretty quickly. The guy who ruined your marriage must be like smelling salts. "What're you doing here?"

"I'm checking on you."

"Why? Where is my . . ."

"Your dad's fine. Some bruises. Stitches on his forehead. Superficial wounds."

I breathe out a big burst of relief, which hurts, like punishment. And that's when I see my right arm. It's in a cast from the wrist to the elbow, lying there beside me like a piece of petrified wood. "Fuck," I say.

"It's broken. Your wrist. Like, broken-broken. For the rest of your life, when it rains, it's probably gonna hurt."

I let this sink in. I've never broken anything before. "Why are you here?"

"This is, like, the fifth time you've been awake. You don't remember?"

I tell him no.

"Makes sense," he says. "You flew out of a truck like a human lawn dart and landed on your head. You're lucky you're not a vegetable right now. Or dead."

I look around the room. No cards or flowers, like my grandpa has. There's an unopened Jell-O cup next to me and a packet of crackers.

"You ever hear of a seat belt, by the way?" says Tyler. "It's a pretty helpful technology they came up with recently."

"What day is it?"

"You crashed two days ago. I've seen worse. A hit like you took? I've seen people out for a week, ten days. You absolutely destroyed Neal's truck, by the way. Nice work finishing that job."

"Shit."

"Yeah. That security guard at your parents' place called it in. Did you know his name is Don Johnson . . . like the actor? Anyway, I was, like, two miles away, so I hit the lights. I get there, and who do I find? *You*, in the grass, next to an inflatable sex doll, in your underwear. What the fuck, man?"

"It was a good plan," I say.

"Clearly," he says.

"Do I have, like, a morphine button I can push?"

"You'll be fine. Take Extra Strength Tylenol for your head. The swelling will go down in a few days. It'll hurt less after that. They might get you some Percocet or something, if you whine enough. When they ask you to rate your pain between one and ten, say eight—maybe eight and a half. Don't say ten. It's embarrassing, and they'll just think you're being a pussy."

We sit there for a while. It's too silent. I wish I had some of the cool machines that my grandpa has, just to add some white noise. "All righty then," I say.

"What?" he says.

"Well, you've checked on me. I'm not dead. Could you send my family in and maybe not be here anymore? You're not exactly someone I want to spend a lot of time with."

He leans forward in his chair. "Relax," he says. "Your family is . . . Well, they'll be back. But I actually wanted to talk to you."

"I don't want to talk to you."

"Stop it," he says. "You owe me."

"For what?"

"For *what*? I brought you here. I stabilized your neck. I made sure they didn't give you a catheter. They wanted to, you know. Trust me . . . You're glad they didn't. You're wearing an adult diaper, by the way. Much better alternative. It's probably chafing like a bitch, though. Use Vaseline."

"OK. We're even, then."

He fiddles with his hands, wringing his fingers. "If I ask you a question," he says, "will you pretend for a second like you don't hate me and just answer it?"

"Can you hand me the phone so I can call security?" I say. "Do they have security at hospitals?"

"Toward the end," he says. "When you knew there was something wrong. With you and Karen, I mean. Was she acting . . . different?"

His stupid, handsome face looks drained and tired. I recognize that expression—I looked at it in the mirror every day the last year of my marriage. "What do you mean?" I say.

"*Different*," he says. "Weird. I don't know. Quiet? Like, you'll say something, and she won't even respond? And if she does, it's like a one-word answer?"

I think of the poor French kid on the garage roof. I think of the others—the list of them. I think of my plate of Sizzling Chili Lime Chicken and "Wake Me Up Before You Go-Go" and the adorable old couple. "Not really," I lie.

"I'm starting to think, maybe she's . . ." He doesn't want to say what he's thinking, so he doesn't.

"She's moody," I say. "She's always been moody. I wouldn't worry about it."

"You think?"

"Yeah," I say.

He stands up, and for a moment he doesn't know how to leave. Men who like each other shake hands or say something funny or rude. But we don't like each other. We're enemies. "So do you want some Jell-O or something?"

That's not something I imagined fucking Tyler would ever ask me.

"No. I feel like I'm gonna barf."

"That's the concussion. It'll pass."

"Good to know."

"Oh," he says. "I don't use bronzer, by the way."

"What?"

"Bronzer. When I pulled you over, you said I got bronzer on your new jacket. But I don't use it."

"Really?" I say. "Your skin just naturally looks like that?"

He nods.

"Well, fuck you, then. What hospital am I in, anyway? I should try to get to my grandpa."

And right then, I know. Tyler's eyes shift to the wall and back. My grandpa is dead, and this is how I'm finding out. Fucking Tyler is telling me.

"He's gone, isn't he?" I say.

"Last night," he says. "Sorry."

It's not a montage this time. It's just a single scene, quiet and lovely. There's Karen and my grandpa dancing at our wedding reception. It isn't planned, like the first dance or the father-daughter thing. The DJ switches from "Bust a Move" by Young MC to a Sinatra song—"My Way"—and the dance floor instantly clears of everyone under sixty. Karen gets up and takes my grandpa's hand, and they dance together while everyone watches. It's a thing of absolute beauty.

When Tyler leaves the room, I hardly notice.

42

And finally, after all this time, after two weeks of summer sun and big skies, we have some ambiance.

We're at my grandpa's church, Sacred Heart, in downtown Omaha, for his funeral, and it's raining like hell.

Our family takes up one whole pew, end to end. I'm sitting between Nancy and Jim. Gina, lovely in a sophisticated black dress, is next to him, and then come Bryce and Emma. They look like two miniature adults in a little shirt and tie and a dress, respectively. I'm disappointed to the point of genuine sadness to see Bryce not wearing his karate gear. At the very end of the pew, as far from my mom as possible, sits my dad. I'm in my new suit. It's sharp, perfectly tailored, but it doesn't look right because of my cast and my swollen face from the accident.

I'm curious what we must look like to all the people here. Are they thinking about my mom and how embarrassed she must be? Are they thinking about my dad with the big Band-Aid on his head, the local philanderer? Are they thinking about me, the damaged son, and asking themselves what in the hell happened to me? I can practically hear them whispering. *He used to sell insurance.*

An old man named Gus, who I recognize from the bocce court at New Beginnings, is at the lectern telling a lengthy story about my grandpa and how he snuck a copy of *Showgirls* into the DVD player a few months ago during movie night. His friends and neighbors have been doing this for a while now, telling Henry stories.

Every few minutes, I look around the congregation, scanning from the front of the house to the back. I'm looking for Daisy—or, well, Stephanie. I don't see her. My mother puts her hand on my knee and gives it a little squeeze. She's caught me.

"You've had a tough year," she says. Her eyes are watering; they have been since we sat down. Her voice is just above a whisper.

"We all have," I say.

"You were my sensitive one," she says. She leans forward, glancing at my brother. "Jim was always, well . . . Jim. You cared about things, though. You always felt things more than he did. I always liked that about you."

"It's actually a huge pain in the ass," I say.

She smiles, and I look around, prepared to apologize to someone because I've just casually sworn in a church. But no one can hear us.

It's only been five days since the Glitter Mafia outed my parents, so to speak. Already she looks different. She's wearing less makeup today. Her hair, somehow, is less electrifying. Or maybe it's just my imagination. A few hours ago, before we came to the church, we were all in the kitchen in our nice outfits. The phone rang. It was her agent calling. Fox News decided to "put her on the shelf" for a bit. They're not sure for how long—at least until things blow over. When she hung up the phone, she went to the cupboard and got an English muffin. These were the first carbs I'd seen her eat since I got here.

Gus is still talking. Apparently this was my grandpa's thing—hijacking movie nights with R-rated things.

"You don't think I'm a villain, do you?" Nancy asks.

"What?"

"I don't care about what *they* think. But I care about what you think. I care a lot."

A few years ago, it dawned on me that in the inevitable future movies about the gay rights movement, people like Nancy will be the bad guys. This isn't a movie, though, and it's not the future, either. It's now. And once again, she's not a symbol. She's just my mom. "No, Mom," I say. "I don't. I promise."

When Gus steps down, a heavy silence falls over the congregation. Everyone looks around, waiting to see if anyone else is going to talk. Emma has found one of the hymnals and is loudly flipping the pages.

"Brooooook," she says. "Staarrrry."

"Shhh," says Gina.

And then I see Mrs. DiGiacomo. I barely recognize her, because she, like Bryce, has shed her uniform, ditching her robe for a long green dress. She shuffles her way up to the front.

"Staaaarry!" says Emma. It echoes from the rafters.

Mrs. DiGiacomo climbs up onto a step stool and spends a good fifteen seconds adjusting the mic. Then she says, matter-of-factly, "I had a crush on Henry."

There's a smattering of polite laughter.

"That's what we used to say—*crush*. Don't know what people call it now, but that's what I had. And don't laugh; he was a handsome man. For an old folks' home in Omaha, Nebraska, he might as well have been Paul Newman."

The laughter is genuine now.

"When you're my age, you can't sit around waiting for a man, because who's got the time? You need to be aggressive. So one afternoon, a few weeks after he moved in, I asked him over for dinner. I told him I'd make him Italian, and afterward he could even watch his ridiculous Cubs. I checked the *TV Guide*, and they had a night game that night. Seemed perfect. But he told me no anyway. He didn't say it mean. He could be blunt—we all know that. Never mean, though. When I asked him why, he said, 'Marie, I haven't eaten dinner with a woman since my wife. She's the only woman I want to eat with, and she's gone.'"

My mother starts quietly crying beside me. I put my good hand on hers.

"So if you believe in . . . *up there*," says Mrs. DiGiacomo. "And it's nice to believe. Let's all try to be happy and not so glum today, because Henry's up there, and he's finally getting to have a nice meal with Dot."

The church falls quiet again. But not for long, because this is the moment Emma chooses to drop the brick-size book onto her foot. The sound—a dull thud—blasts across the church, and Emma screams. She takes a breath and screams again. Gina tries to scoop her up, but she's on the move. She climbs over her shocked brother, her embarrassed parents, and lands in my lap, sending a swarm of bee stings up the broken parts of my body. She wraps her arms around my neck and screams into my ear, and I'm aware of hundreds of eyes on me.

"Emma, honey," says Jim, reaching. "Come here."

She just squeezes me harder. For some reason, she wants me to comfort her. "I got her," I say. "It's OK." I stand up—no easy feat—and I get the hell out of there. It's maybe thirty yards from our pew at the front of the church to the exit, and I cover it like I'm being chased, and then I push through a big, serious-looking door. Out in the wide, stone entryway, it's cool and quiet, and it's just the two of us.

Emma cries into my neck. I feel her heartbeat. And when she starts to calm down, I feel her little body relax. I tell her things that I imagine you tell upset children. "It's OK, honey. You're all right. See? No biggie, right?" She hiccups out a few last-ditch cries. I keep holding her, though. It's quiet out here, and I'm fully aware of the fact that I don't want to go back inside. I don't want to be stared at. I don't want to keep looking for Daisy/Stephanie and not finding her. I don't want to hear more old people talk about my grandpa, because he's gone, he's never coming back, and I'm really starting to miss him.

"Pop-Pop."

It's Emma. She's said something, and, unless I'm mistaken, it was actual words.

"What, honey?" I say.

"Pop-Pop," she says again, pointing.

I turn around, and there's a picture of my grandpa propped up on an easel. He's with me and Jim and Emma and Bryce. He's holding Emma in his arms—because she's just an infant swaddled up like a giant burrito—and he's smiling.

The tangled, jagged barbed wire of pain and regret and directionless emotion that I've been shoving down to the deepest parts of my gut travels up through my body and out of my mouth in one knee-buckling sob. A second follows. I try to fight it, because I don't want to cry here, now, in some church entryway, but it's too much.

Behind me, the door opens. I hear it. I feel the atmosphere change. I feel everything change. Because right here, at the end of the story, in a dress I don't recognize, stands Karen.

She's here to fuck with my head one last time.

We're in her car, parked in the parking lot, the car I helped her buy, her green Ford Escape. I'm in the passenger seat, and Karen is in the driver's seat. Every few seconds, the wipers streak across the windshield and make a sound like a vampire dying.

"I wish you'd stop staring at me," she says.

It sounds mean, but in her defense, that's exactly what I'm doing. I'm staring at the shape of her face. I'm staring at the indentation at the top of her lip. It has some biological name, this weird little spot, but I can't remember what it is. It's lovely, though. I'm staring at the mole above her collarbone where her pulse beats. Time has somehow enhanced these things, as if she's been converted to high definition since I saw her last.

"I've thought about you so much in the last year, I'm having trouble believing you're actually here."

"That's creepy," she says.

Maybe she's right. But it doesn't matter. I can say whatever I want. She can't divorce me again.

"Blarg!"

We both look at Emma, who's standing in the backseat, watching us.

"She turned into a cute little thing, didn't she?" says Karen.

Emma's got a My Little Pony figurine. I have no idea where it came from. Perhaps she pulled it like magic from the ruffles of her dress. One leg of her tights is bunched and twisted. When we test-drove this car a few years ago, the salesman sat where Emma is now and mentioned that there was plenty of room for car seats. "You know, when the time is right."

"I like your suit," she says. "My dad's a pro."

"Thanks. It's half-European."

"Did he really punch you?" Karen says.

"Yeah, but I asked him to, so we're cool."

"You're even, then."

"I guess so."

I should have more to say than this. I should have an entire speech prepared with platitudes and quotes from Taylor Swift songs. But I don't. The little Jiffy Lube sticker at the top corner of the windshield. She's two thousand miles late for an oil change, which is more satisfying than I can even describe. I handled car maintenance in our marriage. Bug killing and garbage removal, too.

"I wasn't ignoring you, you know," she says. "When you showed up at the house. And when you called. I actually wanted to talk to you. It felt mean not to. But Tyler wouldn't let . . . He didn't think it was a good idea."

Fucking Tyler.

"For the record," I say, "he knows you're thinking about leaving him."

She doesn't act shocked or ask what I'm talking about. She just looks sadly out the window, and I have to stop myself from reaching over and rubbing the back of her neck like I used to when she looked troubled.

"You should have just stayed married to *me*," I say. "If you wanted me to landscape the yard, you coulda just asked."

She laughs, and it sounds nice with the drumming rain. "He's not as funny as you are."

"People who look like him can't be funny," I say. "Nature doesn't allow it."

Emma laughs behind us. There's no reason why, she just does.

"I tried really hard to stay in love with you, Andy," says Karen.

The pain from hearing this is delayed. It starts small, like a pinprick, and then it intensifies outward.

"Sometimes, I'd be driving home from work, or I'd be at the grocery store, and I'd say to myself . . . *Why isn't this enough? Why can't I just be happy?*"

"Ever come up with an answer?" I say.

"No. I just knew I couldn't be with you anymore. I couldn't have a baby with you. If I did, that'd be it. That's what I'd be forever. I'd be this . . . *mom*, in Omaha, Nebraska . . . married to . . ."

"Me," I say. "A short insurance salesman."

"I don't mean it like that." She reaches for me, and when her hand finds my arm, I see it, the small sliver of a diamond. And there it is. It should be an agonizing thing to see, but strangely, it isn't. It just feels like the end.

"You're . . . ," I say.

She takes her hand back. She didn't mean for me to see it like that, I guess. "Yeah. I was going to tell you. I thought about writing you a letter."

"Since when?"

"Last month," she says. "He asked me at Memorial Park. A picnic. Kind of cheesy, right?"

Behind us, Emma is tracing streams of water across her window.

"I heard you're with someone," she says. "My mom told me. My dad said she's very pretty."

I stare at her ring, small and shiny. I asked Karen to marry me on a Tuesday evening in the wintertime. I wanted to surprise her, and what could be more surprising than a Tuesday-evening wedding proposal?

"It's weird," she says. "I know I have no right to—I mean, *obviously*—but when I heard that, it hurt me. The idea of you with someone else. Is that crazy?"

I could tell her that I'm not with the girl she thinks I'm with—not even close. I could tell her some shortened version of the truth, but I don't do that, either. Noble or not, mature or otherwise, it's nice to be able to hurt her, if only for a moment.

"Do you love him?" I say.

We watch the drizzle for a while, and she doesn't answer me. It feels weird to sit in the passenger seat of this car. I always drove. Karen always preferred to be driven. There's a minivan parked directly across from us. It has a *Nancy Knows* bumper sticker. "Always Right. Always Right."

"Maybe this time will be different," she says.

I hear organ music coming from inside the church. It's taken me a long time to realize this, but I'm lucky that all this happened. I'm lucky that she failed at trying to love me and left me at Applebee's a year ago. If we'd stayed together, Karen and I, we'd have ended up two unhappy people in some big house somewhere, avoiding one another. And by then, it'd have been too late.

"I hope you're right," I say.

When I take her hand and kiss above her dry knuckles, she looks like she might cry. But then Emma holds her hand out and demands that I kiss that one, too, and it saves the moment for all of us.

She offers me an umbrella from her center console when I step out of the car. I say no, even though I'm pretty sure it was my umbrella once. I flip the seat down and Emma climbs into my good arm. I tell Karen good-bye and she tells me good-bye. She tries to back out, but she realizes she's still in park, and she's momentarily flustered. And then Emma and I watch as the girl who was once the love of my life drives away forever.

The rain is just drizzle now, and the organ sounds even clearer. I'm about to go back inside, but I see a head poking up from behind a Subaru Outback across the street. It's Kenny, the stalker, watching the church. I hold my cast up, doing my best to wave. But when he sees me, his eyes go wide, and he runs away.

43

I'm packing to go back to New York with all the precision with which I packed to come here.

I'm not drunk or concussed this time, but with only one working arm, it quickly devolves into me just jamming crap into my duffle bag. I roll my suit up in my hanger bag, even though I'm pretty sure you're not supposed to roll suits. I throw some odds and ends in, too, like a few Lego men, some Eddie Vedder flannels, my duct-taped Walkman, and some nice pictures of my grandma that I found in the basement.

And now I'm standing over the "Andy & Karen" box, wondering if I should take any of it. In situations like this, I've found that it's best to take nothing, because once you take something you can make a pretty good case for taking everything.

My phone buzzes from the dresser. It's sitting next to the Lego *Millennium Falcon*, which, unfortunately, is too big to pack. It's a text message. It says simply:

    Meet me in the gazebo. Now.

I step out of my room and into the dark upstairs hallway. I hold my breath and listen for sounds of life, but there's nothing. It's after midnight, and this big, quiet house is as quiet as ever.

After some feeling around the kitchen, I hit a switch, and the room lights up just enough to find the bottle of Jack Daniel's I lifted from the funeral reception, and two small glasses. I stop on my way through the living room, doing my best not to wake my dad. For reasons I can't explain, he's sleeping on the couch instead of in one of the extra rooms. Maybe he feels like it's more of a punishment down here with his feet sticking over the armrest.

It's a warm night, but by female standards, I guess it's cool, because Daisy is in fleece pants and a jean jacket. She's reading her Curtis Violet book by cell phone light.

I sit beside her and pour two drinks. "When are you leaving?" she says.

"Tomorrow."

"Oh."

I try to analyze what "Oh" means—the tone and the inflection. This is when you know you're in trouble. This is the moment you know you care about someone, when you're wondering what two letters mean.

"I've been punched . . . twice," I say. "I practically broke my arm off. I destroyed my best friend's truck. I nearly killed my father. I contributed to my mother's humiliation. I buried my grandpa. And I've been at least partially drunk for two straight weeks. It's time to go."

"Mrs. D. told me about your accident. We ate Hot Pockets after the funeral. Watched a little *Young and the Restless*, too. Did you know Victor Newman is currently wanted for murder?"

"They'll never convict him," I say.

"I hope not. I don't know if Mrs. DiGiacomo could handle it."

"I looked for you at the church," I say. "I saw Creepy Kenny. Figured you weren't too far away."

She nods. "I saw you looking for me. It was sweet. I'm good at hiding, though." She taps my cast like she's knocking gently on a friend's front door. "Does it hurt?"

"Constantly," I say.

"I didn't take advantage of Henry," she says. "He was my friend. I felt responsible for him. When he started tipping me more and more, I told him he didn't have to, but he just kept doing it. It goes into this account. It's complicated. It's not like he was just handing me cash. I didn't know about the will thing until Nancy said it at dinner. Honestly. I'm not going to accept it. I'm gonna give it back."

"I'm sure Nancy will appreciate that."

"I'm not doing it for her," she says.

"That apartment where we . . ." I say. "Is that yours?"

"It's a staged apartment. Half that building is empty. A friend of a friend knows the developer. He let me crash there. It was just supposed to be for a few days. I wanted to see Henry in person and say good-bye. Then I saw you in the parking lot that day—in your dad's car. Jesus, you looked so wrecked. That's when I came up with my make-Andy-happy plan. It was a . . . a whim. The whole thing."

We listen to the sounds of the yard at night.

"Do you really teach housewives how to write Vagina Fiction?"

"Online. I'm actually a pretty good writer when I try. I told you the truth more times than I lied to you."

I look at the book in her lap. "Did Curtis Violet really hit on you in Iowa?"

She sighs. "I let him kiss me in the hallway of his hotel. Then I told him to go to bed, and I drove all the way home in the middle of the night by myself. He was a very sad person. He talked about his son a lot, how he wished they were closer."

I look back up at the house, and it's still dark. I refill my glass. I should have a dozen or so more questions to ask her, but I can't think of any right now.

"You talked to her, I assume?" she says. "K-a-r-e-n. I was going to follow you out when you left with Emma, but she beat me to it."

"She's never going to be happy. She's never been happy, actually."

"Good," she says, but there's no bite behind it; it's just a word whispered in the nighttime. "You look better, you know. Well, you look like hell. But you know what I mean. You're on your way back, Andy Carter."

"Maybe that's because of you," I say.

She studies her fleecy knees. I should've brought out a blanket or something. Some hair falls into her eyes, and she doesn't even bother to push it aside, and for one very clear moment all her defenses are down, and I can see how starkly unhappy she is.

"The girl your ex is with now . . . What's she like?"

"She's everything that I'm not."

"Then she must be very, very boring," I say.

When she smiles, I think about how things could be. It's my least painful montage yet. There's her sitting on the rocks in Central Park. There's her petting Jeter's stupid head and wearing her earbuds on the subway and wandering through endless record shops. There's her, two steps ahead of me, climbing the stairs to my apartment. There's me, watching the backs of her knees and wanting to kiss them. And there's us—together—not just pretending.

I ask her if she's ever been to New York. She takes a sip of her drink and tells me that I should stop asking questions.

"It's a cool city," I say. "You can be whoever you want there. That's the big draw. Like, you said you're a good writer? You have any idea how many writers there are in New York? They write mainly in Starbucks, as far as I can tell."

She's looking out into the dark, listening.

"I had this Etch A Sketch when I was a kid," I say. "I used to love that fucking thing. I'd try to draw something, like a bird or a dog, but I was a really shitty artist, so I'd screw up every time. But it didn't matter, because I'd just shake it up and start again."

Daisy smiles. "A mildly complex Etch A Sketch metaphor dropped into casual conversation," she says. "Impressive."

"I went to private school."

She turns to me, resting her elbow on the gazebo railing. She touches the back of my head, swirling my hair with her fingers. She tells me that she can't go to New York. She doesn't tell me that she doesn't want to go to New York or that she won't go to New York. She tells me that she can't.

"Why?" I say.

"I'm still in love with him. I think about him every minute of every day. And if I go to New York, he might not be able to find me if he comes back."

It might be the saddest thing I've ever heard. And I totally get it.

She kisses me on the cheek. "Go home, Andy Carter," she says. "Shake it up. Start all over again. You're ready."

Henry hears his name, close and gentle.

"Henry. Henry."

He feels her, the weight and shape of her body, tucked in beside him. She fits perfectly there, like always, her head on his shoulder, her arm draped across his chest.

"It's me," she whispers.

Of course it is. Finally.

It's too dark to really see her; it's just her outline in her dark sweater, her hair pulled back. She's effortlessly pretty, his Dot, like Audrey Hepburn. That's her specialty, looking good without even trying. That's the first thing he noticed about her. She was some nineteen-year-old girl who looked like she belonged in a catalog.

He says hi, but nothing comes out because he can't talk.

"Shhh."

It feels like he's floating, mostly. He remembers pain, but there isn't any of it now. He smoked grass once in the summer of 1951 with his friend Eugene Speers from Council Bluffs. It felt like this feels. Like floating.

"Sorry I've been away so long," she says.

This reminds him of their hammock. He put it up with two posts in their yard at the place in Bellevue. They lay on it like this together, side by side, on Saturdays and Sundays. A storm took it once—tore it right out of the yard and took it up into the sky. He found it on the roof the next day and put it up again.

"I can't stay for long," she says.

He feels her breath on his ear. He's missed her so much. He closes his eyes and wishes he could talk, so he could tell her not to go. He's been lost without her.

"I've loved you for so long," she says. "Since I was a kid."

He can't say it back. He hopes she knows.

"I'm waiting for you. I've been waiting for you this whole time. So if you want, if you're ready, it's OK to let go. It's OK. Because I'll be there. And then we can go home."

His limbs are so heavy. Everything is so heavy. Maybe she's right. Maybe he should stop fighting it. He wishes he could see her, but it's too dark. If he could talk, he'd tell her he's ready.

"I love you, Henry," she says.

I love you, too.

"I love you. I love you. I love you. I love you. I love you. I lo . . ."

44

"Goddammit, Andy Carter!"

I'm back in New York, at the Underground, working. I've been here for about fifteen minutes, and it's not going well.

"You have any idea how depressing it is seeing a one-armed white man trying to mix a damn drink?"

"Sorry," I tell him. And then I say sorry to the girl standing at the bar. She's holding a wrinkly twenty, watching me fumble and spill my way through her Long Island iced tea.

"Breaks my damn heart," says Byron. Seeing me all busted and helpless has inspired the career bartender in him. He's flipping bottles and dancing around like Tom Cruise in *Cocktail*, and it's every bit as obnoxious as it sounds.

"I just need to get used to it," I say. "I'll be fine."

He laughs. "My third-best bartender, stripped of his essence. You know, if you were a horse, I'd have to take you out back behind the dumpsters and shoot you."

I finally hand the girl her drink, which took me about ten minutes to make, and I'm on to the next one: a gin martini, shaken. Which begs the question: Who in the hell comes to a bartender with a broken arm and asks for a shaken martini?

Eventually, thank God, our small run of drinkers ends, and we get a chance to relax. I use the time to scratch under my cast with a tool I painstakingly built from five stirring straws.

"Motherfucker's itchy, isn't it?"

I tell him yes, and then I take a sip of my ginger ale. Byron noticed when I poured it instead of my customary beer, but he didn't say anything, just lifted his eyebrows.

"What'd you do to yourself, anyway?" he says. "Your arm? Your face? Shit went down out there in the heartland, huh?"

"I crashed my friend's truck," I say. "And I got punched a couple of times."

In a lot of crowds, a comment like this would generate some follow-up questions, but Byron just says, "Thug life," and then eats a handful of bar cherries.

Outside, a swarm of people passes the bar. They're cheering and waving rainbow flags, marching down the sidewalk together. This happens every few minutes. This afternoon, the Supreme Court declared gay marriage legal in all fifty states, and New York is celebrating. The first person I thought about was Nancy. The second person I thought of was Stephen. I pictured him and the boys running through the silent streets of Omaha, Nebraska, happy and validated under that enormous sky.

I got back to New York three days ago. I called Byron and told him I was ready to work. I didn't tell him about my arm. It's not like I was scared to. I just forgot. This throbbing, broken, plastered thing attached to the right side of my body slipped my mind, somehow. That's how I've been since getting back—all spacey and preoccupied. The good news is, I haven't thought about Karen at all. Maybe the movie screen in my head is off for good. Maybe I'm cured. Or maybe I've just replaced her with Daisy. I went online last night. The night before, too. And the night before that. I typed the address, I sat waiting for the page to load, and when all the girls appeared, I scanned each of them for Daisy. But she wasn't there.

"So aside from breaking your shit and busting up your buddy's ride, Ohio was good, then?"

"Oma—"

"Omaha," he says. "Just teasing, man."

A guy with a mustache and a "Legalize It" T-shirt orders a beer. I handle it successfully—easily, even—and Byron smiles. "Tell you what. Until you get that motherfucker off, you're the beer bitch. That's your thing. I'll set you by the taps. People want beers, they go to you. They want real, sophisticated, intellectual adult drinks, they come to me. Problem Solving 101. See? That's manager shit right there."

"I can handle that," I say.

"So the girl?" he says. "The ex. You stay cool, like you promised? You didn't go all white-dude psycho, did you?"

"Byron," I say. "The bitch is dead to me."

"Amen," he says. And then he tells me to go the fuck home. "Beer-bitch duty starts tomorrow night. Nine sharp. And wear something sexy. A nice little pair of shorts maybe. Give the beer drinkers a little something-something to look at."

I'm walking up my stairs again, all four flights of them. I'm carrying Cap'n Crunch, some Diet Dr Peppers, and mint chocolate chip ice cream. When the foreign guy at the corner store saw me this time, he was stone-faced again, completely expressionless. I laughed, which must have looked odd, me, all damaged, laughing.

"Again . . . *you*," he said.

"Again . . . *me*," I said.

"You . . . you should be careful more."

When I make it up to my floor, Jeter is in his spot, whacking his tail against my door. When I got home the other night, there was a pile of dead mice on my mat—and there's a new one there now. "Thanks, buddy," I say.

Inside, we do what we do. He stalks around, getting his cat dander all over everything, and I pour him cereal. I sit on my couch/bed and consider becoming a cat person. I could buy some cat toys, maybe some actual cat food. I could get some cardigans. Drink less. Post pictures on Twitter of him doing mysterious cat things. That sounds like starting over to me—like a clean Etch A Sketch.

My phone rings, and I see that it's Byron. "Hey. Did I forget something?"

"Andy!" he says. "No, but you left like five minutes too soon, man."

"What do you mean?"

"You got a visitor."

My heart speeds up in my chest. For the last year, I've imagined Karen showing up at my door. Frazzled and full of regrets, her hair wet from rain. *I've made a horrible mistake.* But I'm not thinking about my ex-wife. I'm thinking about Daisy. I want it to be her so badly that my voice cracks when I say, "Who is it?"

"Katie!" he says. I am so absolutely confused by this that I don't say anything. Byron laughs. "My sister's roommate, you idiot. The blind date chick. Remember? She stood you up, you left town. I felt like a dick."

"Oh. Katie. I forgot her name. Right."

"Yeah, she didn't mean to stand you up, I guess. Some bullshit about the subway. You know how it goes. Whatever. I sent her your way. Don't worry, I warned her about all your broken body parts. She's prepared for how hideous you look."

"What do you mean you sent her my way?"

"You live like four blocks away. You don't want to come here. This isn't a good first date place. Go outside, meet her in front of your building. She should be there any minute. Take her someplace respectable."

"But I'm—"

"What, you got big plans? A conference call or something?"

"No, but—"

"*But* nothing. Get down there. And don't act like a weirdo. I vouched for you. Plus my sister will be pissed."

When I hang up the phone, I must look strange, because Jeter is staring at me. "Dude," I say. "I've got a date."

Outside, in front of my building, I can hear singing and cheering, people blowing whistles and playing Queen songs. It's coming from a few blocks away. There aren't any bars on my street, just apartments and brownstones, so it's quiet enough to hear footsteps.

A girl is walking my way. She's moving slowly, looking at the building numbers as she goes. Any doubts that it's her are erased when she waves. "Hi," she says.

"Hey."

"Are you Andy?"

"Yep. And you're Katie, right?"

She stops and smiles. She's small and pretty. She's really pretty, actually, and she's wearing glasses. "I am," she says. "I like your shirt."

It's the corncob cowboy. I forgot I was wearing it. "Thanks."

"Are you from Nebraska, or are you being ironic?"

"Both, I guess."

"I'm from Washington, DC," she says. "Well, Arlington, Virginia. I tell people DC, because no one really knows where Arlington is, which is kind of annoying."

I nod, masking my ignorance. I'm an adult male, private school–educated, and I don't know where Arlington, Virginia, is. All this time

I've been quietly judging everyone who doesn't immediately know everything there is to know about Omaha.

"Those are cool glasses," I say.

She touches the frames, straightening them. "They're not real," she says.

"Yeah, they are," I say. "I can see them."

Katie from Arlington, Virginia, laughs. "No, I mean, yeah, they *exist*. But they're just for show. I bought them because I thought they'd make me look smarter. I decided the New York me is going to wear smart-girl glasses."

"Well, it's working," I say. "You look very smart. I actually feel a little dumb by comparison."

She looks at my arm. "So yeah . . . Byron wasn't kidding. How'd you hurt it?"

"It's a long story," I say. "But I owe my friend a truck."

At the end of my block, two cars pass, both of them honking. A few bars of "It's Raining Men" blast from the intersection.

"I'm sorry about our date," she says. "The subway was all . . ."

"Don't worry. It happens."

She shifts her weight from one sandal to the other. They're, like, three-inch heels, at least, and I'm still taller than she is. "Actually, that's not true. I never even got on the subway. I stayed in my apartment."

"What?"

"I chickened out."

"You did?"

"I've never been on a blind date. I was getting ready to come meet you, and I started thinking about all the things that could go wrong. Like, how I could get lost on the way there or maybe we wouldn't like each other or you'd be a jerk. No offense. There are a lot of jerks here. It started to feel hopeless, you know. Does that even make sense?"

"You're a very honest person," I say.

"Maybe. Denisha was so pissed at me. She said her brother said you're this great guy and that I'm stupid. She's been hounding me about it for two weeks."

"I'm glad she did," I say.

Katie smiles. "Me, too, actually. You don't seem like a jerk yet. So that's good. And you don't look nearly as horrible as Byron said you would."

"I like to set the bar really low and then just barely exceed it."

She snort-laughs. It echoes off a million square feet of cement and brick and stone. I take a breath and feel myself relax because, in my experience, there are few things as disarming as a girl who snorts when she laughs. "Maybe we should get a drink," I say.

"OK, cool."

"Great. So you like—"

"Oh, look," she says. "It's a cat."

And there he is. He's on the front stoop of my building, standing on the bricks, his tail slowly wagging, his eyes aglow from the street lamps, his fur as mangy and matted as ever.

"Jeter?" I say. "What are you doing down here?"

"You . . . know him?" she says.

"Yeah. He's mine. Sort of. That's a long story, too. I just officially adopted him about twenty minutes ago. I guess he followed me down here."

"He looks a little . . ."

"I know. I should brush him or . . . something, right? I don't really know how to take care of cats. I need to Google it. I should take him back up, though. He could get lost or run over or something."

She looks up at my building, scaling it to the top with her eyes. "Is this your building?"

"Yeah."

"Do you have access to the roof?"

Now it's my turn to look up. "I . . . I don't know. Should I?"

She laughs. "Really? You don't know if you have access to the roof of your own building? Roofs are, like, half the point of living in New York."

"I have no idea. I've been a little out of it for a while."

"Well, do you want to find out?"

"Really? Like, now?"

"They lit up the Empire State Building in rainbow colors for the Supreme Court ruling. I can't see it from my roof. There's too much in the way. Maybe we can see it from yours."

"OK," I say. "That sounds cool. I'll bring drinks. Oh, wait. I don't actually have drinks. I mean, drink-drinks. I'm trying to drink less. I have soda. I just picked up some Diet Dr Pepper. Apparently, it tastes more like regular . . ."

Her eyes go wide, and I stop talking, which is good, because I was about to start quoting Diet Dr Pepper commercials. "I love Diet Dr Pepper," she says. "It's . . . it's my drink."

Jeter follows us up the stairs, nipping at my heels as we go. When we get up to my floor, I open my apartment door, but he just stands there. "Go in, dude," I say. "You live here now."

He digs his nails into my welcome mat and squints up at me.

"I don't think he wants to go in," says Katie.

"Suit yourself."

She waits in the hallway while I grab two lukewarm sodas from my fridge. When I return, she opens hers immediately, and I do, too. At the end of the hallway, we find a door marked "Roof." There's a hand-drawn sign there that says "Restricted Access," but we ignore it and push right through. For a year now I've lived maybe fifty feet from this door. I've walked past it daily on the way to the garbage chute, and I've never even noticed it.

The dim stairwell smells like God knows what, and the steps are steep and dusty. When we reach the top, four more flights up, we stand for a moment at a rusted, industrial-looking door. There's another "Restricted Access" sign. This one's bolder, somehow more serious.

"You should open it," she says. "That way you'll be the one to get arrested."

"Good thinking," I say.

Humid air and the smells of the city hit us instantly. The roof is soft under our feet, like warm asphalt. There are a few scattered plants up here, an abandoned bird's nest, and a pair of old, faded Fisher-Price binoculars. Jeter leaps up onto the ledge and looks down at the street below.

We're eight stories up, by my count, but we're dwarfed by taller buildings on all sides. We both take turns saying "wow" and sipping our tepid Diet Dr Peppers, because it's beautiful up here. As advertised, the Empire State Building, which we can see if we lean at just the right angle over the ledge, is one enormous, beautiful gay rainbow.

"How long have you been in New York?" I ask.

"Two months," she says.

"Why'd you leave Virginia?"

She looks out at my abbreviated view and sighs. "Because it was time to go."

I wonder what his name is, the guy back in Arlington. I wonder if she hurt him or if he hurt her. I don't ask, though, of course, because it doesn't really matter. She's here now. We both are, along with ten million other people.

"Well, it's nice to meet you, Katie," I say.

We're so fixated on the Empire State Building that it takes us a moment to realize that we can see Freedom Tower from here, too. A sliver of it at least, down a long corridor of looming buildings. It's a good view, all things considered, except for Jeter, who's now a cat-shaped silhouette against all the lights. Katie eventually joins him at the ledge. She pets his head and he lets her, and they both look at the city for a long time.

"It's all so pretty," she says. "But it's kind of scary, too."

And she's right. It's absolutely terrifying.

ACKNOWLEDGMENTS

I want to thank my wife, Kate, for her understanding, patience, and love. Our daughters, too, for going to sleep when they're supposed to, mostly. I want to thank my agent, Jesseca Salky, who's an expert at making me feel like I'm her only client in the world. Thanks to Carmen Johnson, my editor at Little A, for helping me tell this story better than I ever could have on my own. And thanks to the band Wilco for inspiring so much of this book.

ABOUT THE AUTHOR

Photo © Jason Rice

Matthew Norman lives in Baltimore with his wife and their two daughters. His writing has appeared on *Salon*, the *Good Men Project*, and the *Weeklings*. His first novel, *Domestic Violets*, was nominated for a Goodreads Choice Award in Best Humor.

Visit his blog at www.thenormannation.com, or follow him on Twitter @TheNormanNation.